UNTIED LINES

A MICK NASSAU KEY WEST MYSTERY

DL MITCHELL

Black Rose Writing | Texas

The author grants the final approval for this literary material.

First printing

This is a work of fiction. Names, characters, businesses, places, events, and incidents are either the products of the author's imagination or used in a fictitious manner. Any resemblance to actual persons, living or dead, or actual events is purely coincidental.

ISBN: 978-1-68513-647-5
LIBRARY OF CONGRESS CONTROL NUMBER: 2025933755
PUBLISHED BY BLACK ROSE WRITING
www.blackrosewriting.com

Printed in the United States of America
Suggested Retail Price (SRP) $21.95

Untied Lines is printed in Minion Pro

*As a planet-friendly publisher, Black Rose Writing does its best to eliminate unnecessary waste to reduce paper usage and energy costs, while never compromising the reading experience. As a result, the final word count vs. page count may not meet common expectations.

PRAISE FOR
UNTIED LINES

"*Untied Lines* follows Mick as he investigates the injury to his friend, and is soon drawn into a larger conspiracy. Mitchell drops the reader in the middle of the tight knit community of Key West, and surrounds you with the local traditions and landmarks as the story evolves. The characters are as rich and diverse as the Key West culture, and the story builds effortlessly to a surprise ending."
–Gary Gerlacher, author of *AJ Docker Medical Thriller* series

"DL Mitchell delivers a non-stop tale of intrigue, romance, and resilience. Set against the dramatic backdrop of a Key West hurricane, her sophomore novel *Untied Lines* follows former investigator Mick Nassau as he delves into his best friend's suspicious injury while navigating new relationships and personal challenges from a forced retirement. Mitchell masterfully intertwines a gripping mystery with themes of friendship and redemption, creating a story that's as emotionally compelling as it is suspenseful. Five Stars!"
–Cam Torrens, bestselling author of the *Tyler Zahn mystery suspense* series

For my sister, Wendy

SPECIAL THANKS

Untied Lines is my first book—but the third to be published. Like choosing a favorite child, it's impossible to say which novel is my favorite. But I'd be lying if I didn't admit that *Untied Lines* holds a special place in my heart.

My sister, Wendy, was instrumental in helping me get it to the finish line. Her support and enthusiasm, coupled with her plot, character, and editorial advice, mean everything to me. My brother, Jeff—the creative one in the family—inspired me with a mocked-up movie poster, allowing me to visualize what the story could become. My mom, Denise, is a force of nature. Having traveled the world, her adventurous spirit is infectious to everyone around her. My husband, Blair, and daughter, Maddy, are my biggest cheerleaders. Without their loving support, none of this would be possible.

Thank you to Keri and Mark for your generosity and for sharing your beautiful beachfront home with me. I wrote most of *Untied Lines* on your deck, overlooking the Atlantic Ocean. The character Bob the Dog is based on your beloved beagle, Bailey—the sweetest, bravest, and most loyal dog.

My weekly critique group from Scooter's Coffee keeps me focused and ensures that the dialogue and plot make sense. I learn so much from your insights and balanced feedback.

Shoutout to the talented team at Black Rose Writing, with a special thanks to my editor, Mary Ellen Bramwell. I'm grateful every day to be one of your authors.

And last, but certainly not least—mystery readers! Your kind words of support and encouragement fuel me to keep writing.

UNTIED
LINES

CHAPTER 1

Who in their right mind ventures into the eye of a hurricane? Mick had spent the past two hours asking himself that very question. Taking calculated risks had always been his superpower, but the abrupt end to his once-illustrious career as an investigative special agent had left him reeling. Now, standing soaking wet on the deck of Jack's boat, he was forced to reevaluate his own decision-making abilities.

"It's only forecast to be a Cat 1 storm," Jack had said when he called a day earlier to extend an invitation. "My place is like Fort Knox—I've got automated shutters and a brand-new generator. If you're really serious about getting away, you better get packing."

In desperate need of a change of scenery, Mick didn't think twice before racing from his home in Tallahassee to Key West to reunite with his best friend—a hurricane wasn't going to stop him. What did it say about his frame of mind that putting himself in the path of a dangerous storm seemed like the better option?

"Mick, toss over that starboard fender." Jack's voice sounded muffled against the wind as the stinging rain turned sideways. Securing his beloved boat, *Bravo Zulu*, at the marina in deteriorating conditions put them in a race against the clock. Pleasantries and a proper reunion would have to wait. The latest weather update from the National Hurricane Center showed Hurricane Denise strengthening to a

Category 2 while exploding in size. Expected to make landfall later that night, its effects would be felt well in advance.

Mick turned his baseball cap around and planted his feet wide before facing the storm's onslaught. After hanging the fender, he pointed at two dock lines, coiled with precision and sitting near the transom. "What about these?" Everything else that could blow away had been removed or tied down.

Jack leaped onto the deck from the metal gangway. "I'll tie those after everyone clears out of the marina. I don't want anyone to trip over them. Let's head to Turtle Krawls until this rainband passes. Least I can do is buy you a drink after putting you to work the minute you arrived." Jack's favorite waterfront bar was within eyesight—his port in a storm, and the two men dashed for cover.

"That's nasty out there." Mick shook off the excess water from his face and arms. The normally raucous establishment had emptied except for a few weather-hardened locals enjoying a last meal. Mandatory evacuation orders issued by Monroe County kept the tourists away.

"Trust me. There'll be sunny breaks between rainbands, but it'll change quick." Jack's grin filled his face. An enormous man, he stood over six foot three with an ever-widening girth. His thick, light brown crewcut added to his already towering height. He dressed in his unofficial captain's uniform—a garishly loud Hawaiian print shirt, cargo shorts, and old-school Sperry topsiders. Deeply tanned crow's feet, earned from decades on the water, framed his blue, sparkling eyes. A retired Navy captain, he'd returned to Key West to fulfill his lifelong dream of owning a charter fishing boat.

A woman waved Jack over to the bar, handing them each a towel to dry off.

"Thanks, Cassie. Meet Mick—one of my oldest friends in town for a visit."

"Hi, Mick. You sure got bad timing," Cassie said, struggling to hide the flush in her cheeks. Often oblivious to the effect he had on women, Mick could easily be described as tall, dark, and handsome, but his gray-green eyes shaded by thick, black eyelashes had an exponential impact. "You boys look parched. What can I get you?"

"I'll take a pint of whatever local beer you have on tap," Mick said.

Jack nodded in agreement. "Make that three."

Mick turned to look at him. "Three?"

"Jo should be dropping by soon."

"What? She's in town?" The last he heard, Jack's sister, Dr. Joanna Barton, lived in Boston. She had moved there at the start of her veterinary career to be near her then-boyfriend, now ex-husband.

"I have to catch you up. Our local vet hospital closed when the owner died, so Jo used Ellie's inheritance to buy the place. She's been home for a month, but I never see her—she's working day and night to get ready for her grand opening."

Almost on cue, Jo swept into the bar. Jack stood to greet his sister with a hug.

"I know, I know," she said. "I'm late. I had to finish up some last-minute painting in the exam rooms."

Mick hadn't managed a word. That cute, spunky girl he'd last seen years earlier had become a stunningly beautiful woman. Long, sandy-blonde hair cascaded around her face in big, loose curls with a hint of freckles across the bridge of her nose complementing brilliant, blue eyes. Her sporty tank top and cut-off jean shorts showed off her long athletic frame. Jo seemed to notice Mick staring at her and broke the awkward moment by greeting him with a hug as well.

She stood back to look at the two men. "Mick Nassau. It's been a lifetime since I saw you last. Jack is always sharing updates about what you've been up to over the years, so I feel like I've kept up with everything."

"Likewise, Jo. I can't wait to hear about the new veterinary hospital. I imagine it's all-consuming right now," Mick said.

"It's been tough. I knew it was going to be a ton of work but underestimated the time I'd need to get it just right. I wouldn't change a thing, though. It's a dream come true."

Cassie interrupted their conversation when she returned with three grilled grouper sandwiches. "I'm closing the kitchen soon, and this would just go to waste. Lunch is on me."

As they finished their meal, Jack peppered Jo with questions about her storm prep. She assured him the hurricane shutters were secure, and she had ample supplies.

"My offer still stands if you want to bunker down at my place," Jack said.

"I'm good—stop worrying." Jo packed her leftovers in a to-go box and promised to touch base first thing in the morning. "It really is great seeing you, Mick." She looked back to her brother. "I know you've been hounding me to take a break and go diving with you. Let's plan something for later this week while Mick is in town."

"Okay. But you can't back out this time." Jack looked across the harbor. "The weather's lifting. Drink up." They finished their beer and paid the bill, adding an oversized tip for Cassie. As they walked out of Turtle Krawls, the clouds parted, blinding them with sunshine. The steam coming off the dock turned the air into a sauna. Tropical summer rain provided limited relief from the oppressive humidity. Jo said her goodbyes and headed for the parking lot while the two men returned to the marina.

"Let me lock up *Zulu*, then I'll drop you at my place before the weather turns again. I'd never admit this to Jo, but I'm running a little behind on my storm prep. It took longer than I thought to help my neighbors secure their boats."

"What's left to do?"

"My backyard furniture needs to be pulled under cover, and any loose items like potted plants, hanging baskets, and lanterns and stuff have to be put away in the storage shed. Don't want them to become flying projectiles."

"No problem. I'll double-check everything outside."

"And we didn't talk about this yet, but I'm planning to stay with a friend tonight—actually, Bea's more than a friend."

Jack had never been shy about the ladies in his life. His navy career contributed to his bachelor status, but things were different now. He seemed settled and content in a way Mick had never seen before. "When do I get to meet her?"

"Tomorrow, for sure. She owns an art gallery on Duval, so we're around the corner if you need anything." Standing on the dock next to *Zulu*, Jack stopped to watch an approaching vessel. "What the hell?"

Curious about why this hit on Jack's radar, Mick asked, "What's up?"

"Abe, the guy who owns that old boat, never leaves the dock, and I mean never. My last charter took me out near Marquesas Keys, and I saw Abe on Rebecca Shoal with his dive flag up. It's not a normal spot to bring tourists because of the currents. Now, he's out again with a hurricane bearing down. I don't like it."

Jack quickly explained a little more about Abe. He lived aboard his ancient trawler and mostly kept to himself, rarely engaging with his neighbors along the dock. Rumors of a checkered past led to speculation he was hiding from the law. Since he minded his own business and never caused trouble, everyone gave him a wide berth. Key West was a great place to go if you wanted to drop off life's radar.

"Let's do a little reconnaissance." Jack motioned for Mick to follow him to the end of the dock.

CHAPTER 2

The man captaining the boat looked up at his welcoming committee. Abe's thin, pinched lips and narrow-set, dark eyes exuded mean and nasty. He appeared to be in his sixties, which made his wiry frame even more impressive. Short gray hair ringed his bald head, with eyebrows stuck in a permanent scowl.

"Hey, Abe. Let us help you tie off."

Abe said nothing but offered a weak smile before tossing Jack a line. "This is my buddy, Mick."

Abe acknowledged him with a curt nod as a younger man appeared from below deck. Tall and scrawny with a long, stringy ponytail, he wore a Hog's Breath Saloon tank top revealing tanned arms covered in tattoos, including a large dive flag tattoo on his forearm. He avoided making eye contact with anyone, including Abe, and jumped onto the dock with his dive bag.

"Thanks, Abe. Catch you later," the stranger said as he brushed by both Mick and Jack before heading toward town.

"I saw you out diving Rebecca Shoal a few days ago," Jack said. "My fishing charters are always asking for a dive boat recommendation—I'd be happy to send them your way."

Abe didn't reply until after he finished putting out his bumpers, creating an awkward silence. "Don't you worry, Jack. I'm not interested in stealin' any of your prized customers. I was just helping a friend—no need for you to spy on me." Then he turned his back and disappeared into the cabin.

"I guess that's our cue to move along," Mick said. "Charming guy."

"Yeah. He sure rubs me the wrong way." Jack looked up to the sky before checking the weather app on his phone. "We gotta go."

. . .

Mick received the expedited tour of Jack's historic, conch-style cottage, recently inherited from his Aunt Ellie. The Barton siblings descended from true Conchs, the name given to people born and raised in Key West. Their roots traced back to the early settlers made up of pirates, adventurers, shipwreck salvagers, rumrunners, and the original Bahamian immigrants. Aunt Ellie, a beloved Key West matriarch who had contributed to the town's genuine sense of history, had passed away at the beginning of the year.

"You still planning to go back to the marina?" Mick asked.

"Yeah—for a couple hours, but I'll get to Bea's well before the eye comes ashore." He flipped open his laptop. "Help yourself to anything. I'll be here at first light after I check on two of Ellie's friends. They live alone in Old Town, and I look out for them since they don't have family in the area. Then we can go together to the marina. Once this storm business is over, there'll be time for us to do some fishing and diving, and I can introduce you around town."

"I like the sound of that."

"You've got to be kidding me." Jack shook his head in disgust and sat back in his chair.

"Everything okay?"

"It's about my recent charter to Rebecca Shoal, the one I was giving when I spotted Abe. First off, the guy was by himself, which was strange. Most people charter the boat with friends. On top of that, he dressed more for a business meeting than a day on the water. I just assumed he wanted to go fishing, but he had no interest and instead asked me to show him around the west side of Marquesas Key. That's when I saw Abe.

"Carrying on a conversation with this guy was painful. I asked him about his interests, but he responded with vague answers and quickly shifted the topic. We toured around the area all day, and he tipped well, but why charter a fishing boat if you aren't interested in fishing?"

"That is weird. Don't you charge around a thousand dollars a day?"

"Yup. But there's more. He just emailed me to charter another full day on the boat. He even asked if we could go out first thing tomorrow morning—only hours after Denise makes landfall."

"All the hotels have emptied. What sane person wants to go boating in a hurricane?"

"I offered to reschedule for next week. It's the slow season, so I can't turn down any business. But I won't be disappointed if he doesn't rebook."

The winds intensified, signaling the imminent arrival of another rainband, prompting Jack to head for the door.

"You'll be safe here, Mick. This remote controls the motorized hurricane shutters—you can leave them closed till I get back. And the generator will automatically kick in to power the fridge and A/C. Help yourself to anything. And thanks for finishing up my work outside. I'll see you in the morning."

■ ■ ■

Mick spent the next hour securing the exterior of Jack's place before showering and grabbing a bite to eat. He settled in front of the TV with a cold beer, distracting himself from the worsening conditions by flipping between the local news and the Weather Channel.

He noticed a framed photo displayed on the bookcase, showing Jack sitting next to a woman with her head resting on his shoulder. Her dark hair cut into a fashionable bob complemented her Mediterranean features. Bright, intelligent eyes mirrored the warmth and kindness of Jack's. She was a natural beauty, and the two of them seemed to fit together. Assuming the woman was Bea, Mick thought they might be more serious than Jack led him to believe.

It wasn't long until the howling winds became constant, causing the lights to flicker before they went out. The generator kicked in to power the essentials, but the TV didn't rate as a necessity. Despite living his whole life in Florida, he had never experienced a hurricane landfall. He felt secure at Jack's place—or as secure as you can be when winds gusting to one hundred miles per hour are bearing down. The groaning sounds coming from the nearby trees kept him on edge.

Despite his exhaustion after a long drive and a few hours of labor, Mick paced the room using a flashlight to navigate the darkness. He listened to the sound of a distant transformer blowing as the winds intensified. Tempted to look outside, he knew better than to open the front door.

Mick moved into his bedroom, resigned to a sleepless night as he lay still, eyes wide open, holding his breath each time flying debris battered the metal hurricane shutters. When the eyewall moved on land, the cottage began to shimmy and shake. The winds reached a crescendo, sounding like a freight train running through the front yard, then in an instant—it was quiet. The calm weather inside the eyewall lasted only minutes before the backside of the hurricane roared ashore, leaving him convinced the damage had to be considerable.

When the storm's wrath moved north, Mick, who was grateful to have a roof overhead, forced his body to relax in a desperate need for sleep. He decided against surveying outside in the dark of night in case of downed power lines and would venture out first thing in the morning.

●●●

Mick woke to a persistent, forceful knock at the front door. It took him a moment to remember where he was since the hurricane shutters kept the room in total darkness. He threw on some clothes then stumbled to the door. Daylight streamed into the cottage, blinding him, but once his eyes adjusted, he saw the woman from Jack's photo standing alone.

"Bea?"

"Jack never came home last night. Is he here?" She walked inside, dark circles under her eyes as they darted around the room.

"He dropped me off around six and was headed to the marina for a couple hours before going to your place."

"I talked to him after that. He said he was leaving soon, but then I lost power and cell service. I'm worried sick. It's just not like him. I keep telling myself something must've happened with *Zulu*, forcing him to stay."

"Let me grab my keys, and we'll head over to the marina together. I'm sure he's okay. He's the most seaworthy sailor I know." Mick put on a brave face, ignoring the uneasy feeling growing in the pit of his stomach.

CHAPTER 3

Bea climbed into Mick's Jeep as he cleared the driveway of storm debris, giving him a minute to collect his thoughts. Jack's golf cart parked at the back of the house looked undamaged at a glance. A more detailed inspection would have to wait.

Ever since their early days in the Navy, his friendship with Jack had been built on a lifetime of shared adventures and mutual respect. That's how he knew Jack would never leave Bea alone in the hurricane. Not if it was within his control.

"I'm sure you're right about Jack," Bea said as Mick buckled his seat belt. "He's probably helping a neighbor—always the hero. He was going to check on Earl and Betty since they were nervous about the hurricane—their sailboat is docked across from *Zulu*." Bea forced a smile, but her hands woven together in a tight grasp gave away her true emotions.

They drove in silence so Mick could concentrate on navigating around downed trees, palm fronds, garbage cans, and unidentifiable obstacles on their way through the deserted streets of Old Town. A few storm-weary locals wandered outside to inspect their homes and businesses for damage. Strict Florida building codes prevented against catastrophic loss, but Mick noticed missing siding and shingles and canvas awnings torn from their frames.

Closer to the waterfront, flooded low-lying roads forced them to make multiple detours. When they reached Front Street, two blocks away from Jack's section of the historic Key West marina, Bea's phone beeped, startling them both.

"Mick, my cell service just came back on. There's one text from Jack—it says he only had a couple things to do before heading to my place."

"What time was that?" Mick asked.

"Around eight o'clock. I'm so scared something's happened to him."

"Let's not get ahead of ourselves. This is Jack we're talking about. He's indestructible."

When they turned into the marina lot, they saw Jack's truck parked in its usual spot. Before Mick could come to a full stop, Bea jumped out and started running for the dock, calling Jack's name. Mick followed suit, catching up to her in time to board *Bravo Zulu* together. Ocean debris littered the deck. They continued to call out for Jack as they entered the cabin. Mick saw him first, laying on the floor, not moving, as Bea rushed ahead of him.

"No!" Bea screamed.

Mick ran to his side. "I can feel a pulse, Bea. He's alive. Call 911."

He avoided moving Jack based on his awkward body position since it was impossible to rule out a spinal injury. Blood matted in his hair appeared to be coming from a wound on the back of his head. Jack's pale face and cold extremities showed signs of shock, so Mick grabbed blankets off the bed to cover him. He placed his hand above Jack's mouth, counting each breath. They were slow and shallow but seemed steady.

"The ambulance is on its way," Bea said, "but the operator warned me they're handling a high volume of calls because of the hurricane." She knelt beside Jack, holding and stroking his hand. "Don't leave me, honey," she whispered. "We're all here for you. Just wake up. Wake up, please." Tears streamed down her face.

Mick had undergone extensive first aid training during his career as a Navy JAG lawyer and later at the Florida Department of Law Enforcement. Yet now, it all became useless—there was nothing he could do but sit and wait for the paramedics. He had never felt so helpless. Jack, who was always bigger than life, looked broken and frail.

The sound of approaching sirens assured them help was near.

"Bea, stay here, and I'll run out to the road to meet them."

He sprinted to the street-side of the marina, directing the ambulance to park as close as possible. The paramedics grabbed their gear as Mick urged them to hurry, leading the charge to get back to Jack. After entering the cabin, the first responders asked Bea to step aside in order for them to assess Jack's vitals. Mick held Bea to support her and could feel her entire body shaking. He found another blanket in the cabin and wrapped it around her shoulders.

"What's wrong? Will he be okay?" Bea asked.

"Ma'am, his breathing is weak, but his pulse is steady right now. We won't know more until we get him to the hospital. Does he have any medical history, or is he taking any medications?"

"He's healthy as an ox," Mick said. Bea confirmed with a nod of her head.

One paramedic placed an oxygen mask over Jack's face and started an IV, while the other man returned to the ambulance for a stretcher. Once monitors were connected, Mick relaxed as he listened to the steady beeping sound tracking Jack's heart rate.

The paramedics carefully and systematically moved Jack onto a spinal board before carrying him to the stretcher on the dock. With only one hospital in Key West, there was no question where they were headed.

"Bea, can you go with Jack in the ambulance?" Mick asked. "I'll get Jo, and we'll meet you there."

Bea nodded. "I need to be with him right now."

"Wait, I don't have her contact info. Can you give me her address? I think it's best if I tell her in person, plus her phone might not be working."

"She lives in the apartment above the vet hospital. Her door's at the back of the building. Just hurry, please." Bea followed the paramedic into the ambulance. A minute later, they pulled out of the marina with sirens on.

Mick bolted for his Jeep, relieved to see a weak cell phone signal. He'd spent enough time with Jack in Key West over the decades to have a general idea of how to find the vet hospital, so he didn't need to rely on GPS.

The adrenalin coursing through his body left him feeling anxious and a little numb. He took long, slow breaths to calm his nerves as he drove through Old Town. The streets were empty, and he had to focus to avoid hitting debris on the road. His decades of training kicked in, allowing him to keep a level head in the face of chaos. But it wasn't easy. Not when it involved his best friend.

CHAPTER 4

As Mick pulled into the narrow alley running behind the veterinary hospital, he saw Jo walking a dog. She stopped and pulled the dog close to her. When Mick realized she wouldn't recognize his car and his presence appeared threatening, he stepped outside, waving at her. "Jo, it's Mick."

She relaxed her stance, smiled, and resumed walking toward him. "How did you fare during the storm?"

He stood still, struggling to find his words. Oblivious to the reason for his visit, Jo closed the distance and greeted him with a hug.

"What are you doing here so early? Where's Jack?" She tilted her head to look around him at the car, but when she turned back, Mick couldn't hide the fear on his face.

"I'm sorry, Jo. He's been hurt and is on his way to the hospital in an ambulance right now. Bea's with him. The paramedics said his vitals are stable, but we don't know anything else."

Jo took a step back, her hands flying to her mouth. Mick reached for the dog's leash as she let go.

"What happened?" She grabbed his arm for support.

"I have no idea. We just found him on the boat a little while ago. He didn't make it to Bea's last night, and she came looking for him this morning. He was unconscious, and it looks like he has a head injury."

"Oh, no. We need to leave now. Let me put Bob in his kennel, and I'll be right back." She disappeared inside the hospital, returning a minute later, then jumped into Mick's idling Jeep.

Except for Jo's navigational directions, they drove to the Lower Keys Medical Center in silence. Mick kept glancing in her direction to check on her. It helped him focus and kept him from thinking ahead about worst-case scenarios.

He parked as close to the emergency doors as possible. They ran into the waiting area and found Bea staring at a clipboard full of medical paperwork. Her hands were shaking, and so far, she'd only filled in Jack's name. Jo sat beside her, gently taking the forms and pen from her hands before Bea crumbled into a sobbing heap in her arms.

Bea fought to collect herself, wiping her tears to dry her face. Mick, wanting to help, handed her a bottle of water he purchased from a lobby vending machine.

"Have they told you anything yet?" Jo asked.

"No, I wasn't able to stay with him after we arrived, and nobody's been back since." Her voice sounded thin and raspy.

Mick stood up. "I'll go see what's happening." The admissions clerk assured him the doctor would be out as soon as possible, and she had no updates to share.

In what felt like forever, but was probably only ten minutes, the doctor came out to speak with them. Jo presented herself as Jack's family and his medical power of attorney.

"I'm sorry to meet you all under these circumstances," the doctor said. "Jack has suffered a traumatic head injury and is in a coma right now. His vital signs are stable, and I've ordered a CT scan so we can determine if there's any intracranial hemorrhage or swelling. He also has a hairline fracture of his skull."

They took a moment to absorb the news.

"How long will it take to get the results?" Mick asked.

"Within the hour. We're not a level one trauma center, so depending on the CT, he may need to be transported to Jackson

Memorial Hospital in Miami. It's the closest hospital with the specialties to manage this type of brain injury."

"Can we see him?" Jo asked.

"Soon, but only for a moment. I know you have lots of questions, but we may need to act fast. Take this time to make a plan since only one of you can accompany Jack on the air ambulance. I need to go, but I'll update you shortly."

"Thanks," Mick said to the departing physician.

"I really want to go with Jack," Jo said. "But I just left Bob in the kennel without feeding him and ran out the door. I haven't talked with any of my staff this morning, and I need to find out if they're okay."

Bea stood, pushed her shoulders back, and cleared her throat. "Jo, I can go with Jack. I can do this, and I promise to update you the whole way. Go take care of your patients and staff, then you and Mick can drive to Miami together." Bea turned to Mick, looking for support for her plan.

"I'm here for whatever you need. I think driving is the fastest way to get there since the airport's likely still closed."

The anguish in Jo's face made it clear she was torn between her responsibilities and her desire to be with her brother. "I'm still hoping the CT will be clear, and he'll wake up any moment."

"I want that too, but you know Jack," Mick said. "He would want us to take care of business first. He'd be mad as hell if we were all running off hysterically in multiple directions."

"You're right. We have a plan, but hopefully we won't need to use it." Bea took each of their hands in hers.

Time seemed to stand still as they waited. They all jumped to their feet when the doctor came through the doors, waving for them to follow. He hurried to the treatment area of the ER, forcing them to run to keep up.

"Jack has a subdural bleed—a type of brain hemorrhage. Right now, it's not a surgical emergency, but he needs to be monitored closely by specialists. He's been intubated to secure his breathing before air transport. It's a standard precaution with head injuries, and I don't want you to be alarmed when you see him. You can stay with him for just a minute because we need to prep him for airlift to Miami. The chopper is inbound and will leave again as soon as he's on board. Have you decided who will go with him?"

"I'm going," Bea said.

"And we'll be right behind," Mick added. "Jack was in the Navy for over twenty-five years. Jo, I can get you the contact info to have his medical records transferred to Jackson Memorial." She nodded, but the vacant look on her face told him she hadn't heard a word he said. Mick turned to the doctor. "Would that help?"

"Yes, thank you. The Monroe County Sheriff's office confirmed the highway is open all the way to Miami. There's some storm damage between Summerland Key and Big Pine Key, but it should be clear after you pass that area."

The doctor led them into a private area of the treatment room, and all three gasped when they saw Jack lying in bed. He didn't look like Jack. Never in their wildest imagination could they picture him as anything other than strong and full of life. Monitors and IV lines connected to his body were nothing compared to the dehumanizing breathing tube and respirator. They were grateful for the doctor's warning, but it was still a shock. His head wound had been treated and bandaged. Thankfully, Mick thought his color looked better since finding him only an hour ago.

Jo rushed to his side, no longer able to hold back her emotions as her eyes filled with tears. Mick's heart went out to her. Jack was her big brother and always took care of her and everyone else, for that matter.

"Oh, Jack," she cried. "You need to hear me right now. I need you to be okay. We all need you to be okay. I love you, big brother. Please wake up." Bea and Mick stood on either side of Jo, to support each other and be close to Jack.

It wasn't much longer before the doctor came back in and told them it was time to go. Bea and Jo struggled to let go of Jack's hand as he was wheeled out of the room.

"Please be safe driving," Bea said. "If anything happens to either of you—" Her voice broke as she tried to hold back her tears. "I'll send you constant reports."

"You just worry about Jack, and we'll be there soon," Mick called out to Bea as she hurried to the waiting ambulance.

They thanked the emergency doctor then sprinted to the Jeep. Jo called her hospital manager but had to leave her a message. Concerns about how her staff had fared in the storm and whether their cell service was still down were allayed when her manager called back only a few minutes later. She'd been up on her roof to secure a tarp but would meet Jo in fifteen minutes to get the keys to her apartment.

"I'll drop you off, then go home and grab some supplies and a change of clothes. I can be ready when you are," Mick said.

As they turned onto U.S. 1, the sound of an overhead helicopter drew their gaze upward. Mick reached for her hand as they followed the air ambulance's flight path until it disappeared from view. The realization hit him like a physical blow—his best friend was on board, fighting for his life.

CHAPTER 5

Mick walked in the front door of Jack's cottage, fully aware he had limited time, but stood frozen in place—surrounded by photos and mementos highlighting a life well lived. He couldn't fathom a world without Jack Barton. He suppressed those fears and emotions for the moment and packed only the essentials. The lights were flickering on and off, so he left the door open to allow the sunlight to illuminate the front rooms, especially since the hurricane shutters kept the place dark. After deeming the coffee machine an essential appliance, he used the generator's power source to fill two travel mugs. He completed a quick walk around the property and concluded the hurricane had caused no major damage—there would be lots of clean-up to do when they returned but nothing urgent.

Before heading back across town, Jo texted to ask him for the Navy Medical Records contact information so she could arrange the transfer of Jack's files. Even if there was a delay in accessing his medical history, Mick doubted it would affect Jack's immediate care. He sent her the requested info and raced out the door.

A short while later, he parked behind the veterinary hospital and knocked on her door.

"Come on in, Mick. I'm upstairs."

Her apartment appeared to be a work in progress. Decorated with vintage mid-century furniture, walls showcased samples of paint colors, and all flat surfaces were covered with books and papers. "Jo, I'm here."

She popped her head out of the bedroom. "I'm almost done. My hospital manager is meeting me downstairs in five, then we can leave."

When she walked into the living room, bag over shoulder, Mick saw she had been crying. Only Jack's complete recovery would take away her pain, so he chose not to offer hollow platitudes.

Instead, she asked him, "How are you holding up?"

He smiled through strained eyes but struggled to find his voice.

"I know. I'm barely hanging on right now," she said before grabbing her keys and leading the way downstairs to the treatment area. "Mick, this is Amber, my friend and hospital manager." Amber waved at Mick from a nearby office. "I want to check on Bob one more time before we go."

Jo waved for him to follow then pointed to a large kennel. "You remember Bob from this morning? A local brought him in yesterday after finding him wandering around Stock Island. He didn't have a collar or a microchip, and we can't find his owners. Half the staff voted to name him Bo, and the other half voted for Bailey—they compromised on Bob, which morphed into Bob the Dog. The good samaritan posted signs in the area where she found him, but I'm not hopeful we'll locate his owner. Too often, people move out of town and leave their pet behind. It's horrific but a reality. The person who brought him in couldn't keep him because they have cats, but so far, he's the sweetest boy and young and healthy based on his exam."

Bob, a forty-pound mixed breed dog, had wiry, tan and brown fur. Distinctive black markings over large, brown eyes mimicked eyebrows, allowing his face to take on human-like expressions. He sat watching them, tilting his head to the side, as if he understood what they were saying. Mick thought he looked like Benji, the dog from the movies.

"Can I pet him?"

"Of course. Here are a couple cookies. He'll shake a paw for you."

Bob wagged his tail and stood when Mick walked into the kennel, accepting a head rub. He then sat without a command, gently taking the treat.

"What a great dog. It's hard to imagine someone's not out looking for him."

Amber joined them. "Don't worry about him, Doc. I'll be here all day, and I'll take him home with me each night. We can always postpone our grand opening if we need to."

"Let's hope it doesn't come to that. And thank you." Jo tugged at Mick's arm, pulling him away from Bob. "We've got to go." She threw her bag in the car's backseat, and they began their journey to Miami.

. . .

Any other day, the Overseas Highway through the Florida Keys would be a bucket list road trip. The clear, turquoise waters stretching across the Gulf of Mexico to the Atlantic Ocean straddled the narrow road, creating awe-inspiring views. The power of Hurricane Denise pushed all the moisture and bad weather north, leaving behind a crystal-clear Florida day—the consolation prize for surviving the storm. There'd even be a break from the humidity in these first few days.

A hurricane evacuation order issued by Monroe County, mandatory for tourists but voluntary for residents, resulted in a deserted U.S. 1. The only road in and out of the Keys would normally be full of bumper-to-bumper traffic.

Mick handed Jo a thermos of coffee. "I wasn't sure if any businesses would be open. There are a few granola bars in the glove box if you're hungry."

"I can't eat right now." She took a sip of coffee. "But thank you for this."

He nodded but wasn't sure what to say, so they continued in silence. After a few minutes, Jo leaned her head back against the seat and closed her eyes. He kept glancing at her, worried about her, but it was more than that. Dr. Joanna Barton captivated him. She seemed to sense his constant surveillance and opened her deep blue eyes, turning to him with a muted smile. He instinctively looked away.

"Thank you for driving. I'm such a mess right now. I can't get the image of Jack lying in the hospital bed out of my mind."

"It didn't look like him."

"I agree. And I'm worried about Bea. She's strong, but it's a lot for anyone."

"Jack and I didn't have much time to catch up. He put me to work at the marina the moment I arrived yesterday afternoon. It seems things are pretty serious with Bea." It was more question than statement.

Jo's smile extended, lightening her face. "They are. Jack is so happy. I wouldn't be surprised if he asks her to marry him."

"Wow. That's a big deal."

"What about you, Mick? Are you married?"

"No. I've come close twice."

"You're not one of those fear of commitment guys, are you?"

"Don't think so. I just haven't met the right person. My career hasn't helped. I'm away a lot, and the hours can be relentless. Or I guess I should say *were* relentless. I'm sort of retired."

"How can you be 'sort of retired'?"

"Long story, but if I didn't take early retirement, I was going to be fired. I guess I'm still wrapping my head around it."

"Oh, that's right. Jack told me you had some dust up with the governor. What's that all about, if you don't mind me asking?"

"No, that's fine. For the past decade, I worked as a special investigator with the FDLE, focused mostly on organized crime and racketeering cases." He didn't want to divulge all the details of the case but admitted recent subpoenas issued for a real estate developer and major donor to the governor's reelection campaign set off a firestorm.

"I'm sure I should know this, but what does FDLE stand for?"

"Florida Department of Law Enforcement."

"So, like an FBI agent but for the state?"

"Exactly. We work cases that cross over multiple jurisdictions. I considered fighting to keep my job, but the new commissioner made it clear he'd sideline me with busy work to keep me out of the governor's line of sight. I'd be forced to watch as less experienced agents struggled with dangerous cases with real-life consequences—I would have been miserable. In the end, it was time to go."

"I'm sorry. It sounds like you really miss it."

"It's all I've done since leaving the Navy. I'd never even thought about retiring, but I've got to figure it out. That's why Jack invited me to Key West. He could tell I needed to get my mind off things."

"That's Jack. I've been divorced for a year now and floundering in Boston. That's where my ex is from. When Ellie got sick, I started traveling back home whenever I could. Jack reminded me Key West was where I belonged. I'm still getting over losing Aunt Ellie. I can't lose Jack, too." Her eyes welled up with tears.

"Jo, my gut tells me he'll be okay. And I always trust my gut."

She nodded and wiped her face. They fell back into a comfortable silence until they passed Islamorada, and Jo's phone buzzed with an incoming text.

"It's Bea. They've landed and Jack's in the ICU. She asked when we'll be there."

"GPS says ninety minutes. Thankfully, the road is wide open. Did she say how he's doing?"

"He's the same, but she'll call us soon."

To distract from their darkest fears, they talked about day-to-day stuff. Jo shared her plans for the hospital grand opening scheduled for Monday. She could postpone it if she had to, but invitations had been sent, and the local paper committed to cover the event.

They pulled in for gas at the first station open for business along the Overseas Highway in Key Largo—a sign that things were getting back to normal. The residents faced an extensive clean-up process, but they'd been here before, and nothing would derail their recovery. Mick filled the tank while Jo grabbed them something to drink. The slow pace through the Keys would change once they hit the open road on the Florida Turnpike.

Jo kept checking her phone, desperate for word about Jack. When they passed Homestead, Bea called.

Jo dropped her head and listened. Eventually, she asked, "Can I speak with his doctor first?" Mick couldn't hear the conversation, but the tears rolling down her face told him everything. "Okay, I'll wait for his call. Please tell Jack I love him." She hung up, taking a moment to find her voice.

"What's happening?"

"They did another CT scan, and Jack's hemorrhage has worsened. They're scheduling him for emergency surgery. Bea said they can't wait until we get there, but the doctor will be calling in a few minutes." She dropped her face into her hands, unable to hold back the tide of emotions.

Mick remained silent—nothing he could say seemed adequate for the moment. Gripped by fear but not wanting to burden her with his own emotions, he did the only thing within his control. Turning his attention to the road ahead, he accelerated, pushing well past the limit, as he sped north toward Miami.

CHAPTER 6

Minutes after exiting the turnpike, Jo received a call from Dr. Marcus, the neurosurgeon at Jackson Memorial. He shared the essential details of the latest scans showing an urgent need for surgery to relieve the pressure on Jack's brain in order to avoid permanent damage. Jo's medical background allowed her to ask questions beyond Mick's comprehension. Her verbal consent provided the go-ahead to prep for surgery. "Do everything you can to save Jack's life."

As soon as Jo hung up, Bea called, and Jo put the phone on speaker so Mick could hear.

"I'm scared," Bea said.

"Me too. Dr. Marcus made it clear we don't have a choice. I understand why they can't wait for us—but I really wanted to see him first."

"I'm going to splash some water on my face, then I'll be in the main reception lounge outside the ICU—where he'll be coming back after surgery. Just please get here as soon as you can."

They drove the last few miles with their own thoughts. Despite breaking all speed limits, Mick had failed to get there in time. He felt as if he had let Jo down.

They pulled into the hospital parking deck and hurried inside to find Bea sitting alone in a quiet corner of the ICU lounge, staring out the large windows. The bright, cheerful space felt at odds with the anxious mood of those waiting for news about their loved ones.

Bea stood when she saw them, prompting Jo to run across the room. They held each other then turned to pull Mick into their embrace, acknowledging his status as an honorary member of the family.

"Did the doctor say how long the surgery would take?" Mick asked, the lump in his throat making it painful to speak.

"He did, but to be honest, I didn't register all of what he was saying. It's like time stood still ever since we boarded the air ambulance."

Jo shifted her chair next to Bea's and put her arm around Bea's shoulder. "It's a lot. Thank you for handling everything."

Mick, a man of action, felt helpless as he was forced to sit around and wait. He had to get his emotions under control. Expressing his anger at the situation wouldn't help anyone, and he really wanted to be there for Jo and Bea.

"I'm going to find us something to eat and drink. Any requests?" he asked.

They both declined food but welcomed a coffee. Mick knew better—if they didn't take care of themselves, they'd be no help to Jack. Amazingly, the hospital cafeteria had an authentic Cuban coffee shop, so he loaded up with three café con leches and guava pastries. The most that even he could stomach right now.

"Thanks, Mick." Jo accepted the delicacies with a smile. "I didn't think I was hungry, but these look delicious."

They savored their sweet treats and caffeine boost as they waited for word about Jack. Jo occupied herself by researching traumatic brain injuries on her phone, but Mick couldn't sit. He paced up and down the hallway, checking back every few minutes. With each passing hour, their hopes for a speedy recovery were fading.

"I can't take this much longer." Jo turned her phone face down on the table. "I really need to see him with my own eyes, to know he's going to be okay."

"The doctor said he wouldn't be awake right after surgery." Bea stopped talking when she noticed a man walk into the waiting room. "That's Jack's doctor—Dr. Marcus."

All three jumped to their feet. Dr. Marcus put them at ease with a kind smile, but they continued to hold their breath.

"Jack's surgery was successful. He's in recovery, and his neurological status is stable. We removed the hematoma, but we'll have to keep him in an induced coma for the next 24 to 48 hours. It's a necessary precaution to control any risk of swelling. His brain needs time to rest and heal."

"What happens after he's out of the coma?" Jo asked.

"We'll continue to monitor and support him, and our goal is for him to wake up quickly."

"But what if he doesn't?" Bea asked, barely able to choke out the words.

"We go hour by hour and day by day. Right now, there are no indications why he can't make a full recovery, but we won't be able to fully assess him until he wakes up."

"Can we see him?" Mick asked.

"Soon. But only one at a time while he's in the ICU, and you'll need to keep your visits short."

"Okay. Thank you, Doctor Marcus. We appreciate everything you've done for Jack," Jo said. "When will you update us again?"

"Jack will be under constant monitoring, and I'll contact you if there's a change. The ICU nurse will come and get you when it's okay to see him."

"We'll be here around the clock until we can take Jack home with us," Bea said.

The three of them sat together in the waiting area not saying much. They were all in their own personal head space thinking of Jack.

When the ICU nurse appeared, she greeted them, advising they could go in one at a time, so Jo went first. When she returned, her face was red from crying, but she was smiling.

"How is he?" Bea asked urgently.

"Well, it's a lot. His head is completely bandaged, and he's hooked up to a bunch of machines and monitors. It's really hard to get close to him. He looked peaceful though. I read that coma patients can hear what's going on around them, so I talked to him and held his hand. Deep down, I felt he was going to be okay. It might be my Barton gut instinct talking to me. Jack always said it was one of our greatest family traits. Bea, you can go in now if you're ready."

"I'm so worried. If there's a chance Jack can hear me, I want to be strong for him."

"He already knows you're strong. You'll feel better once you see him," she said reassuringly.

As Bea walked away, Jo turned to Mick. "You've been taking care of the both of us, but I know this is really hard for you, too."

"I think I'm in denial. Like this is happening to somebody else. I don't do well when I'm forced to wait around."

Jo smiled. "You and Jack are two of a kind. That would also be his biggest frustration right now."

Bea returned, signaling Mick was next. "Being able to tell him I love him made me feel better. I just wish I could've stayed."

He took a deep breath and walked into the ICU. Seeing Jack lying motionless, surrounded by a multitude of life-support machines, hit him like a gut punch. He felt awkward and uncertain about what to do. He wanted Jack to wake up and joke around with him—like old times. He eventually found his voice, recounting one of their funniest and most famous navy stories. They'd each told the tale a million times before, but he was certain Jack would enjoy hearing it again. Ten minutes flew by when the nurse kindly asked him to leave.

In between visits, they devised a game plan. Mick found a hotel only a couple blocks away. They would need to rest and shower, and this way, they could go in shifts. He paid for an early check-in and returned with keys.

"It's an extended stay hotel. There's a separate bedroom with two beds and a pullout for me in the living room. I stocked the mini kitchen with snacks and drinks."

"Thanks, Mick. But I can't imagine leaving the hospital right now," Jo said.

"Me either," Bea said.

"I understand, but it's only a five-minute walk. We don't know how many days we're going to be here, and I wanted to have a place if we need it."

"You're right. Bea and I spoke with our teams, and they have things covered back home. I've put the grand opening on hold for now."

They fell into a strange sort of routine. Brief visits doled out every few hours kept them tied to the lounge. During his third run to the coffee shop, Mick glimpsed his disheveled appearance in a mirror. He couldn't convince the others to take a break, so he headed to the hotel for a quick shower and change of clothes. By the time he returned, it had only been half an hour, but he'd missed the latest update from Dr. Marcus.

"He sounded optimistic," Jo said. "Jack's stable, and there are no further signs of bleeding. They're keeping him in the medically induced coma until he's reassessed in the morning."

It really was the best news they could hope for. Late into the evening, Mick convinced them to get some rest while he stayed put, but it was like pulling teeth. They eventually relented, leaving the hospital together. Jo was the first to return, close to midnight.

"Hi." Jo surprised Mick as he dozed sitting in an uncomfortable chair.

"Hey. Were you able to get some sleep? Where's Bea?"

"I had a quick nap and a long hot shower. Thanks again for the room. Not having to think about all that was a gift. Bea finally fell asleep, so I left her a note and said I would call her in a few hours to check on her."

"I'm glad. I think she went into shock this morning when we found Jack. It didn't help that she'd been up all night waiting for him to come home. She hasn't slept in two days."

"I didn't even think about that," Jo said. "We're all in survival mode, I guess."

Bea reappeared at dawn wearing a change of clothes Jo had packed for her. She carried a tray of coffee. "I think you all need this more than me."

They were contemplating a refill when Dr. Marcus walked into the lounge.

"There's been no further swelling or hemorrhage, so we've started the process to bring him out of the induced coma. After that, it's a waiting game."

"We understand, Doctor. Do you have any idea how long it will take him to regain consciousness?" Mick asked.

"That's up to Jack. It's not an exact science—it could be hours or days. I'm sorry I can't offer you more reassurances."

Jo pulled the doctor aside to consult with him privately. Mick watched as she did most of the talking. Her expressions and body language relaxed as she ended the conversation.

"What was that all about?" Bea asked.

"I wanted to get more information about what to expect once Jack wakes up. Traumatic brain injury cases that make full recoveries still need physical and occupational therapy support. It could even include speech therapy. Thankfully, Jack's cottage is all on one level, and he has that huge walk-in shower. I think it would be easy to set him up at home since Key West has a neurologist to manage his care and the services he might require."

"Oh, I hadn't thought about all that," Bea said.

"It's okay—we can handle it. And Jack has an army, or should I say, a navy of friends to lend a hand."

"Jack and I never talked about it, but I can stick around until he's ready to kick me out." Mick smiled.

"Thanks. That means so much to both of us," Jo said. "Knowing that you're with him. We would love for you to stay at the house." Discussing their plans for the weeks ahead brought hope. Planning Jack's recovery gave them purpose and tamped down the fear that would creep back in as they waited. They needed him to wake up.

CHAPTER 7

Jo sat upright in her chair. "I just realized we haven't told Wayne and Michelle about Jack's injury. They'll be devastated to hear the news." She picked up her phone and connected with them right away.

Mick leaned over to Bea to ask, "Is she calling Wayne Michaels?"

Bea nodded. Mick had met Wayne, Jack's closest friend in town, on previous visits over the years but had never met his wife.

"Thankfully, they weathered the hurricane with no serious damage," Jo said after hanging up. "I had to talk them out of jumping in their car and driving to Miami. I understand—I'd want to do the same thing. But Wayne offered to check on Jack's cottage, which was nice of him. He and Jack have spare keys to each other's places in case of an emergency.

They continued to take turns visiting with Jack, hoping their familiar voices would help guide him back. When Jo returned to the lounge with a smile on her face, they realized something was different.

"I noticed Jack's eyes flutter, so I squeezed his hand and kept talking, and then it happened—his fingers moved. I called for the nurse, and she said those were very encouraging signs. They're assessing him now."

Bea sprang to her feet and hugged her. "I've been holding my breath since I got on that helicopter with Jack. Now, I feel it in my bones—he's going to be okay," Bea said.

"He's too stubborn and strong to be anything else," Mick said grinning and finally allowing his shoulders to relax.

They found it difficult to sit and wait, Mick most of all. He walked outside for a change in scenery and to continue his pacing. When he returned, Dr. Marcus had just entered the waiting room.

"Jack is out of his coma, and his initial neurologic assessments are positive—he's stable, and we've removed his breathing tube."

Bea hugged the doctor then stepped back and grabbed Jo and Mick with shaking hands.

The doctor smiled before continuing. "We often can't fully determine the status of his injury until he's completely awake. He was a little agitated during his evaluation, which is normal, so we've given him a mild sedative. Jack will probably cycle in and out of sleep as his recovery progresses. For now, he'll be staying in the ICU."

They were overjoyed, as if the weight of the world had been lifted. Dr. Marcus warned them to expect Jack to be disoriented when he woke up. To help keep him calm, it would be ideal for one of them to be there around the clock.

"I knew it!" Jo pumped her fist. "He *was* waking up. But I need to see his eyes open and hear his voice, then I'll know everything will be all right."

Bea put her hand to her heart and took a deep breath. "You were right, Jo. It's a miracle."

Mick agreed. "I'm sure he'll be bossing you around in no time."

Jo chuckled, and Mick felt relieved to see her laughing again.

■ ■ ■

As they took turns at Jack's bedside, they became convinced he was aware of their presence. Occasionally, he would open his eyes and look at them before falling back asleep. In the early evening, Jack woke up briefly, and after seeing Jo, he said her name and managed half a smile. She told them it was the best sound in the world. They each had similar experiences to report.

In need of a caffeine boost, Mick volunteered for a coffee run. While balancing three hot drinks and bottles of water, he fumbled the carrying tray then scrambled to keep them from spilling. The coffees remained upright, but the water bottles toppled on their side. And that's when images of Jack's cabin on *Bravo Zulu* flashed before his eyes. The realization stunned him, and he sat to collect his thoughts.

As best as he could recall, none of the cups or items sitting on Jack's galley counter had been knocked over. How was that even possible? A hurricane strong enough to throw a huge man like Jack across a room would also topple lightweight items that weren't anchored down.

He focused hard, trying to picture the cabin that morning. Finding Jack had consumed all his attention, so he couldn't trust his memory. Perhaps he'd overlooked other items scattered around the cabin—but he doubted it. Years of experience as an investigator had trained him to take in details in an instant. He would have to wait until he got back to the marina in Key West to know for sure.

Mick entered the lobby and found Jo on the phone. He assumed it was her hospital manager on the other end because she mentioned Bob the Dog.

Jo hung up and looked at him. "Sounds like the power and services are mostly back on in Key West," she said. "A lot of superficial damage has been reported but nothing catastrophic."

"That's good. Is Bob okay?"

Jo smiled at his concern for the dog. "He's fine. My grand opening is in two days. What should I do? I've been advertising the event, and I'm worried clients will show up, and we'll be closed."

"Jo, I understand how Jack's brain works well enough to say that he'd be furious if you missed your big day."

"I don't disagree. But I can't leave him right now."

Bea joined them having apparently overheard the tail end of their conversation. "All Jack's been talking about for weeks is how you're fulfilling your dream. Why don't you two drive home tonight so you can be there for your event. I can hold down the fort until you get back. Jack knows we're here and even responded to me just now, even though he keeps his eyes closed most of the time. Go in and talk to him about it."

"This is an impossible decision. I'll go and see Jack then decide." The pained expression on her face made it clear how tormented she felt about leaving her big brother right now.

After Jo left the lobby, they continued to make plans under the assumption she would be returning to Key West that night. Since Bea would be staying with Jack, day and night, she went to the hotel to lie down for a few minutes as Mick had suggested.

While waiting for Jo, Mick closed his eyes and tried to replay the morning after the hurricane. He struggled to recall the state of the cabin, and it bothered him. He'd assumed Jack suffered a horrible accident, but what if that's not what happened? He wouldn't know for sure until he could get back to the marina and see for himself.

"Mick." Jo put her hand on his shoulder.

"Oh, sorry. I didn't see you."

She'd been crying but smiled through her tears. "You were a million miles away just now. Anything to share?"

"No, just tired. What did you decide?

"Jack was sleeping, but I told him all about my plans for the grand opening. He tapped my hand with his finger, I think to get my attention, then grinned at me and told me to go. That's all he said—just 'Go', then he squeezed my hand and fell back asleep. I really think he'd been listening to me and took it all in."

"I'm sure he was, and he made his wishes known. Jo, you have to be there—we can figure out the rest afterward."

"I'll go. But I need to talk with Bea first. I don't feel right about leaving her all alone."

At that moment, Bea reappeared with two bags in hand. One was Mick's travel bag and the other was Jo's.

"Did I hear my name?" she asked.

They didn't have to worry about her. In front of them stood a brave, strong woman who loved Jack completely. He was in good hands.

"I'm upset I'll miss the hospital's grand opening, but I know it's going to be a huge success." Bea handed them their bags. "I've packed up your stuff. Mick, here are the keys to the boat and truck. Jack had them in his pocket when he was admitted. You've got a long drive ahead, and you need some rest before your big day."

"What about your gallery? What's going to happen while you're here?" Jo asked.

"My assistant has everything under control. She can keep the place open for me indefinitely. I don't have any events on the calendar this month. It's the slow season, and we can cut back our hours and operate on a shorter day." Bea reassured them she'd be able to handle any gallery business from Miami and would keep them updated about Jack.

Jo failed to hold back her tears as she hugged Bea tight. She grabbed her bag and followed Mick to the parking garage, but then she stopped and turned to look at Bea over her shoulder. He wondered if she'd changed her mind about leaving until she hurried to catch up to him.

Mick volunteered to drive and she didn't argue. He listened in as she called and spoke with all her staff members. She shared the terrific news about Jack regaining consciousness and discussed last-minute details that had yet to be handled before the hospital doors reopened to the public.

By the time they exited the turnpike for U.S. 1, heading south, Jo fell asleep. Although Mick was hungry and needed a pit stop, he didn't want to risk waking her, so he continued through to Key West. When he pulled up to the back of her hospital, Jo's eyes slowly opened.

Yawning, she said, "Thank you for driving." She grabbed his arm, pulling him close to kiss him, her lips lingering on his cheek. "Don't worry about Bob," she whispered. "I'll keep him upstairs with me until we reopen."

They locked eyes, she smiled then reached into the backseat to grab her bag. By the time she was halfway to the hospital door, he'd recovered from their moment and rolled down his window.

"Ring me anytime tonight if you get news about Jack."

"I will. See you tomorrow." She waved then disappeared inside.

What was he thinking? How could he even consider starting a romantic relationship with Jo? She was Jack's sister, and that dynamic alone was fraught with pitfalls. The possibility of dating Jo had never come up before. She'd either been away at school, engaged, or married ever since Mick first met her. What would Jack think? That would be an uncomfortable conversation he'd rather not contemplate. It would be smart to wait and see how things unfolded before acting on his feelings for Jo.

CHAPTER 8

Traffic was light through Old Town. Restaurants and shops had reopened, but it appeared many of the tourists who were forced to cancel their vacation plans because of the hurricane had yet to return. Live music streamed from the bars on Duval Street, but Mick couldn't help wondering who the musicians were playing for.

He would have loved nothing more than to head straight to Jack's place and collapse into bed, but he wouldn't be able to rest until he'd double-checked things on *Zulu*. He couldn't remember whether he'd even closed the door to the cabin when he and Bea rushed to follow the paramedics as they loaded Jack into the ambulance.

He turned right onto Front Street and slowly drove the last few blocks before reaching the marina parking lot. He dreaded returning to the boat without Jack. He'd done his best to avoid reliving the traumatic memory of finding him unconscious only two days ago. Watching over Jo and Bea gave him a necessary distraction, even though neither of them needed taking care of. Actually, if he was honest with himself, he hadn't dealt with his own emotions. He mastered the art of pushing away his feelings, a true lesson in avoidance. Jack was his best friend, and he couldn't imagine this world without him.

The streets were too dark to discern if there'd been any notable hurricane damage to nearby businesses. He parked next to Jack's truck and, after checking the exterior of the vehicle, turned on the engine. It started on the first try. He then used his phone's flashlight to navigate the darkened pathway to the waterfront. Normally well lit, the effects of the storm persisted with spotty power outages.

Glancing across the marina, it appeared every third boat had its deck and cabin lights on. Any other evening, people would be sitting outside, visiting with their neighbors. It was certainly quieter than the lively place he was accustomed to.

As he approached *Zulu*, his mind's eye played out the scene as he remembered it. He'd been desperate to find Jack and had failed to take in any other details, including the debris scattered around the deck. Shocked to discover he'd had the wherewithal to lock the cabin door, he pulled Jack's keys from his pocket and stepped inside.

He pictured Jack lying lifelessly next to the dining table—a bloodstain on the floor marked the exact location. Mick quickly turned away, preferring to deal with it after he had his bearings. Details he'd failed to notice while he rendered first aid now stood out to him.

The cabin was spotless, as it always was with Jack. Most things inside a boat were battened down, but the few loose items that had been sitting on the galley counter or next to his bed in the main berth were exactly where you'd expect—likely where Jack had placed them. Nothing had fallen over, and no items were knocked on the floor of the cabin other than Jack's water bottle and his sunglasses. Mick assumed he would have kept those specific items close to him as a regular course of business.

His head swam, bad enough he had to press his hands against the wall to steady himself. When he moved outside on deck for some fresh air, his breathing edged closer to hyperventilating. He forced himself to take deep breaths. The faint sound of music coming from Turtle Krawls distracted him from the panic rising inside. He used the music to shift his focus as he tried to decipher what tune was playing. And it worked. His heart rate slowed, and his mind cleared.

The upside of his long, successful career in law enforcement meant he was good at his job. But there was a downside. He had a suspicious mind, often seeing deception and ulterior motives where they didn't exist. It likely contributed to his status as a bachelor. He found it hard to let his guard down even when surrounded by his closest friends.

That mind was working overtime right now. There was no way a storm packing enough force to throw a huge, muscular man across a room resulting in life-threatening injuries wouldn't also toss much lighter items around the cabin. Absolutely no way. So, why were magazines, salt and pepper shakers, a drinking glass, and a teakettle sitting exactly where they belonged. It made no sense, unless something else happened on board that night.

He wished he could speak to Jack and ask him directly. Perhaps there was an innocent explanation for it all, but until Jack said otherwise, he would stay convinced this wasn't an accident.

Mick glanced across the dock to see if any neighbors were around but didn't see anyone. Bea had mentioned Jack's plans to check on his friends, Earl and Betty, before the storm. They owned the sailboat across the dock, but their cabin lights were dark.

Eventually, he'd have to go back in and clean up Jack's blood but not tonight. He couldn't face that task right now. The moonless sky combined with minimal lighting meant he'd have to wait for daylight to inspect the hull and exterior of the boat for damage. With nothing more to do, he locked the cabin door and left the marina.

Instead of walking toward his car, Mick wandered along the Key West Historic Seaport. The smell of garlic and seafood permeated the air. Despite the late hour, most of the restaurants were still open. He couldn't remember if he'd eaten lunch, and now it was past dinner. His stomach growled in protest. The walkway eventually made a hard right at the end of Elizabeth Street, landing him in front of the Conch Republic Seafood Company. The large open-air restaurant glowed with warm lighting, accented by the elevated tropical fish tank that stretched the length of the dining room. Mick sat at the bar, picking a spot absent of patrons on either side of him. He wanted solitude and a quick meal.

"What can I get you?" the bartender asked.

"I'll have whatever local ale you have on tap and a cheeseburger with fries." He didn't have the energy to look over the menu.

The bartender pulled a pint and placed it in front of Mick. He took a drink and turned to face the harbor, staring out past the boats moored in the marina. This part of town had some foot traffic thanks to its proximity to Duval Street and the large, upscale hotels near Mallory Square. A few pedestrians gathered along the dock, watching as giant tarpon swam through the glow cast by the underwater transom lights of a fishing boat.

He set down his empty glass just as his food arrived.

"Get you another?" the bartender asked.

Mick waved him off. "No, thanks. But I'll take an iced tea."

As he finished the last bite, his eyes grew heavy. Sleepless nights and raw emotions had drained his battery. He paid the tab before he was too tired to get up off the bar stool. The walk seemed longer back to his car, but that was likely his full belly slowing him down.

When he pulled into Jack's driveway, he noticed the porch lights were on and the hurricane shutters had been opened. All the debris that had been strewn across the front yard had miraculously disappeared. He assumed Wayne had been there to check on things. The back yard was only accessible through the house, but an inspection of that area would have to wait until morning. Mick stumbled in the front door, dropped his keys on the counter, plugged his phone into the charger, then landed face down and fully clothed on his bed. Sleep came in less than a minute.

CHAPTER 9

Mick woke at dawn, feeling unsettled and disoriented. The details surrounding the scene inside Jack's cabin that had been nagging him since his epiphany in the hospital cafeteria lingered. But after running on pure adrenalin and limited sleep, he struggled to organize his thoughts.

Sunlight streamed through the bedroom window, forcing him out of bed. After a hurricane blew through town, it typically left behind a clear and sunny day. That glorious weather did nothing to counter his exhaustion. He'd slept for only a few hours over the past three days, and it would take more than a night's sleep to catch up.

He kept checking his phone for updates about Jack, but there was nothing. He told himself that no news meant things were stable, and since it was still too early to call, he dragged himself to the kitchen and brewed a pot of extra-strong coffee. He'd be better off if he stuck to his morning running routine, but he didn't have it in him, instead opting for a long, hot shower. It helped, but nothing could erase the effects of recent days. After finishing his third cup, he redirected his limited energy to making a mental checklist.

Even though Wayne had cleared the debris in the front yard, he wanted to survey Jack's property for any storm damage. After leaving in a rush for Miami, he couldn't be certain whether he'd missed something. To help take his mind off things, he'd focus on tasks and keep busy. Mick did a detailed inspection of the cottage and surrounding fences, and everything appeared to be intact. He concentrated his efforts on picking up fallen limbs from a banyan tree in the backyard, and when he'd piled the last load into a garbage can, Jo called.

"Hey. I just spoke with Bea and Dr. Marcus. Jack is more awake this morning, but he keeps slipping between sleep and wakefulness."

"Is he in any pain?"

"No. She said he's comfortable and seems to be aware of stuff going on around him. They'll assess him again this afternoon, so we should get more details later."

Mick didn't understand how she did it. Her voice sounded positive and full of energy.

"That's the best news. I've been awake forever, worrying—I think it's the *not knowing.* I wish we could be there to see him for ourselves."

"I'm planning to drive back to Miami as soon as the grand opening wraps up. Jack said my name this morning, and when Bea reminded him where I was, he nodded and gave her a thumbs up. He asked about *Zulu,* and when he found out you were taking care of everything at home and the marina, he said, 'Good,' and fell back asleep."

"We might not be by his side, but I believe he's aware we're here for him. And I agree with Bea. He'd be disappointed if you didn't go ahead with your hospital plans."

"I have to believe that so I can be at my best for this event—but it's hard."

"You've got this, Jo. All your work will pay off."

"Thanks. How about getting together for an early dinner?"

"Sounds great."

"It shouldn't take too long, but I have to swing by the pharmacy and pick up a prescription for one of Ellie's friends. Jack's been taking care of her, helping around the house, going grocery shopping, and driving her to doctor's appointments."

"Doesn't surprise me. I'm heading over to the marina. I only stayed on board last night for a few minutes—to check the cabin lock and make sure the boat's still floating. I'll be there all day cleaning up. And I want to look around since I didn't take it all in the morning we found Jack. Being back on the boat might help me make sense of his injury."

"Okay." Jo paused before continuing. "Sometimes bad things happen to good people. It may never make sense. Accidents rarely do. What do you expect to find?"

"I'm not sure. It's probably the investigator in me, needing to check all the boxes before moving on." He didn't want to tell Jo yet about his suspicions that the storm had not been the cause of Jack's accident. He first needed to piece things together for himself.

"*Bravo Zulu* is Jack's baby. Thanks for taking care of her. I'll text you when I'm heading your way."

■ ■ ■

Mick walked to the marina so he could drive Jack's truck home when he was done. As far as he could tell, it seemed like business as usual. A tourism slogan described Key West as *Close to Perfect and Far from Normal.* The town had its own quirky, tropical vibe. Most of the vacationers had returned, and the cruise ships were back in port. Early morning crowds filled the shops and restaurants along Duval Street as the Conch Tour train resumed transporting tourists through the historical highlights of Old Town. Resilient locals understood their entire economy had been built around tourism, and they weren't going to let the weather impede their livelihood.

As he approached the waterfront, he expected to see more damage from the storm surge, but he found limited signs a hurricane made landfall only a few days before. Any debris around the docks had been removed.

Bravo Zulu, a navy term meaning a job well done, was now Mick's responsibility, at least until Jack returned. When Jack bought the forty-three-foot Hatteras, Mick knew he'd fulfilled a lifelong dream. Its navy-blue hull, polished to a high shine, showcased the sleek lines of the sport fishing yacht upgraded to meet Jack's exacting standards.

Mick passed by tourists walking along the dock to check out their options for a sunset cruise or snorkeling trip. Before he could board *Bravo Zulu*, some of Jack's neighbors approached him. Earl and Betty were the first to introduce themselves and inquire about Jack. Everyone on the dock was aware of his injury but were otherwise speculating about his status.

Earl's brow scrunched up with worry. "I can't believe what's happened. He spent all that time helping us get ready for the storm. I hope that's not why he was here so late working on his own prep."

"Not at all, Earl. He wanted to wait until everyone had cleared out of the marina before tying his last few lines, as they would become a tripping hazard on the dock once he was finished. Jack wouldn't put anyone in danger, including himself," Mick replied emphatically.

"How long will he be in the hospital?" Betty asked.

By this time, a few more of Jack's neighbors joined in on the conversation. Even Abe ventured over to the group. It became obvious Abe didn't normally socialize with the gang based on the looks of surprise they gave each other as he approached.

"We're taking it day by day. Jack's recovering from a coma and a serious head injury. His doctors will continue to assess him. He's in the ICU, and Bea is there with him."

"We're so sorry, Mick. Is there anything we can do? Can we visit him?" Earl asked on behalf of the group.

"Oh, I wasn't clear. He's not at the Key West hospital. They airlifted him to Miami on Friday morning. We're hoping to get him back home as soon as possible."

The update had a sobering effect on Jack's neighbors as the seriousness of his injury sunk in. Everyone offered to help any way they could, then the group dispersed, leaving Mick standing alone with Abe.

"So, Jack's still in a coma, or is he wakin' up yet?" Abe asked matter-of-factly, no hint of concern in his tone.

"He's no longer in a coma." Mick didn't volunteer any more details.

"Oh. Well, best wishes to Jack." He turned and walked back to his boat.

Mick tried to reconcile Abe's interest in Jack's health with his first impression of the guy. He sounded disingenuous. Jack's easygoing personality meant he was often misjudged, especially by guys like Abe. Jack said he preferred it that way—it gave him a tactical advantage. In reality, Jack's fierce intelligence meant nothing got past him unless he wanted it to. And he had made it clear he didn't like Abe. Mick shrugged off the conversation as he boarded *Zulu*.

Plant and ocean debris cluttered the deck, but everything important appeared to be in its place. Mick stared at the cabin, mustering the courage to step back inside. He held his breath as he unlocked the door. Overcome by a flood of emotions, he forced his feelings to the side.

After walking through the cabin, he drew the same conclusion he had the previous night. He couldn't reconcile how only Jack had been thrown so forcefully. It defied logic and science. And Bea had confirmed he planned to take shelter at her place before the worst of the storm came ashore. People often underestimate the power of a hurricane, but Jack wasn't most people.

It was in Mick's nature to tackle the hardest jobs first—get them out of the way. He second guessed that approach as he looked at the bloodstain on the cabin floor. There was no way he'd let Jo come on board and see it, but years spent working to preserve crime scene evidence dictated his next steps. He meticulously photographed the entire cabin and interior before using cleaning supplies from the galley to remove all signs of Jack's trauma. He cleaned only the blood-stained floor directly where Jack had been laying and left the rest of the cabin untouched.

Once he'd finished, he moved on deck to recalibrate before tackling the next task. He preferred a day of hard, physical labor to the job he just completed. Mick looked around and noted the lines Jack had tied before the storm were still secure. On the stern deck, he found two lines hidden under a palm frond, still partially coiled. These were the two lines Jack specifically waited to tie off until after everyone had left the marina on the night of the hurricane. Why would he leave these lines untied if the strongest part of the storm was bearing down? Jack's injury must have occurred before he finished securing *Bravo Zulu*. It was the only explanation. Accidents can happen, but Jack was that guy who took precautions to ensure accidents never happened.

Mick walked over to Earl and Betty's sailboat and found them sitting on deck.

"Can I ask you a question?"

"Sure, Mick."

"What time did you return to the marina after the storm?

"It probably wasn't long after you left with Jack. We passed an ambulance on the way into town," Betty said.

"When you arrived, did you notice whether any of Jack's lines were still tied across the dock, blocking your access? I'm trying to figure out if somebody untied his lines after the storm."

"His lines were just like they are now," Earl said. "None of them crossed over the dock. We talked about going on board to clean *Zulu*, but Jack's so particular, and we didn't want to mess anything up."

"Were you the first ones back on Friday, or were other people here already?"

"We were first and have been here ever since except leaving for a couple meals at Turtle Krawls," he said. "Why do you ask?"

"It's probably nothing. I guess I'm just trying to make sense of the senseless."

Earl had a puzzled look on his face. "Do you want us to give you a hand with *Zulu*?"

"I may take you up on that offer. Let's see how far I get today. Jack's sister, Jo, is coming by later. Her hospital grand opening is tomorrow, then she's heading back to Miami to be with Jack. I'm not sure if I'll be going with her. Can you keep watch over things when I'm not around?" Mick handed them his business card with contact numbers. "Call me anytime."

"Of course. Anything for Jack. Please tell Jo congratulations from us."

...

Mick had spent enough time on boats to know the routine: rinse, scrub, wipe down, repeat. As the sun moved overhead, the oppressive heat and humidity climbed. Mick turned the hose on himself to cool down.

Jo messaged him with her plan for the day. The hospital staff were busy prepping for tomorrow's grand opening, but she still planned to come by the marina for an early dinner. That gave him the day to work on *Bravo Zulu*. Mick took great care in detailing the exterior, giving it the same attention Jack would have given her. Throwing himself into the work helped calm his mind. Sitting around worrying about Jack wouldn't help anyone. Before carting a load to the marina dumpster, he grabbed the boat keys hanging on a hook in the cabin. Then it hit him. Where was Jack's cell phone?

CHAPTER 10

Jack's belongings, including his keys and wallet, had been returned after his ER admission but no phone. Mick searched the cabin and the cockpit but didn't find it. Jack would have kept his phone in the deep pocket of his cargo shorts like he always did, especially in storm conditions. He'd want it handy in case Bea or Jo needed anything. He called Jack's number, but it went straight to voicemail. He dialed repeatedly, listening for any telltale ringing or buzzing, even though it would likely have run out of power by now or been turned off.

Maybe Bea had picked it up when the paramedics were there, so he called her but had to leave a message. Likely she was sitting with Jack and had turned it off. He would check with her later. By midafternoon, he dropped the last load of debris in the marina dumpsters, then walked to the Half Shell Raw Bar, a favorite of Jack's, and ordered their fresh catch sandwich. Good food takes time, so while he waited, he made a call.

"Hi, Bea. How's Jack doing?"

"About the same. The neuro team is with him right now, so I'm hoping for an update soon. My gallery manager said things in town are pretty much back to normal. What about the marina? Is everything okay with *Zulu*?"

"Like nothing happened. You can tell Jack I detailed the boat today."

"That'll make him happy. Thanks, Mick. For everything." Bea's voice cracked.

"Have you been able to sleep?"

"A little here and there. I'm fine. I just want him to come home."

Mick agreed wholeheartedly but worried about her managing long days and nights at the hospital on her own.

"Bea, do you have Jack's cell phone?"

"No. It wasn't with his stuff they collected at the hospital."

"Okay. I'll look around again, so don't mention it to him. I don't want him to worry."

. . .

Back at the marina, Mick spent the next hour searching every square inch of *Bravo Zulu* for the phone. He had to be certain whether it was missing. Jack had used his phone when he texted Bea around eight o'clock. It bothered him he couldn't find it but forced himself to stop looking so he could finish polishing the steel railings.

Pleased with his day's work, Mick sat on deck enjoying a cold beer when Jo called.

"Hey, Mick. I'm wrapping up and should be there in an hour. Want me to pick something up or go out to eat?

"I've spent the day cleaning the boat—I'm a little ripe."

"Why don't I grab some takeout from Garbo's Grill. It's that fancy Airstream food truck on Caroline Street. We can sit on deck and have dinner watching the sunset."

"Sounds perfect. You pick for me. I'll eat anything. And thanks, Jo. I'm so tired I can't think of moving right now."

"No problem. I'm not up to being around a bunch of people. See you in a few."

Mick watched as a Fury catamaran sailed out of the marina, its deck packed full of eager tourists who waved at every boat they passed. Key

West sunsets attracted enormous crowds, and without a cloud in the sky, tonight would not disappoint them.

He'd been staring at sunsets his entire life, hoping to glimpse the elusive *green flash*. Legend says the exact moment the sun drops below the horizon, a green flash of light will streak across the sky. Mick doubted if the flash really existed—maybe it was some old tale passed down by generations of fishermen. An eternal optimist, he kept staring.

But the serene water view did nothing to tamp down the feeling gnawing away at him. Something about Jack's injury didn't add up. After decades of investigating crimes, Mick wondered if he was seeing things that weren't there. Old habits die hard. He'd talk with Jo about it since she would have a less biased point of view.

Mick didn't notice Jo arrive until Bob the Dog jumped onto the deck.

"Hey, buddy." Bob wagged not only his tail but his entire body. "This is a nice surprise." Bob sat in front of Mick, accepting his petting.

"Hope it's okay. He needed some exercise." Jo set down a portable water bowl and filled it before passing a couple dog treats to Mick so he could reward the well-behaved rescue dog. "You were miles away right now." Her voice had a note of concern.

Mick nodded. "Just lots on my mind. Dinner smells great. What do you have there?"

"Kobe beef kimchi hot dogs. They're amazing!" Jo's smile transformed his mood.

"What do you want to drink? There's beer or wine."

"I'll take the coldest beer in the fridge, please."

Bob followed Mick to the cabin, and while they ate, the curious dog wandered the deck, sniffing every surface until he lay down, resting his head on Mick's shoe. Jo finished first, sighed, then leaned back in her chair.

"I totally get why Jack chose this way of life," she said longingly.

Mick laughed. He couldn't imagine the Navy advertising gourmet food and cold beer in their recruitment posters.

Jo looked at Mick with a smirk on her face. "I didn't mean lounging around on deck. I mean being outdoors on the water."

"I know what you meant." He smiled. "If they served these hotdogs in the galley, I might never have left. Thanks for getting dinner."

"No problem."

"Any word from Bea or Jack's doctors? Oh, and how are Ellie's friends—everything okay with them?" Mick asked.

"They're a little shaken up after the hurricane but otherwise all good. I told them to call me if they needed any help until Jack gets back. I also talked with Bea while I waited for our food. Jack's been more alert today. Dr. Marcus ran a bunch of tests, but they won't finish his evaluation until tomorrow. He's still confused and groggy, so they can't do too much at once. Bea noticed his speech is slow, and he sometimes has a tough time finding his words. She thought it might be caused by his medication, or it could be from his injury. But the best news is they're planning to transfer him out of the ICU. At least we can talk to him on the phone if he's in a regular room."

"I wish I could see him." Mick struggled to picture Jack stuck in a hospital bed. "Are you still driving to Miami after the opening?"

"That's my plan. Do you want to come with me?"

"I'm not sure. Can I tell you in the morning?"

"Sure." Jo stared at him with a puzzled look on her face.

Mick didn't want to worry her but needed to explain his hesitation. "Listen, Jo. A few things are bothering me." He ran through all the details about finding the untied dock lines, the intact cabin, and the missing phone. "Saying it out loud only convinces me something isn't right, even though I recognize there could always be a simple explanation."

"Is there anything missing from the boat other than Jack's phone?" Jo asked.

"Not that I can tell, and Bea said his wallet was in his pocket when he went to the hospital. Jack showed me all the onboard bells and whistles, so I think I would notice. If anyone was going to steal something from the boat, there are dozens of items more valuable than Jack's cell phone. Plus, he contacted Bea around eight to tell her he'd be leaving soon. The outer bands from the hurricane were definitely onshore by then, but I can't imagine they were so strong to have violently tossed him in the cabin, especially without jostling everything else inside."

Jo sat quietly until Bob nudged her hand for a pet, drawing her back into the moment.

"Mick, I know we all think Jack is indestructible, but it could've been an accident." Jo didn't sound convinced.

"Maybe." He shrugged.

"What aren't you telling me?"

"While sitting on deck tonight, I noticed a few surveillance cameras aimed at this part of the marina. It's getting late, but I want to check them out in the morning to see if there's any footage of *Bravo Zulu* during the storm." Mick glanced over his shoulder toward town. "I can see a camera outside Turtle Krawls—there's a chance it picks up this dock."

"And if the video footage only shows a storm blowing through the marina, then we'll know nothing else happened. Is that what you're thinking?"

"That's as far as I got sitting here drinking my beer before you arrived. I'm also going to check on Jack's laptop back at the house to see if he has the *Find My Phone* app turned on. He gave me his password so I can log in."

"Do you really think it could be something other than an accident?" Jo asked.

He shrugged. "My job taught me to prepare for the worst-case scenario. I can't help but be suspicious. I spent my entire career chasing criminals. During those years, I learned to trust my little voice. I rely on my gut instincts all the time, and they almost never let me down."

"Okay, I get it. Don't forget about my Barton gut instincts. I trust them too. The most important thing is that Jack is improving. Hopefully soon, he can tell us himself what happened that night, then we can all move on."

Mick nodded. "If Jack is lucid enough to fill in the details before your grand opening, I'd love to drive to Miami with you."

"Deal." Jo stuck out her hand to shake on it. "I'll call Bea in the morning between my early appointments, and I'll let you know what she says."

Mick gripped her hand, holding it longer than expected for a transactional handshake. Her hand relaxed in his, and neither of them moved for a moment. She smiled in a way that made Mick think she also sensed the energy between them.

They had another drink on deck to watch the fireball of a sunset as it dropped below the horizon. As the sky transitioned to shades of purple and blue, the exhaustion set in. Mick would have been happy sitting with her late into the evening. Not only beautiful and smart, Jo entertained him with childhood stories of Jack. She made him laugh, which was a welcome distraction from the worry. Mick walked her and Bob to their car and said good night. Before going their separate ways, Jo pulled him close and kissed him gently on the cheek.

"Thanks, Mick." And then she was gone, leaving him filled with a mix of emotions as he stood in the parking lot.

Was it their shared trauma drawing them close? Mick thought it was more than that, but she was his best friend's sister, and he needed to take it slow.

On his way home, Mick passed by the famous Blue Heaven restaurant. Even though he was tired and dirty, he went inside and ordered a slice of key lime pie, which he ate while sitting at the bar. A large banyan tree shaded the small, quaint courtyard during the day, but by night, it transformed into a magical place with twinkling lights, live music, and chickens running around under the tables. The acclaimed restaurant had become famous for their key lime pie. Each time a server brought a slice to a table, the neighboring patrons gawked at the sight—the meringue on top stood six inches tall. Mick wished Jack was sitting next to him—like old times. They'd shared many meals at this same bar over the years. He missed his friend and wished it could all go back to the way it was before the hurricane. One day at a time, he told himself. One day at a time.

CHAPTER 11

"What the hell?"

Jarred from his sleep by the crowing of the free-roaming roosters, Mick took a minute to orient himself. Key West had a reputation as a late-night party town, so the roosters must have become background noise for many of the locals who routinely slept late.

Days had passed since his last morning run, prompting him to lace up before the extreme heat and humidity set in—still stinking hot but tolerable for a Floridian. Whenever he needed to work through a problem, running allowed him to clear the clutter and focus. And it saved him tons of money by avoiding therapy.

Mick weaved his way through the narrow sidewalks of Old Town, his route under constant invasion from the dense foliage spilling over white picket fences from postage stamp-sized front yards. Only ninety miles from Havana, Cuba, the tropical climate of Key West felt more like a Caribbean Island. Defined by an independent streak and set far off the beaten path, its residents attempted a coup in the eighties to secede from the U.S. mainland and create their own nation, The Conch Republic. The tongue-in-cheek uprising lived on, symbolized by the flag representing the fledgling new Republic now flown from flag poles and plastered on tourist memorabilia.

After a sluggish five-mile run, he returned to Jack's place and sat on the porch till he stopped sweating then jumped in a cool shower. Two cups of coffee later, he was a new man. He began formulating a plan for the day when Jo called.

"Morning, Mick." She sounded rested and cheery.

"Where do you get your energy from?" he asked. "I'm better after my run but nowhere near as recharged as you sound."

She laughed. "I think I'm operating on pure adrenalin. My first appointments are coming in this morning before the grand opening. I originally scheduled them for after the event, but I want to leave as soon as possible for Miami. It's an important day for me, and I wish Jack was here to celebrate."

"He's so proud of you, Jo. You should have heard him going on about everything you're doing."

"Thanks. Did you find any information about his phone from the laptop?" she asked.

"No luck. I searched his *Find my Phone* app. The last location pinged at the marina before the storm, but now, it's turned off or the battery is dead."

"Okay." She paused. "Well, I have good news and bad news. I just talked with Bea, and Jack can follow conversations and answer questions about the details of his life—simple things like his address, career, family, and stuff. And he's been moved out of the ICU. I cried when she told me. The bad news is that he has no memory of the events leading up to and immediately after his head injury. The doctors told Bea it's normal for brain trauma patients not to recall that period, and it may or may not come back to him."

Mick said nothing.

"Are you still there?" Jo asked.

"Yeah, sorry. I was thinking about what I'm going to do today. Are you okay driving to Miami on your own this afternoon?"

"Sure. Are you still planning to track down whatever surveillance video you can find?"

"I think so. I really want to see Jack, but maybe I can leave later—after I confirm it was just an accident," Mick said.

"Well, I plan to be on the road by three or four, so let me know if you get any new info. Will I see you at my opening?"

"I wouldn't miss it."

. . .

Set inside a small, weathered-gray building in the middle of the marina, the Key West Dockmaster's office bustled with activity. An assistant pointed Mick toward the fuel dock where he could see a short, muscular man wearing a wide-brimmed, fishing hat. Mick introduced himself and presented a business card identifying him as Special Agent Mick Nassau. In the end, his expired credentials were unnecessary since the dock master happily offered to help after hearing the news about Jack.

Unfortunately, he could only offer words of support. None of the security cameras captured the area near *Bravo Zulu*. They were directed at the office building and towards the main port channel and fuel docks. The marina offered twenty-four-hour security, so they didn't need a high-tech camera system. In this small, close-knit community, everyone looked out for each other.

Having struck out with the dockmaster, Mick walked along the harbor, stepping around the crowds huddled outside restaurants. Many of the bars in town had cameras aimed indoors to stream live videos of tourists drinking and partying on their vacation. None of that helped to recreate what happened during the hurricane. His best chance of finding what he needed would be to check at Turtle Krawls since it was located opposite the dock leading to Jack's section of the marina. The manager on duty, Cassie, recognized him immediately and waved for him to sit at the bar.

"Hi, Mick. I'm so sad to hear the news about Jack. How's he doing?"

"He's slowly improving, and he's now out of the ICU."

"What a relief. It's not the same around here without him."

"Cassie, can I ask a favor?"

"Sure. Any friend of Jack's is a friend of ours. What do you need?"

He told her about his search for video during the hurricane.

"I can show you the cameras we're using right now. There's one pointed at the bar area where the main cash register is located and one centered over the front part of the restaurant where the band sets up. That's the one we keep running on our online webcam. We have two other outdoor cameras that might help."

"That would be great," Mick said. "Do you save your security recordings?"

"Of course. The system saves one week at a time to the cloud and records over the previous dates. We should still have what you're looking for." Cassie motioned for him to follow her.

"Perfect. I can't thank you enough. It'll mean a lot to Jack, too."

Cassie stopped and turned to face him. "Is there something going on that I should know about?"

"Nope. I'm looking to document how the storm affected Jack's boat around the time of his injury—for the insurance company," Mick said. He wasn't going to elaborate on his theory with the manager. He didn't want local gossip impeding his fact-finding mission.

Cassie sat at the desk to access the security cameras. "Here's the angle I think you're interested in. The equipment is so old. Sorry. The quality sucks."

Mick squinted at the grainy image on the left then pointed to the screen. "This camera picks up the entry to Jack's dock. Would it be possible to get a copy of the recording from this past week? Please." Mick offered his most charming smile.

"Like I said. Anything for Jack. But you need to promise if you see anything sketchy, you'll share the information with me. Okay?"

"I will," he said. "I really appreciate this."

"Sure thing," she said. "It'll take me a few minutes to make a copy. Why don't you stay for lunch? We have hog snapper on the menu—caught fresh today."

Although he wanted to get back home to review the video, it would be rude not to accept Cassie's invitation. After skipping breakfast, the mention of a fish sandwich had him salivating, so he grabbed a spot at the bar and ordered an iced tea along with the snapper.

Staring out at the marina and the Gulf beyond, Mick's mind wandered. With everything that had happened since he arrived in Key West, it had become easy to avoid the original reason for his visit—a reset. Newly unemployed—he refused to call himself retired—he had no hobbies other than running and the occasional fishing trip with his workmates and friends, Frank and Bryce. His last serious relationship ended over six months ago, like they all did. Mick's career focus kept getting in the way, and eventually, the women grew impatient and moved on.

Did he have a fear of commitment like Jo suggested? He didn't think so, but after a string of failed relationships, he had to wonder. It seemed like forever since the end to his once storied career, but the upside of all this free time meant he could stay in Key West to help Jack.

The bartender set the grilled hogfish sandwich in front of him, breaking his train of thought. It was easily one of the tastiest meals he could remember. Cassie returned to the bar with a USB drive of the requested video as he finished his last bite.

"Thanks for this." Mick nodded to the drive now in his hand.

"I expect to see you back in here real soon." She squeezed his arm and smiled before returning to the hostess stand to seat a waiting group.

Mick paid his bill then walked to Jack's golf cart he had parked nearby. Despite the horrible video quality, he would at least be able to make out the basic silhouette of a human form to determine if anyone had entered or exited the dock ramp to *Bravo Zulu*. He planned to watch from the time Jack returned to the marina and move forward from there.

Mick had been suppressing his feelings of guilt for leaving Jack alone on the boat that day. Of course, he did so at Jack's request in order to finish securing the cottage. At the time, he had no heightened concerns about his friend's safety, but he had to wonder if things would be different if he stayed at the marina. Using hindsight to second-guess himself could be destructive, as he would likely make the same decision again under similar circumstances. Guilt could be all-consuming and wouldn't help him right now, so he pushed those thoughts aside.

After arriving at the cottage, he loaded the video to the laptop and fast forwarded the footage until he saw Jack walk onto the dock. He then slowed the recording to watch for anything out of the ordinary. While it would have been great to have a view of *Zulu*, the entrance to the dock marked the only way to and from that row of boats.

As the rain and wind intensified, any foot traffic around the marina became infrequent. Based on the timestamp, about the time Jack had called Bea, there had not been a single person captured moving into view for over half an hour. He paused the video to rest his eyes and grabbed a drink from the fridge. When he sat back down, he had to focus.

Minutes later, Mick saw a man exiting the dock leading away from *Bravo Zulu*. Despite the horrible quality of the video and decreased visibility from the driving rain, he immediately recognized the guy with his scrawny frame, long ponytail, and tattoos. It was the same guy he had seen getting off Abe's boat earlier that day. His tattooed arms were visible in the video, specifically the dive flag on his forearm, and he carried a small duffle, not his large dive bag.

Mick hadn't remembered seeing this guy return to the marina after their first interaction, but they were busy securing *Zulu*, and he could have easily slipped past. After rewinding the security feed, he captured the tattooed diver's return, coinciding with the time Mick and Jack were back at the cottage.

"Bingo!" Mick said out loud as he jumped from his chair.

Now he had a place to start. With Abe's help, he should be able to track down the diver and find out if he saw Jack on deck that night. Likely a long shot but worth pursuing.

He continued working through the remaining video, advancing it slowly until another man stepped off the dock. The weather had worsened as the ominous storm cover darkened any remaining daylight. After rewatching the footage many times, Mick was certain he didn't recognize this second guy. That meant little, since he had only been in town for less than a day. The stranger wore casual pants with a polo style shirt—not the normal Key West attire of shorts, t-shirts, and flip-flops. He had a medium build, dark hair and appeared to be middle age. He kept his head down so only part of his face could be seen.

After saving and printing the best images of both men, he continued. The ferocity of the hurricane ensured nobody else came on camera until Bea ran into the frame the following morning in search of Jack.

Mick pressed stop when he saw himself run onto the dock. Trying to prepare for what came next, he walked to the kitchen, grabbed a beer from the fridge, and took a long swig before pressing play. He watched as the paramedics arrived, followed by Jack being wheeled away on a stretcher. It seemed so surreal, like watching a TV show. He saw the painful expression on his own face and the fear on Bea's. He powered through the remaining video until Earl and Betty arrived to the marina. Just like they said, they were the first ones back the morning after the hurricane. He'd had enough and closed the laptop. Jo's event started in thirty minutes, and he didn't want to be late.

CHAPTER 12

The Key West Animal Hospital buzzed with activity. Cars overflowed the small parking lot, spilling into the back alleyway. People mingled on the sidewalk outside the front entrance while their dogs enjoyed bowls of water and bone-shaped cookies. Clients circled the front desk to schedule their first appointment with the new veterinarian. Jo's staff passed out refreshments and took turns conducting hospital tours. The pet owning population of Key West had been eagerly awaiting her grand opening.

Mick became transfixed, watching Jo across the lobby as she greeted her guests. Unaware of the effect she had on everyone she interacted with, her beauty and confidence were matched only by her authentic charm. Clients hung on her every word, laughing together as they shared stories about their pets. She turned her head, made eye contact with Mick, and smiled before waving him over to join her.

I'm in trouble, he thought to himself. Her smile took his breath away. Mick couldn't remember the last time a woman had this effect on him. But then, Jo wasn't just any woman. "Careful, Mick," he said under his breath.

He stood at the back of a long line of enthusiastic clients waiting to meet the new veterinarian and introduce her to their four-legged family members. Eavesdropping on their conversations, he learned they loved the new hospital decor and were very impressed with Dr. Joanna Barton. It took a while for him to make his way to the front and garner her undivided attention.

"Oh, Mick. I'm so glad you're here." She hugged him, holding on for a few seconds before letting go. "Isn't this turnout amazing?"

"It's phenomenal. You should be proud, Jo."

"I am. You just missed Wayne and Michelle. He asked for you to call him." She reached into her pocket and handed him a business card. "They came early so we could talk privately before my clients arrived, but they're now on their way to Miami. I just wish Jack and Bea were here," she said.

"I saw a local reporter taking pictures and interviewing a few of your clients. It looks like they'll be able to read about it in the paper."

"That was my staff's doing. They've been taking care of all the details over the past few days and invited the local media here for the event. I'd be lost without them."

"Where's Bob the Dog?" Mick asked.

"He's in the kennel. We had him out in the lobby earlier, but it got too busy. Would you be able to take him for a walk?" she asked.

Mick smiled in response to her rhetorical question. When he entered the kennel, Bob stood and wagged his tail, likely excited to see the leash hanging in Mick's hand. They left out the back door, and when they approached the first intersection, Bob sat down and looked up at Mick. The light turned green, Mick nodded, and the two resumed their walk. Every passerby stopped to pet the friendly dog, commenting on his unique appearance. It was hard to understand why his previous owners wouldn't be frantically searching for him.

When they returned to the hospital, Mick filled Bob's bowl with fresh water as Jo walked into the kennel.

"The clients are gone." She handed him a couple dog cookies. "These are Bob's favorites."

Bob accepted the treats with a gentle mouth, then Mick closed the kennel door. "What's going to happen to him?"

"We put his picture on our website, but so far, nobody contacted us to claim him. We'll make sure he ends up in a wonderful home."

"He really is an exceptional dog. Whoever gets him will be lucky."

"You *do* realize he's up for adoption?" Jo smiled and nudged his arm. "Do you have any pets?"

"I've always wanted one, but with my career and travel schedule, it wouldn't be fair, even to a goldfish."

Jo raised her eyebrows and tilted her head. "But things are different now."

Being reminded of his current employment status struck a chord. He had to stop thinking of himself as Special Agent Mick Nassau. He was just Mick, and he had no idea what his future looked like. To change the subject, he asked about her plans for managing the hospital when she was in Miami.

"I've talked with the staff, and we're going to operate half days for the next week. I can't think beyond that right now. The hospital is normally closed on Saturdays at noon until Monday morning, so I need to concentrate on getting through the next few days. This way, I'll be available for medical or surgical appointments but can still see Jack. When I'm gone, the staff can answer clients' questions, refill medication, and book appointments. I want to make sure the doors are open every day."

"It sounds like a good plan but exhausting. How are you doing?" Mick asked.

Jo smiled at his concern. "I should ask you the same thing."

"Just need a bit more sleep. Before you go, do you have a minute to look at a couple photos?"

Jo's eyes narrowed. "Is this about Jack?"

He nodded, so she grabbed his arm to lead him to her office for a private conversation. Mick pulled the two printed photos from his pocket and handed them to her.

"This guy is a scuba diver Jack and I saw on the day of the storm. The second guy left the dock later that same night."

She studied the images and shook her head. "I've been away for so many years, I can't keep track of all the changing faces. Where did you get these?" She handed the printouts back.

"Security camera from Turtle Krawls. Both these guys were at the marina during the hurricane, on the same dock as Jack. I'd love to ask them if they saw anything. It's a long shot, but it's my only lead."

"Jack has a buddy who's been the bartender at the Green Parrot as long as I can remember. His name is Jim, but people call him Little Jimmy, and he knows everyone in town. He's a big, tall, bald guy. I'd ask him."

"Great. I'll do that."

"I'm seeing one quick appointment, then I'll be on the road. I'll call you with an update when I get to Miami."

"Tell Jack not to worry about *Zulu*. Everything's great, and I hope to see him soon."

Mick checked on Bob the Dog before leaving out the back door. Now that the hospital had reopened, he hoped Jo could find him a new home.

• • •

Time to get to work. Mick stopped at the cottage to change his clothes and print additional copies of the surveillance images then drove over to the marina in the golf cart. He parked in the usual spot near Turtle Krawls, hoping Cassie might still be on duty.

"Hi, Mick! You're back fast. Is there anything else I can help you with?"

"Thanks again for sharing your security video. Could you look at something for me?"

"Sure."

Mick handed her the printed images. "Do you recognize them? I've seen the skinny guy with the tattoo around here once before, but I don't recognize the other guy."

She stared at the pictures. "Man, we've got to get some new cameras. Sorry about the horrible quality."

"That's all right. Have you come across either of these guys before?" he asked again.

"No. Sorry. I've never seen them around town, and they don't come in here to eat."

"I appreciate you looking." He put the photos in his pocket. "See you later." Mick crossed through the restaurant, exiting onto the boardwalk nearest *Zulu*.

Next order of business—Abe. Mick stood on the dock opposite his trawler but didn't spot him outside. After calling his name and receiving no reply, he stepped from the gangway onto the deck. "Abe," he shouted one more time.

"Who the hell do you think you are?" Abe exploded out of the cabin, his face furled in anger.

Mick instinctively reached for the gun holster on his belt, which of course wasn't there. He had to return his weapon when he retired. His next best decision was to deescalate the situation, so he raised his hands in the air.

"I called out first. I just have a quick question—it's important."

"I don't give a shit if my boat's on fire. This is private property. You've got no right."

Mick dropped his arms and took two steps toward Abe, who responded by taking two steps back. Bullies like Abe always crumbled when confronted. Mick wasn't going to put up with his posturing, but he still needed his help.

"Trust me. It won't happen again."

Abe glared at him without speaking. Mick had seen that look before and understood exactly what it meant. Abe was calculating whether he'd be successful at using physical force to get him off the boat. Could he take him or not? Mick put his hands on his hips and moved another step closer. Abe apparently decided Mick could hold his own and relaxed his arms at his side.

"What is it and make it quick."

Mick handed him the two pictures. "This looks like the guy you had out on your boat on the day of the hurricane, coming back from a dive trip. Could you tell me his name? Also, wondering if you recognize the guy in the second picture?"

Abe refused to take the photos and only glanced at them for a second.

"Don't know them," he grunted his reply.

Mick thrust the skinny guy's picture closer to Abe's face. "Look again. I'm pretty sure this guy was one of your recent charters."

"I already told you, I have no idea who they are. Why don't you ask Jack? He's always messing around in everybody's business."

"I can't. He's still recovering and doesn't remember much from that day."

Abe's brow lifted, and he leaned back against his cabin. "Well, I can't help you, so if you don't mind…" Abe pointed toward the dock—the implication clear.

Recognizing a dead end when he saw one, Mick turned and left. Jack had good reason for keeping an eye on this guy, and Mick planned to do the same.

Leaving Abe's, he walked throughout the marina, showing the pictures to anyone he could find. After striking out with the harbormaster, he returned to *Zulu* and noticed Betty and Earl sitting on their deck.

"Hey, Mick. You look like you could use a drink. Why don't you join us for happy hour." Earl stood and grabbed another chair.

"Thanks. I could use one. A beer sounds perfect."

"Take a seat. I'll be right back."

Mick sat next to Betty on deck, and they chatted about the storm and updates on Jack while Earl busied himself in the galley.

"Here you go." He handed Mick a bottle wrapped in a koozie and set a plate of food on the table between them.

"Thanks."

"What do you have there, honey?" Betty asked her husband.

"That amazing smoked fish dip from the market and some crackers. Dig in, everyone."

"Mick just told me Jack's out of the ICU. Isn't that wonderful news?" She pressed her hands together as if in prayer. "We miss him."

"Jack's our anchor down here. He's the reason Betty and I call this place home," Earl said.

Mick nodded. "I'm hoping to see him in the next day or two." He took a long drink then asked, "Can I get your help with something?" He gave them the printed photos, and they examined them closely.

"Do you recognize either of these men? I know the images aren't very clear."

Betty shook her head, but Earl kept staring at the skinny guy's photo.

"Earl?" Mick asked.

"I don't know who he is, but I'm pretty sure I've seen him before. I'm trying to place him, but my mind's coming up blank. Is that taken from the end of our dock?" Earl pointed past *Zulu* toward the Harborwalk.

"It's from a camera mounted outside Turtle Krawls. These two men were here during the hurricane, and I'm trying to find out if they remember seeing Jack or anything else out of place that night. I saw the skinny guy getting off Abe's boat earlier the same day."

Both Earl and Betty set their drinks down and turned to Mick. They were no longer smiling, and Earl removed his sunglasses before asking, "What aren't you telling us?"

He wanted to assure them they had nothing to worry about, but he owed them an honest answer. So, Mick shared everything that had been bothering him about Jack's injury, including his missing cell phone.

"Could he have dropped it overboard during the storm?" Betty asked. "It happens all the time."

"It's possible but not likely. You know Jack," Mick replied.

"You're right," Earl said. "It's upsetting to think this could have been something other than a horrible accident. What can we do?"

"Well, if you remember anything about this guy in the photo, call me. Also, if you can keep watch over *Zulu* while Jack's in the hospital, I'd really appreciate it. Jo's overwhelmed with juggling her reopening and trips back and forth to Miami. Everyone's spread thin right now."

"You can count on us."

Earl shared their contact info before Mick left. He double-checked the systems on *Zulu,* then sat in Jack's captain's chair to finish his beer. Looking out over the marina, he caught Abe watching him from inside his cabin. Mick returned his stare until Abe disappeared behind the curtains.

CHAPTER 13

Mick stayed on deck through early evening. A sunset cruise catamaran sailed past loaded with sunburned tourists out for a booze cruise. Fishing charters returned to port with the day's catch as crews rushed to clean the boats before heading to the local bars with their tips.

It'd been a frustrating afternoon, striking out repeatedly as he showed around his surveillance photos. He still needed to track down Little Jimmy at the Green Parrot, though he doubted it would lead to anything. In hindsight, he should've just driven with Jo to Miami. At least then, he could see Jack with his own eyes. As if reading his thoughts, Jo called.

"Hi, Mick. I'm glad I caught you—I have a surprise. Just a second."

"Hey, buddy," Jack said. His voice sounded quieter and less animated than usual, but still distinctly Jack.

"Jack! How are you doing?"

"Well, better," he said. "It's tough being stuck in bed all day. They're getting me up to walk, but I'm still pretty weak. They keep telling me it's normal so I don't get too frustrated."

"You were in a coma a few days ago. You need to give yourself time. I can't tell you how good it is to talk to you."

"You too, Mick. How's *Bravo Zulu*?"

"Well, I'm sitting on her deck right now. She looks great. And Betty and Earl are watching over her when I'm not here."

"They're the best. And Mick, thank you for everything. Bea and Jo keep singing your praises. I'm going to let you go now, buddy. I'll talk to you tomorrow." His voice trailed off, and the phone went silent.

"Mick," Jo said. "Are you there?"

"I'm here. He sounds good. A little quiet for Jack but still good."

"He's doing so much better, but he tires easily. They removed his bandages this morning. It was a bit of shock to see the incision—most of the back of his head has been shaved, and there's a long line of staples."

Mick tried to picture Jack's incision. "That would be shocking."

"We'll meet with the physical and occupational therapists in the morning, and hopefully, they can provide us with a better idea about when he can be discharged and what type of assistance he'll need going forward."

"Are you still returning home tomorrow?" Mick asked.

"Yeah, that's my plan. Wayne and Michelle will be here with Bea on the days when I'm working. I going to stay until after his therapy appointments."

"Has Jack mentioned anything about the night of the storm?"

"No, sorry. Give me a second." An increase in background noise signaled Jo had changed locations. "I'm in the hallway—I didn't want to talk in front of Jack. Every time I prompt him to remember that night, he gets frustrated, and I end up dropping the subject. I think the memory loss is harder to deal with than any physical challenges. Did you learn anything during your investigation?"

"I wouldn't quite call it an investigation, more of an inquiry, but no—I struck out. Can I text you the images of the two guys from the marina to show Jack and Bea in case they recognize them?"

"Sure. Jack is half asleep, but Bea is here.

"I'm sending them now."

"Okay." A minute later, Jo came back on the phone and confirmed that Bea didn't recognize either of them.

Being able to talk with Jo helped lessen the frustration of yet another roadblock. Feeling connected to her allowed him to process his own emotions and focus on the end goal—getting Jack home.

. . .

Famous for its great live music and casual atmosphere, The Green Parrot, an iconic Key West dive bar, had become an anchor for locals and tourists alike. People out for a late-night Duval Street bar crawl stopped in for a drink but often stayed till closing. The buzz of partying tourists standing shoulder to shoulder streamed through open windows as Mick approached. Despite it being the slow season, the crowd packed the place. He immediately noticed a tall, bald guy behind the bar and hoped he'd found Jimmy. He waited until the bartender finished making drinks for a large group of girls out to celebrate a bridal shower then ordered a beer.

"You Jimmy?" he asked after taking his first swig.

"That's me. What can I do for you?"

"My name's Mick. I'm a good friend of Jack Barton's. His sister, Jo, told me I should talk to you."

"Yeah, I heard Jo was back in town. Where's Jack tonight?" Jimmy asked.

Mick told him about Jack's injury and explained that he was taking care of things for Jack until he returned home. Jimmy's face dropped after hearing the news.

"We've been friends since we were kids." He shook his head then grabbed from a stack of clean bar towels to wipe his brow. "I can't even imagine him lying in a hospital bed." It seemed everyone had the same reaction of pure disbelief trying to imagine Jack as anything other than his larger-than-life personality.

"I'm trying to track down the name of a guy I've seen in town. I have a couple photos I'd like to show you. Hoping you might recognize him."

"Sure. Let me finish taking care of these thirsty customers, then I'll take my break. We can go out back where it's quiet, and I can have a smoke."

"Thanks, Jimmy. No rush."

Mick welcomed being forced to sit still for a few minutes. It felt like ages since he last experienced the carefree feeling of being on vacation, yet it had been less than a week since he and Jack reconnected. In that short time, his entire world had turned upside down.

The band returned from their quick break when Jimmy signaled for Mick to follow him out the back of the bar. He led him through the staff door to a picnic bench in a side yard.

"Thanks for waiting. Things slow down for a few minutes once the band picks back up. Smoke?" He offered Mick his cigarette pack.

"No thanks."

"So, you said you wanted to show me a picture."

"Yeah. The picture is blurry. This guy's real skinny, about five foot ten, and in his thirties. He wears his hair in a long ponytail and tattoos cover his arms, specifically a tattoo of a dive flag on his forearm. I saw him down at the marina getting off a private dive charter. Do you recognize him?" Mick asked.

Jimmy furrowed his brow as he scrutinized the photo. "I'm not one hundred percent sure, but based on your description, it sounds like a guy named Skiff." He tapped the image in his hand. "Yeah, Skiff."

"Skiff? That's his name?"

He nodded. "He's been in and out of town for about a decade. Kind of a lowlife. He comes in now and then, but I think he mostly hangs out at a few local bars outside town. He's a professional diver, working salvage and stuff like that."

"I assume his parents didn't name him Skiff. Do you know his real name by chance?"

"No, sorry. Is it important?"

"I'm not sure yet. He was at the marina at the time of Jack's injury, and I want to talk to him to find out if he saw anything suspicious."

"He better not have anything to do with Jack getting hurt, or I'll make sure he's run out of town." Jimmy stamped out his cigarette butt with force.

"I don't want to scare him off before I talk to him. Is there any way you could help me find out his real name or the name of the bar where he hangs out?"

"I think so. After closing, I'll be meeting up with a few of my bartender buddies. We keep late hours. How about I get back to you tomorrow?"

"Sure thing. I appreciate any help you can give me. Here's my cell phone number." He handed him an old business card. "Call anytime."

After looking at the card, Jimmy whistled. "Special Agent, is it? Cool. It was real nice meeting you, Mick. I'm glad you're looking out for Jack. Can you pass along a message to him for me?"

Mick nodded.

"Tell him he better get his butt out of bed and back to town, pronto." Jimmy flashed a wide gapped-tooth smile.

"I will. Listen, I know you've got to work, but can I show you one more picture? This guy was also at the marina around the same time." Mick handed over the photo of the preppy guy in the polo shirt.

"No, sorry. He looks like any other random tourist. If you want to leave these with me, I can show the gang later tonight. Between the bunch of us, we cover most of the watering holes in town."

"That would be great." He shook Jimmy's extended hand before walking out the back laneway toward Jack's golf cart.

It was getting late, and Mick realized he hadn't eaten since his early lunch, so he stopped by the food truck for a repeat of their takeout kimchi dog. Piled high with toppings, he ate at a garden table before resuming his short ride home. Grabbing a beer from Jack's fridge, he distracted himself with sports highlights. It didn't work because he kept replaying the events of the day. What began as an innocent, fact-finding mission ended with a deep pit in his stomach.

So far, the details only supported the theory that Jack had suffered a terrible freak accident. But something felt off. The pieces didn't quite fit together. He couldn't shake the feeling he was overlooking something critical. Determined, he resolved to keep digging into the investigation, even if it led to more dead ends.

He'd take another run at Abe in the morning, and in the meantime, he hoped Little Jimmy might have some new information to share. With nothing else to do, he flipped between baseball games, but the Green Parrot's music, the chatter of tourists, and the distant hum of boat engines played in his head. All a reminder of Jack's vibrant life in Key West. He hoped he'd be back soon to enjoy it, but until then, Mick would keep searching for answers. That nagging voice inside his head wouldn't leave him alone.

CHAPTER 14

He woke up on the couch in the middle of the night, groggy and disoriented. After turning off the TV, he stumbled to bed and resumed his fitful sleep, shifting in and out of dreams that bordered on nightmares. His sleep mirrored the unsettled feeling that had been building up inside of him all day.

"Aaagggh!" Mick growled. The roosters didn't seem to notice his outburst and kept on crowing. "I can't catch a break."

He tried his best to ignore them, but their relentless "cock-a-doodle-doo" forced him to accept defeat. After finishing a quick cup of coffee, he did the only thing that worked to clear his mind and headed out for a run. After almost circumnavigating the entirety of Key West, he landed back on Jack's front porch completely exhausted and invigorated, all at the same time. His running routine, and the surge of endorphins it brought, helped him stay focused—a necessity for navigating the complexities of any investigation.

During moments like this, Mick realized how much he missed the daily camaraderie he had shared with his workmates, Frank and Bryce. They were each other's sounding board. He'd texted a few times after the storm to let them know he was safe and to give them a brief update on Jack, but he owed them a call.

"Hi, Bry," Mick said. "Can you talk?"

"Sure. Frank and I are in the car right now, heading to an interview. You're on speakerphone."

"Hey, Mick. What's the latest on Jack?" Frank asked.

"He's out of the ICU and is improving every day. I drove back to Key West with his sister, Jo. She's a veterinarian and in the process of reopening one of the few vet hospitals in the area."

"I bet it was hard for both of you to leave Miami," Bryce said.

"It was brutal, but his girlfriend, Bea, is with him. Since I got back to town, a few things have happened, and I wanted to run them by you guys."

Mick wondered if he'd been disconnected when the phone went silent until Frank asked, "What's on your mind?"

"We left during the aftermath of the hurricane, so I came straight to the marina to check on Jack's boat and start the cleanup. Something kept bothering me, but I couldn't put my finger on it. I wanted to understand what could've happened on the boat that night to cause such a severe injury. All the dock lines held during the storm, so I couldn't imagine the boat moved with such force to throw Jack across the cabin, causing him to hit his head. He's a huge guy. On top of that, nothing else in the cabin had been knocked over. Just Jack. It didn't make sense. That's when I noticed it. He'd prepared a couple extra dock lines he planned to tie off after everyone left the marina that night. When I got on board, the lines were still coiled on deck."

"What if he changed his mind?" Bryce said.

"No way. Remember, he's a Navy captain. More lines are always better, and he told me he planned to tie them after the marina emptied—they would've crossed the dock and been a tripping hazard."

"Okay, but isn't it possible he had an accident and didn't get to finish?" Frank asked.

"It's possible but hard to fathom. If the eye of the hurricane was close to making landfall, he would've already tied the lines and moved to Bea's place to ride out the storm. Since his injury occurred prior to that decision point, I don't think the force of the rainbands alone could have tossed him around in the cabin with that amount of force. And he texted Bea around eight that night to tell her he was wrapping up and heading her way. Am I overthinking this?"

"Maybe, but I've never known you to let your head get in front of the facts," Bryce said. "Your instincts are always right."

"Thanks. I needed to hear that. I've barely slept in days and been second guessing if my mind was playing tricks on me."

Frank, the pragmatic investigator, asked, "Has Jack been able to fill in any of these details?"

"No. Unfortunately, he's lost all memory of the time just prior to the injury until he woke up from the coma. The doctors say it might come back to him, but there's a chance it doesn't. I guess that's a normal thing with head trauma. But there's something else. We can't find Jack's cell phone. He would've had it in his hand or his pocket, and as best as I can tell, it's missing."

"It sounds like you need to figure it out, or it'll eat at you," Frank said. "I assume you already have a game plan or you wouldn't have called us."

"You know me too well. I've tracked down surveillance cameras pointed near Jack's section of the marina. It captured two men leaving the dock that night, just before the storm came ashore and shortly after Jack sent his last text. Nothing else moved around that area until I arrived the next day, other than the wind and rain, of course. I have a lead on one guy, and I'm hoping to get more info about where to find him this morning. It's possible one or both men talked to Jack that night and can shed some light on what happened. Nothing would make me happier than to find out it was just a stupid accident."

"Is there anything we can do to help?" Bryce asked.

"Just listening to my suspicions is help enough. I've been able to bounce some ideas off Jo, but it's not the same as having you guys around."

"Are you going to be in Key West for a while? Everyone at Tucker's has been asking."

Mick missed the gang at his favorite after-work bar. "No idea. I committed to being here to help Jack if he needs me. I'll know more once he's out of the hospital."

"From what you've told us about Jack, he sounds like the type of person to work hard at his recovery," Bryce said.

"He's tough and stubborn and smart. A perfect combination. Thanks again, guys. I'll keep you posted if I turn up anything interesting."

"Be safe. We can't cover your back from up here in Tallahassee," Bryce said. "And remember—you're supposed to be retired."

Mick had been partnered with the rookie, Bryce Taylor, four years ago. They quickly became one of the most effective teams in the field. Over the years, there were countless times they had to rely on that partnership to get them through some dangerous situations. The lead up to Mick's so-called retirement had been excruciating, but it had been equally tough on Bryce. When he agreed to leave, Mick's only request was to have Bryce partnered with Frank De Lucca, another stand-up guy. Bryce had a brilliant career ahead of him if he could avoid following in Mick's footsteps.

Talking everything through with his friends helped clarify his plan for the day.

■ ■ ■

Mick had just stepped aboard *Zulu* when Betty and Earl came over for an update on Jack. He had nothing new to share until Jo called after his back-to-back therapy sessions.

"We haven't seen either of the guys from your surveillance pictures," Earl said.

"We take turns staying on deck," Betty added. "We don't want to miss anything important."

"Thanks. I might drive to Miami to see Jack tomorrow. Jo has to be back in her hospital later today."

"We'll take care of everything here while you're away. You tell Jack there's nothing to worry about, okay?" Earl said.

"I will. Thank you."

"If you're going to be around for a while, Earl and I would like to make a quick run to the grocery store for provisions. We can pick up anything you might need."

"I'm good. You two take care of your errands. I appreciate you staying on duty when I'm not here, but you need to live your lives, too."

"Jack is family," Earl said. "We'll be on alert until he's back safe and sound or you tell us, with complete certainty, we have nothing to worry about."

Mick wondered if he'd made a mistake sharing his suspicions since it seemed he'd turned Jack's neighbors into covert agents. "I'll be here for another hour."

"Quick, grab the keys, Earl."

Once they had left, Mick walked to the end of the dock. Having learned his lesson from their last interaction, he stayed put this time. He didn't see Abe but could hear someone in the galley.

After twice calling out Abe's name without getting an answer, he shouted, "Abe. It's Mick. I know you're in the cabin. I can hear you. I'm going to stay here until you come out and talk to me. I've got all day."

A couple minutes later, Abe shuffled out of the cabin with a surly look on his face.

"What now?" he glowered at Mick.

"When I was here yesterday, I showed you a picture of a guy, and you told me you didn't recognize him. His name is Skiff, and I know he was on your boat last week. You need to stop lying to me." Mick spoke using his most official tone.

"What are you gonna do about it? I dare you—set one foot on this boat." Abe planted his feet firmly, a defiant stance.

Mick instinctively stepped forward then caught himself. Making enemies at the marina wouldn't help get the information he needed. "I have no quarrel with you. I just want to talk to the guy. Skiff's a local, so you must have an idea about where I can find him."

"Even if I did, I wouldn't tell you. People are allowed to keep their own personal business private," then he moved toward the cabin door.

"This is a small town, Abe. It's your choice. Just remember, what goes around, comes around."

Abe turned and sneered at Mick. "You can take your Welcome Wagon and get the hell outta here."

Mick shook his head as he walked back to *Bravo Zulu*. It would be a waste of time to continue the conversation. Pissed off after wrangling with Abe, he sat on deck until he'd calmed down. Why was Abe pushing back so hard? Did he have something to hide, or was he just an asshole recluse with anger management issues? By the time Earl and Betty returned, pushing their dock cart, he'd cooled off.

"It looks like you're provisioning for an ocean voyage."

"Well, we want to be prepared, you know. That way, we don't need to leave for anything while you're out of town," Betty said.

"Jack's lucky to have you as friends." He helped them unload then went in search of a big, indulgent breakfast.

▪ ▪ ▪

Mick sat at the bar at Blue Heaven to avoid a long wait. He ordered key lime eggs benedict. Thankfully, dessert was available all day, so Mick added in a slice of their famous pie to finish his meal. Whoever made up the rule that dessert wasn't served with breakfast was misguided. It was a good thing he put in a long run that morning. He'd have to call that brunch because he wouldn't be hungry again until dinner. Just as he pulled back into Jack's driveway, his phone rang—it was an unknown caller.

"Mick, it's Jimmy from the Parrot. Do you have a minute?"

"Absolutely. Did you find out anything new about Skiff?"

"A little. His real name is Scott Bain-something. My buddy wasn't sure if it was Bains, Bainstreet, Bainsbridge, but Bain-something. He's a diver for hire and has done some contract work on salvage boats over the years. Supposedly, he's super skilled but a pain to work with."

"Why's that?"

"Well, word is that he's a big talker, and a few of the dives he's been on have had equipment go missing. Nothing was ever proved, but people always wondered if he had a side business on the go."

"Do you know where he lives or where I might find him?"

"No idea where he lives, but he hangs out at a bar called the Hurricane Hole on Stock Island. I think that's likely your best chance at tracking him down."

"Thanks, Jimmy. Tell your friends I really appreciate the help. Did you have any luck with the picture of the other guy?"

"No, sorry. Nobody recognized that guy. Like I said, he looks like your everyday tourist."

"I figured. Listen, if you hear anything that might be helpful, call me."

"Sure thing, Mick. You tell any of the bartenders you talk to that Little Jimmy from the Parrot sent you. That might get you a foot in the door."

Finally, the break he needed. He would drive over to Stock Island at lunch and ask around for Skiff. Hopefully, the locals at the bar would be friendlier and more helpful than Abe had been. In the meantime, he needed to lie down and digest his breakfast. After last night's sleeplessness, it only took five minutes before Mick was sound asleep on the couch. It was a good thing Jo called him an hour later, waking him up. He may have otherwise missed his chance to track down the diver.

CHAPTER 15

According to Jo, Jack had spent an exhausting morning with both the physical and occupational therapists. Still weak but improving every day, he used a walker to get around on his own but had some weakness in his hands that affected his ability to manage fine motor activities like writing. Occasionally, he searched for his words, but the therapists reassured them it should not be a long-term problem.

Jack impressed everyone with his hard work, tenacity, and overall positive attitude. Only Jo and Bea could see his frustration, but he didn't let it show to the surrounding team. Provided there were no further complications, the doctors thought he could be released within the week. Any future therapy sessions could be continued back in Key West.

"How are things at home?" she asked.

"Good. And thanks for that suggestion to talk to Little Jimmy at the Parrot. He didn't know about Jack and was real upset."

"Yeah. They've been friends forever. He's a good guy."

"I've got a lead on one man from the photos, and I'm going out to Stock Island at lunch to see if I can track him down," Mick said. "Have you been able to show Jack the two pictures I sent?"

"I did, but he didn't recognize either of them. He stared at the one with the skinny guy for a while but came up blank. Same with the other, but the picture is hard to make out. Sorry. I know you were hoping for more."

"No, that's okay. Until we can figure things out from this end, keep showing him every day. There's always a chance it'll spark his memory. Are you driving right now?"

"Yeah, I'm passing through Big Pine Key, so I should be home soon. I have a few appointments at the hospital starting midafternoon, but do you want to catch up over dinner?" she asked. "The only thing is I'm not exactly sure when I'll be done."

Mick would wait if it meant enjoying a meal with Jo. He'd been feeling isolated since leaving Miami and looked forward to reconnecting.

"No worries. Text me when you're wrapping up. I can meet you somewhere or can pick up dinner and eat in. Whatever you prefer."

"Takeout sounds perfect. I'm wiped out and not up to a crowded restaurant—let's eat at Jack's place. That'll give me a chance to look around to see if there's anything we might need to change or adapt for him before he gets home. Like bars in the shower and stuff like that. Talk to you later."

Mick grabbed the keys to the truck and rushed over to Stock Island before the lunch crowd cleared out. The Hurricane Hole, a classic, open-air Florida Keys restaurant overlooking a marina, offered various preparations of the fresh catch of the day. He walked through the place but didn't spot Skiff at first glance. He wasn't hungry after his huge breakfast but sat at the bar and ordered a bowl of conch chowder and an Arnold Palmer. It would be easier to start up a conversation when the staff had to return to check on him.

While Andra, the bartender, refilled his drink, he asked, "I'm looking for a guy I was told likes to hang out here. His name's Skiff. Do you know him?"

The bartender stared at him as if sizing him up. Mick quickly added, "Little Jimmy from the Green Parrot told me to ask here."

Her facial expression immediately softened. "Why are you looking for him?"

"I need to hire a diver for a small job, and he came recommended." He wasn't sure she believed him, but her raised brows gave away her curiosity.

"Well, he comes in here every couple days. If you want, I can give him your name and number next time I see him."

"I'm eager to get started with my project. Do you have his phone number or address? Are any of his buddies here right now?" Mick stopped, concerned his probing sounded too much like an interrogation.

"Sorry, no. I think he lives near here because sometimes he rides over on a bicycle." She passed Mick a piece of paper and a pen. "I'll make sure he gets your message."

"Okay, thanks." Mick left her his number too—in case she had info to share. He contemplated showing her the photo of the polo shirt tourist but thought that would set off alarm bells. It was the best he could do for now. After finishing his chowder, Mick topped up his check with a hefty tip. Hopefully, the enticement would encourage Andra to follow through for him.

Roadblocks in an investigation were to be expected. He'd left his own file of cold cases behind in Tallahassee. But operating without the backing of a law enforcement agency had stalled his progress. He decided it was time to enlist some local help. Mick certainly didn't have any reciprocal privileges now that he was retired, but a professional courtesy could be extended to a fellow officer of the law, past or present.

. . .

He had worked with the Monroe County Sheriff's Department during his early career, when his Miami field office had been tasked with investigating a case involving excessive use of force by a rookie Key West cop. A tourist had become belligerent at closing time of a local bar when the police were called to assist. The fall-down drunk stumbled toward the door, yelling and flailing his arms, then fell or lunged at one officer at the scene. That young police officer mistook the movement for an attack and fired his taser.

Unfortunately, instead of only subduing the drunk, the man died. It got worse when they identified the drunk as a member of the Georgia House of Representatives in town for a fishing derby. A coroner's inquest confirmed a history of serious underlying heart disease—he had suffered a massive coronary, unrelated to the taser. In the end, the police officer had been reinstated, but it created a lot of bad blood. Mick hoped everybody involved understood he was only doing his job, but he definitely left town without making friends.

The sheriff's office was on Stock Island, so he dropped in since he was close by. He parked in a visitor's spot and noticed a sign on the building listing the sheriff's name, Ron Wheeler. That name rang a bell, but he couldn't be sure if he'd met him before.

Mick presented the information officer at the front desk with his old business card. He could explain his retirement status later, but until then, he would use his former credentials to get his foot in the door. The officer listened to his request then excused herself. When she returned, she asked him to take a seat. He waited almost an hour before she instructed him to follow her.

Surprisingly, he was taken directly to meet with the sheriff. Before he walked into the room, he looked through the office window at the person sitting behind the desk and immediately remembered why the name "Ron Wheeler" sounded so familiar.

"Shit," Mick muttered under his breath. The current sheriff was the same young police officer he had investigated all those years ago. Though twenty pounds heavier and sporting a receding hairline, his face was still unmistakable.

"Mick Nassau. I never thought I'd hear that name again." The sheriff stood and walked around his desk, extending his hand.

"Sheriff." Mick happily accepted his welcome greeting and spoke using his most conciliatory tone. "I appreciate you making time considering I didn't have an appointment." Unsure whether to address the conflicted history between them, he followed the sheriff's lead.

"What brings you to Key West—this time?" Those last two words hung in the air as he took his seat behind his desk, motioning to a nearby chair.

"Well, I'm visiting an old navy friend of mine who lives in town. He sustained an injury during the hurricane and is still recovering at Jackson Memorial in Miami. His name's Jack Barton."

"I know Jack. He's a friend. This is news to me, but it's been a little chaotic around here since the storm. Will he be okay?" he asked with genuine concern.

"He's doing much better, and we're hoping to get him home this next week. He'll need some time to make a full recovery, but considering we didn't know if he would make it during those first few days, it's the best outcome."

"Well, that's a relief, but it still doesn't explain why you're here."

"Jack suffered a head injury on his boat that night. You're probably aware it's docked at the Key West Bight Marina. I noticed some anomalies that didn't sit quite right with me. Jack always puts safety first. I find it hard to believe he made a mistake and stayed on the boat too late that night. He'd been watching the radar all day and tracked the timing of the strongest rainbands and when the eye was expected to make landfall. It would've taken a lot of force to cause this injury, and if that's the case, it doesn't explain why nothing else inside the cabin shifted out of place."

The sheriff continued to stare at him but said nothing, so he continued.

"In trying to understand what might've happened, I tracked down surveillance photos of two men leaving the same dock at the marina possibly around the time he got hurt, but I'm having some difficulty finding out who they are. I want to talk to them in case they saw him or anything out of the ordinary that night. Just trying to tie up loose ends, I guess."

Sheriff Wheeler put down his pen, crossed his arms, and pushed his chair away from his desk.

"Let me get this straight. You're investigating something in my back yard without running it by me first?" His tone left Mick waiting for the other shoe to drop.

"Not really investigating, more like checking things out for a friend."

"Well, I'm glad you said that because while you were sitting in the lobby, I did some checking of my own. Imagine my surprise to find out that business card of yours isn't legit. My contact in Tallahassee informed me you don't work there anymore. They also told me you didn't leave on the best of terms."

Oh, boy. Here it comes.

"I had no intent to mislead anyone. I'm only showing around a couple pictures of the two men I picked up on camera that night. I think one of them may have come into contact with law enforcement in the past when some equipment from a job he'd been working on went missing. That's why I thought you might help. I only want to talk with them, then I'm done."

"Do you have the pictures with you?"

He passed the photos to Wheeler.

"The skinny guy's nickname is Skiff, and supposedly, he's a contract diver in the area. His legal name is Scott Bain-something, and according to a few locals, he hangs out at the Hurricane Hole. I haven't been able to identify the other guy in the polo shirt."

Wheeler studied the images. "You can leave these with me, then you need to explain the actual reason it's so important you talk to them."

Mick decided full disclosure was the only way to play this. He told the sheriff about Jack's injury and how it would be so out of character to put anyone, including himself, in an unsafe predicament. Reconciling the untied dock lines, the tidy cabin interior, and the missing cell phone also posed a challenge. When he finished his story, the sheriff stared at him with a furrowed brow.

"That's real thin. It sounds to me like Jack underestimated the storm that night. It's hard to think of our friends as being fallible, but sometimes that's just the way it is."

"Maybe, but maybe not. I have a gut feeling about it."

"Well, I make investigative decisions based on more than just feelings. I'm not okay having you interrogate any of our local citizens. It didn't end so well the last time you came to town."

"Listen, Sheriff. I'm not here to cause trouble. I'm only looking out for my friend. I might point out that same friend is an upstanding member of your community. You don't owe me anything, but I'm hoping you'll help me out—for Jack's sake."

"I'll be in touch." The sheriff stood, signaling the end to the conversation. Mick nodded then left the office without saying a word.

"Damn it," he grumbled as he walked across the parking lot to his car. Of all the people to end up as sheriff, it had to be that guy. He assumed that'd be the last time he heard from Sheriff Ron Wheeler and accepted the fact he was on his own to find Skiff.

CHAPTER 16

Just a few miles east of Key West, Stock Island felt like a world away. This densely populated suburban town offered affordable housing for the employees servicing the tourist trade in Old Town. Mobile home parks, art studios, live-aboard marinas, and restaurants all tightly packed together gave this working-class town its personality. New eclectic, waterfront resorts boasting large marinas helped to make the island a destination in its own right.

Throughout all his years visiting Jack, he had never spent time there. They usually went out on the water, fishing and diving. He thought Wayne, a full-time resident, might direct him on where to look next, since waiting for Andra at the Hole to pass along a note was not a viable plan.

"Hey, Wayne. It's Mick. Are you in town?"

"Just. Michelle stayed in Miami with Bea, but I came back this morning. Why?"

"Long story. I'm on Stock Island and need some help to get the lay of the land. Could you meet me for a beer, and I'll fill you in?"

"Okay. Jo told me you've been poking around. Is this about Jack?"

"Yeah."

"I'll be at the Hogfish Bar and Grill in ten."

. . .

The dead-end road narrowed as Mick weaved through a busy, mobile park neighborhood. A water view opened up on the right, and as he followed the curve in the road, he arrived at the Hogfish Bar, its thatched roof and sun-bleached directional signs blending in with the working marina. Lucky to find a parking spot, Mick wondered if he'd stepped back in time as his eyes adjusted to take in the restaurant's décor. Framed pictures on the wall told the story of decades of adventure and comradery.

"Mick." Wayne gestured to catch his attention.

"This is quite the place." Mick shook his hand. "Great to see you. What's it been—about five years?"

"Longer, I think. Last time you were in town for a tournament at the Key West Golf Club. One of Ellie's fundraisers."

"That's right—" The bartender interrupted to take their order. Though not hungry, Mick forced himself to order the hogfish sandwich after Wayne endorsed it as the best in town.

"So, Jo showed me your surveillance photos this morning. Michelle and I didn't recognize either of the men. What's going on?"

"To be honest, I'm not sure anything is going on." Wayne listened as he elaborated on all the details that had happened since he returned to town, including his history with the sheriff. "What do ya think?"

Wayne pushed his plate away and took a long drink before speaking. "Jack always bragged about your career successes. Any time a case you were working on made the news, he'd forward the article. If you think something might've happened that night, that's all I need to hear. Jack trusted you, and so do I. What can I do to help?"

Wayne volunteered to show the surveillance photos around the island. Having lived in town for decades, he was familiar with many of the business owners. Suspicious of outsiders, the locals would be more likely to talk with someone they recognized.

"Leave it to me. I'll make the rounds this afternoon, starting with the manager here. I saw him come in while we were eating. I'll probably have more luck if I talk to him alone."

"Thanks. I'm heading back to the marina after I do one more walk-through at the Hurricane Hole." Mick reached for his wallet until Wayne waved him off.

"Lunch is on me."

. . .

After striking out again at Skiff's favorite bar, Mick texted with Jo to see if it would be okay to drop by and take Bob the Dog for a walk. He needed time to unwind and seeing them both would help turn his mood around.

When he arrived at the Key West Veterinary Hospital, he noticed Bob's adoption sign still posted at the front desk. The receptionist waved Mick through as she managed client phone calls and two boisterous Golden Retrievers in the lobby.

"Hi, Mr. Nassau." Jo's head tech walked past him carrying a Pomeranian. "Dr. Barton's in back-to-back appointments, but she wanted me to thank you for walking Bob."

When he entered the kennel, Bob moved to the front of his run, wagging his tail at high speed.

"Hey, buddy." Mick opened the kennel door to pet him. Bob sat with his paw on Mick's shoe, leaning into his leg while he enjoyed an extended ear massage. "Let's go." He attached the leash and they left through the back door.

The cheerful dog greeted everyone they passed. Mick expanded their route but not too far to risk overheating Bob. When they returned, Mick freshened Bob's water bowl and sat on a chair in the treatment area while Bob enjoyed a few of his favorite cookies.

Jo walked out of the nearby exam room. "Mick and Bob, together again. He's happy to see you."

Mick stood to greet her, pleasantly surprised when she kissed him before stepping back.

"How are you holding up?" he asked.

"Treading water, really. I try to be present and focus on the moment by shutting everything else out, whether I'm with Jack or here at the hospital. I guess I'm sort of in survival mode. What about you?"

"That's a long story. I'll fill you in over dinner. Do you have a favorite place I should order from?"

"I'm craving some comfort Italian food. Antonia's, on Duval Street, has amazing Bolognese pasta."

"Sounds good to me."

"I should finish around seven and will meet you at Jack's." Her vet tech interrupted to inform her the next patient was ready. "I have to get back to work, but I'll see you in a few hours. And thanks again for walking Bob."

Mick smiled down at the well-behaved dog while petting his head. "My pleasure." Bob's dinner awaited him back in his kennel, providing a distraction that made it easier for Mick to say goodbye. This way, he didn't have to face the guilt of Bob staring at him when he left.

■ ■ ■

He had a list of things to do before Jo arrived, including a quick stop to get some beer and wine. It'd been a week since he checked in with Mrs. Beckman, his house sitter, who handled things when he had to be out of town for extended periods. After verifying with her that everything was fine, he called Bryce, who was glad to hear about Jack's progress. He listened as Mick recapped his day, detailing Abe's evasiveness, the search for Skiff, and the unfortunate encounter with the sheriff.

"You sure have a knack for getting caught in the middle of things. Do you still think something's off?"

"I don't know. I might be slipping into old habits—once an investigator, always an investigator." He questioned his instincts, wondering if his pursuit of Skiff was driven more by losing his job than by the facts surrounding Jack's injury.

"Be careful, okay. I'm not around to back you up."

Mick wanted to change the subject. "How're things going at work?"

Bryce kept it brief as he updated his former partner on the latest drama involving the commissioner and the governor. Mick's firing hadn't stopped the press from pursuing an investigation into the governor's campaign finances, including his unscrupulous connection to a corrupt real estate developer. The truth always found its way to the light of day. Mick felt vindicated knowing justice had a chance.

...

With the afternoon fading, he showered and sat down to watch the Marlins game on TV as he scrolled through the online menu for Antonia's. He added a shrimp pasta to Jo's request. Dinner would be ready for pickup before seven.

While driving to Antonia's in the golf cart, he received a text from Little Jimmy who had new intel on where Skiff might be staying. He'd be in touch later if he had anything to share. Mick told him to call, day or night.

He could sense his luck changing—Little Jimmy's new lead topped off by an evening with Jo. Tonight wasn't an official date, but that didn't matter. He looked forward to spending time with her. She wanted to inspect Jack's place before his return home, but Mick wondered if she felt the same way he did. Whenever they were together, electricity flowed between them. Emotions were raw after the past week's events, but there was something deeper going on.

He became intoxicated by the smell emanating from Antonia's kitchen when he walked in the restaurant's front door. They were in the middle of their busy dinner seating, so Mick waited a few minutes at the bar for his order. Once he'd paid and was back in the golf cart, it took all of his willpower not to grab one of the garlic rolls out of the bag. He texted Jo to let her know he had the food and would be home soon.

He pulled into Jack's driveway, parking the golf cart at the back to leave room for Jo's car. He juggled the takeout bags while searching for the front door keys when he caught movement in his periphery, coming from the shadows. He turned to look but not quick enough to react before being blindsided by a powerful blow to the back of his head. Mick dropped the bags as he fell to the ground. The last thing he heard before losing consciousness was his attacker growling in his ear, "Back off."

CHAPTER 17

He was out long enough that when he came to and tried to sit up, he heard Jo calling his name. She sounded far away at first. He blinked hard as he tried to bring his eyes into focus.

"Mick! Are you okay?" She ran to his side and caught him before he fell back to the ground.

It took a minute before he could speak. His head was killing him, and he could feel the warmth of fresh blood on the back of his neck.

"I was attacked. My instincts were right," he whispered—his voice barely audible.

"What do you mean?" She held on to keep him from standing. "Mick, just sit, please. I'm calling 911."

Jo propped him against Jack's exterior wall, but he kept leaning over on her shoulder for support.

His vision was blurry, and he didn't have the strength to argue against calling for help. Within ten minutes, both the police and EMS arrived. His head cleared, but he agreed to go in the ambulance to be evaluated at the ER in order to appease Jo. The police officer on the scene would get Mick's statement after he had been treated. Jo picked up the food and golf cart keys and followed behind in her own car. Once again, they were heading to the Lower Keys Medical Center—the second time in a week.

It was close to an hour before the nurse brought Jo back to see Mick. He lay in a hospital bed, surrounded by a privacy curtain, in the bustling treatment area of the ER.

As soon as he saw her, he smiled. Jo Barton was a sight for sore eyes.

"Oh, Mick. Are you all right?" she asked in a quiet, worried tone, taking his hand in hers.

"I've been better. They gave me something for the headache, and thankfully, it's kicking in. I have a few stitches, but it's nothing more serious than that." He could see the look on her face and wanted her to know he'd be okay. "Just a mild concussion, nothing at all like Jack."

A doubtful look crossed her face. "Are you sure? I'd like to talk to the doctor."

"He said he'd be back to go over my discharge instructions. It's the same doctor that treated Jack last week. He's a good guy."

"I'm sure he is, but he's going to wonder about us if we keep this up. Let's all promise to stay out of the ER for the indefinite future."

"You won't get an argument from me."

Just then, the nurse stepped around the curtain followed by the officer who'd arrived first to the emergency call. Mick gave his statement but left out the important parts. He never mentioned the attacker's warning or that Mick had been asking uncomfortable questions around town. He omitted the links to Jack's injury, Skiff, and Abe. Until Mick had more information, he didn't want the local police to get involved, or if he was being completely honest, he didn't want them to get in his way.

The officer concluded he likely interrupted a robbery in progress before anything was stolen. Petty crime occurred in town, just like any other tourist destination. The officer told Mick he would follow up tomorrow to make sure nothing new came to mind but admitted he wasn't hopeful they would ever catch the guy. Mick disagreed but kept that thought to himself. His attack was personal, and the only thing someone would want Mick to "back off" of was his search for Skiff. That wasn't going to happen.

After the police officer left, the doctor came in to review the discharge instructions. Since Mick shouldn't be alone over the next twenty-four hours, Jo confirmed she would monitor him for any complications. The doctor discussed the care of Mick's stitches and symptoms to watch for with a concussion. Unfortunately, they both had become all too familiar with the signs associated with a head injury.

"Let's get you home," Jo said.

. . .

She pulled her car up to the ER door as a nurse wheeled Mick out in a chair, a common precaution. His first few steps were a little wobbly, but he declined any help. Jo stopped at the pharmacy on their way back to Jack's, picking up his pain medicine.

Mick preferred to lie down in the living room, so she got him set up on the couch where he would be comfortable. Neither of them had eaten since lunch, but Mick declined any food, and a few minutes later, he fell asleep while watching Law and Order reruns. Jo scrounged around the kitchen and made herself a grilled cheese sandwich. Unfortunately, the takeout food had been sitting in her hot car and had to be tossed out.

She slept next to Mick in the recliner chair but bolted awake when she heard him groaning as he attempted to stand.

"Wait, wait. Let me help you."

"I'm okay. Just have a splitting headache."

"It's about time to take your next dose of meds. Let me grab them. You really should try to eat something."

"I could handle a piece of peanut butter toast, please."

Jo made him a snack and got him to drink some water. As they sat in the darkened room, Mick said, "That attack tonight was meant as a warning. It was personal."

"When I found you, you said something about your instincts. What did you mean?"

It took some time for him to fill her in on all the details, starting with confronting Abe and ending with his chat with the sheriff, their history, and the hope that Little Jimmy would have more information to share.

"My gut told me something was off about Jack's injury, and getting hit on the head tonight proved I was right."

"If that's all true, that means you're not safe," she said. "And neither is Jack."

"I'll be fine. Nobody's going to get the drop on me a second time, and Jack's safe in Miami, surrounded by Bea and the hospital staff." Deep down, Mick realized he needed to sort this out before Jack came home.

"Can I convince you to go to the police? I get that you have a history with the sheriff, but that doesn't mean you should shut him out," she said.

"Actually, I kind of need him now. I normally prefer working on my own, but I want him to process Jack's boat as a crime scene. Not sure if he'll agree with me though."

"Sheriff Ron Wheeler's little sister, Lily, is one of my good friends. I'm going over to talk with him in the morning. If he's not willing to look into this, then there'll be hell to pay." She began pacing around the room.

Mick cracked a smile. She was even more beautiful when she was angry.

"I mean it, Mick. This has gone from being a horrible accident to a dangerous unknown."

"You're right. We'll both go together to talk to him. Okay?"

She nodded. "You need to get some rest. I'll stay here, and we can sort everything out in the morning."

He needed little convincing. The pain meds started doing their thing, and he quickly fell back asleep. Jo sat wide awake watching him until she eventually nodded off. Just before dawn, they were both awakened by a knock at the door. She jumped to her feet and looked through the peephole, shocked to see Ron Wheeler standing there.

"Sheriff." Jo opened the door and invited him in. "Let me get the lights on and some coffee brewing."

Mick struggled to a sitting position then motioned for the sheriff to take a seat.

"Is it common for you to do personal follow-ups with all the mugging victims in town?" he asked.

"No. You're special."

"Good to know," Mick quipped back.

"But you'll imagine my surprise when your name popped up on an incident report. And right after you informed me about your off-the-books investigation."

Jo walked into the living room, and her presence helped tamp down the obvious tension between the two men.

"Sheriff, we're glad you're here. We were going to come see you this morning," Jo sent a warning glance in Mick's direction. "We have a story to tell you, and we're hoping you can help us out."

Once again, Mick recapped the entire series of events that culminated in his attack last night. The sheriff responded with anger after learning Mick hadn't been upfront with him at the office, or with the police officer who took his statement at the hospital. When Mick closed his eyes and rubbed his head, the sheriff backed off and lowered his voice.

"Okay. I'll look into it, but you both have to promise me you'll stay out of it and let me do my job." He turned to Mick. "You don't have any jurisdiction here—or anywhere else, for that matter. You need to leave it to the professionals."

He understood the sheriff was intentionally trying to provoke him, so to keep the peace, he agreed. Judging by his expression, Mick didn't think the sheriff believed him, but he nodded anyway.

"I have one more request," Mick said. "I'd like you to treat Jack's cabin as a crime scene. Besides me, only the paramedics and Bea have been in there since his injury, and you can get our fingerprints for exclusion."

"I think you're one step ahead of yourself. Let me look into things first. I can't just send my crime technicians into the field on a witch hunt. I need more evidence or probable cause."

Mick would have said and done the same thing, but it didn't reduce his annoyance that no action was being taken.

"Will you commit to telling us if you find out anything that relates to Jack. Anything at all?" Jo asked, her attempts to diffuse the conflict were obvious to both men.

"I will as much as I can. That's the best I can do. I'll be in touch." He stood to leave. "Jo, it was nice seeing you again. We're all excited to have you back in town and congratulations on the new hospital."

"Thanks, Sheriff. I need to reconnect with Lily. Tell her once Jack is settled back home, I'll call her."

"Will do." He let himself out the front door.

CHAPTER 18

"What am I going to do with you, Mick? You're not going to leave this alone, are you?"

"Nope."

"Well, I can't babysit you 24/7. The doctor said you should be monitored today, but I have to be at the hospital soon—my schedule is packed. Why don't you come and hang out with me at work?"

"I'd love to spend the day with you and Bob, but I doubt that's the best place for me to recuperate. How about Plan B? I'll stay here, and I promise to call you if I feel any worse."

"That won't work for me. We need a better plan."

"I'll reach out to Wayne to see if he can come over. Would that suffice?" Mick asked.

"Sure, but I want to talk to him myself." She called Wayne and filled him in on yet another head injury. He'd started out for Jack's place before she finished their conversation.

"I'm going to take a shower." He held onto the couch to steady himself, and once the dizziness subsided, he shuffled to the bathroom. Still shaky on his feet and with a pounding headache, he allowed the hot water to run over his body until he felt recharged enough to move forward with his day. Jo instituted wellness checks every few minutes, calling through the door to make sure he was okay. When he eventually returned to the kitchen, Wayne had arrived, and Mick overheard them discussing his current predicament.

"That was fast. Thanks for coming," Mick said.

"I've already told Wayne when you're due for your next dose of medicine, and he's agreed to keep you out of trouble, at least for today. I'll call later, and I'll be back after work. Please don't do anything reckless."

He nodded. If he didn't say the words out loud, then he wouldn't be breaking his commitment to her. She shook her head, gave him a tight squeeze, and hurried out the front door.

"You don't want to piss her off, Mick. She means business."

"I know. Listen, Wayne. If you've got stuff to do, I'll be fine. Really."

"No way. You're stuck with me," he said. "I had a blast playing the role of a private investigator yesterday afternoon but had little luck. The dock shop manager at The Perry Hotel marina recognized the skinny diver guy and knew his name was Skiff, but that was it. Sorry, Mick."

"No worries. I thought I might drive to Miami today to see Jack, but that was before I was attacked. There's no way I'm leaving town now."

"Jo filled me in on everything that happened since I saw you last. If you need me to do anything to help, just say the word."

Mick had a few things he wanted to take care of. First, he stepped outside to call Bryce and update him on the events of last night. He planned to continue with his investigation, and he hoped Bryce could access the resources of the FDLE to get background info on Skiff. It was asking a lot, but Bryce didn't hesitate.

"I'll see what I can find out. You said you've got someone there with you, right?"

"Yes. Jack's friend, Wayne, is here."

"Promise me you won't try to offload him somewhere and go out on your own."

"He's not going anywhere."

"Okay, I'll talk to you later. Be safe."

Mick joined Wayne in the kitchen when his phone vibrated—a text from Little Jimmy letting him know he had some new information to share. Eager for a break, Mick called him right back. Skiff supposedly lived at the Tropical Seas Mobile Park, in a trailer home on Stock Island. Jimmy didn't have the unit number but thought the manager on duty could help. Mick thanked him profusely for the tip.

Wayne raised his eyebrow in question when Mick disconnected the call. "Sounds like you have a lead."

"I do, and I need to check it out. I don't want to put you in an uncomfortable position. I'll be fine handling this on my own."

"No way—Jo would kill me. Consider me your chauffeur for the day. Where to?"

"Okay then. We're headed to Stock Island, but I need to eat first."

"And take your medicine—as per Jo." He put his hands in the air to signal, *Don't shoot the messenger.* "Let's pick up a breakfast burrito from the Cuban place on South Street. I haven't been there in a while."

■ ■ ■

Mick opted for some huevos rancheros enchiladas and a hit of caffeine in the form of a cortadito—a necessary jolt of espresso and sugar. It was the perfect choice. Except for the giant knot on the back of his head, he felt almost human again by the time they'd finished eating.

Wayne had heard of the trailer park where they were headed but had never been there before. The exorbitant cost of housing in Key West forced many people that worked in the service industry to live in mobile home parks. They were often the only affordable choices, considering their incomes.

They pulled into the Tropical Seas and parked outside a building marked with a manager's office sign in the window. Mick entered the small room and presented his business card authoritatively, compensating for the fact he no longer held the position of special agent. The manager seemed wary of giving away residents' personal information, but Mick's charming personality and her judgment of Skiff as a deadbeat convinced her to cooperate. Skiff, aka Scott Bainbridge, lived in the yellow trailer at the end of Tahiti Street, on the left. Mick thanked her and promised there would be no trouble. He just wanted to ask a few questions.

Skiff's trailer stood out as one of the shabbiest in the park. A broken-down plastic lawn chair and a few empty beer bottles littered the seashell driveway in front. They exited the car and called out his name.

"Wayne, can you stay back? I really don't know what to expect with this guy."

Wayne ignored him and followed behind.

"Skiff, are you in there?" Mick shouted as he approached the door. "I got your name from a friend. I have a dive job I want to talk to you about." There was no answer.

He knocked a few times, then checked the handle—it was unlocked.

"What's that smell?" Wayne exclaimed, covering his nose and mouth with his hand as he took a step back.

Even before Mick cracked the door open, the stench hit him like a wave, overwhelming his senses and bringing tears to his eyes. Only his years of experience at crime scenes allowed him to suppress the urge to retch.

"I'll just have a quick look," Mick said. He didn't hear a sound, which led him to believe the place was empty.

Mick hadn't moved more than two feet inside the front door when he saw Skiff lying on the floor of his tiny kitchen. It looked like a gunshot wound to the back of the head. He swatted away the buzzing flies and checked for a pulse, just to be certain.

"Crap."

"What?" Wayne asked. "Is that horrible smell what I think it is?"

"Yup. He's dead. Just stay there, Wayne—we need to avoid messing up the crime scene."

"Oh shit. Do you want me to call 911?"

"No. Give me a minute, and I'll call the sheriff myself."

He left Wayne standing outside the door and did a quick walk-through of the trailer. It was essentially a one-room space with a small lounge, kitchen, and sleeping loft at the far end. On the dining counter sat a strange, large tank or tub with a bunch of pumps, wires, and equipment attached to the sides. The tank was only half full of water and didn't have any fish in it. Other than the weird tank, the only other thing out of the ordinary were the nautical maps tacked to the wall and marked with hieroglyphic-like scrawls. Mick had to get out of Skiff's place and avoid touching anything. It would be bad enough he had to call the sheriff and break the news but could get worse if he contaminated the crime scene more than he already had. He took photos of the interior, the tank, and the maps before leaving the space.

When he exited the trailer, Wayne asked, "Can you tell what happened to him?"

"Yeah. Someone shot him in the head."

"What's going on here? Does all this have something to do with Jack?"

"I'm afraid it does, but I have no idea what the connection is yet. Wayne, could you walk back to the manager's office to let her know the police will be arriving soon. I don't want her to be frightened when they come charging in."

He then placed a call to the sheriff but had to leave a message, which prompted an immediate return call. After being yelled at for a minute, Mick agreed to stay on site and keep the crime scene secure until a team could get there. He wasn't looking forward to explaining himself, yet again. He'd been explicitly warned against pursuing leads on his own. Hopefully, the sheriff would now take everything Mick had told him more seriously. He could handle any blowback, as long as it led to an official investigation into Jack's case, which he now believed should be upgraded to attempted murder.

CHAPTER 19

The first cars to arrive at the trailer park were patrol cars, lights on but without their sirens. The officers must have been told to look for Mick because they asked for his identification then informed him to remain at the scene until the sheriff arrived. A young officer entered Skiff's trailer, likely to confirm that he was indeed dead and there was no other immediate threat. He didn't last long, quickly running from the trailer with a hand covering his mouth.

Minutes later, the sheriff arrived. His face flushed crimson, and he scowled as he stepped out of the car. He walked past Mick and Wayne, without acknowledging them, in order to speak with the first officer on scene. After the sheriff did a quick survey of the trailer, he ordered the area to be cordoned off. Some neighbors had made their way over to Skiff's, forming a small crowd of spectators. Mick could hear the sheriff let out an enormous sigh before turning and walking in his direction.

"Here it comes," Mick said under his breath.

"So, can you please explain to me how you ended up as the first person at my crime scene?" The sheriff's tone made it perfectly clear he wasn't kidding around.

"Listen, Sheriff. I just came by to talk to the guy. He's the one I showed you from the surveillance photos taken near Jack's boat on the night of the storm. Skiff's real name is Scott Bainbridge." He needed to answer the questions asked of him but decided against embellishing beyond the basic facts.

The sheriff looked back and forth at both men before asking, "Did the two of you go inside the trailer?"

"No. Just me. My fingerprints will be on file in the system for exclusion," Mick said. "Wayne stayed outside. This is Wayne Michaels, a friend of Jack's."

"I know Wayne. How did you get mixed up with him today?" The sheriff pointed in Mick's direction.

"Well, Ron, I volunteered to be his babysitter after Jo left for work. I guess I failed at the task." Wayne's attempt to lighten the mood didn't work.

"Mr. Nassau, please tell me if there's anything else I need to understand about what's going on here." The sheriff's request sounded more like a demand. "I asked you to stay out of it, but clearly, you weren't listening."

"There's nothing left to tell. This guy was near Jack's boat that night, and now he's dead. I don't understand how or why, but these two things are connected," Mick said. "I was asking questions around town, and I ended up in the ER because of it. Isn't it about time you treated Jack's accident as an assault, which means processing the cabin on *Bravo Zulu* as a crime scene?"

"Fine. You win. I'm sure you realize my crime scene techs will be tied up here for a while. I'll call your cell when they're ready to head over to the marina so you can give them access to the boat. I'll also need to get your formal statement either today or early tomorrow. Is all that acceptable to you, *Ex-Agent Nassau*?"

Mick ignored his snide comment. "Yes. But you might also want to talk to a guy with his boat docked near Jack's. He took the dead guy out on a diving charter, yet he denies having ever seen him before. The guy's name is Abe, and I'm sure he's hiding something."

The sheriff's jaw tightened as he ground his teeth together. "What's his last name?"

Mick proceeded with caution when he noticed a bulging blood vessel over the sheriff's right eye. He didn't want to listen to another reprimand or be accused of running a renegade investigation.

"That I don't know, but the marina must have all his information since he's a liveaboard."

"I'd appreciate it if you both left the area now. I'll call you later with details about timing. Wayne, I wish you luck keeping tabs on Mick. I'd tell your friend to go home if I thought it would make a difference." The sheriff walked back toward the trailer.

"That's our signal to leave," Wayne said. "Where to next?"

"Why are you assuming there's a *next*?"

"Well, I've only been hanging with you for a day, but I'm quite certain you're going to keep pushing until you sort this out."

"Am I that obvious?"

"Yeah, but it's okay. This needs to be settled before Jack comes home."

"Agreed. I have a couple pictures I want to show you, but let's get out of here first. How about I buy you a drink at the Green Parrot?"

"I think we both could use one after this morning. Should I check with Jo to see if you can mix alcohol with your meds?"

"I wouldn't make that call if I were you. I promise to nurse my beer."

■ ■ ■

The Green Parrot seemed unusually quiet, even for a weekday lunchtime. Mick knew Little Jimmy would be working from his earlier phone message. They grabbed two stools at a quiet corner of the bar and waited for him to come by.

"What did you want to show me?" Wayne asked.

Mick pulled up the pictures from the crime scene and handed over his phone.

"Here. This was in Skiff's trailer. It looks like some special type of tank. I have no idea about the purpose of all these pumps and wires or what the tank would be used for."

Wayne scrolled through the images, then his face lit up.

"I'm not sure, but I might've seen something like this before. Stay here. I'll be right back." Before Mick could reply, Wayne had jumped off his stool and walked out of the Parrot. "Send those pictures to my cell phone," he shouted through the open window before disappearing toward the harbor.

That's strange, Mick thought. He disliked being stuck in a holding pattern—waiting to hear from the sheriff and now waiting for Wayne to return. He might as well order that beer while he sat in limbo.

"Hey, Mick, did I just see Wayne leave?" Jimmy asked.

"Yeah, he should be right back. I'll have whatever's good on tap."

"Did that lead pan out on Skiff?" He poured him a pint.

"It did. Thanks. Look, you'll probably find out about it soon enough, but you need to promise you'll keep what I'm about to tell you to yourself for now. For Jack's sake, okay?"

"I can keep a secret."

"I just found Skiff—dead—out at his trailer. He'd been murdered."

"What? Holy shit. He wasn't exactly a straight shooter, but I had no idea he was involved in any serious criminal stuff. At least nothing that would get him killed."

Mick kept the cause of death to himself, in case the sheriff planned to hold back that key piece of evidence from the public.

"The reason I'm telling you, Jimmy, is that I really need to speak to any of his friends or previous coworkers. I think Andra, the bartender at the Hole, knew a few but wouldn't give me their names. I'm willing to pay for good info."

"I'm on it." Jimmy stepped away from the bar to make a private call. He returned a few minutes later.

"I talked with Andra, and she's going to pass your number along to one of Skiff's buddies right away. I promise—I didn't say anything about his murder, but she already knew about it. News travels fast on the island."

"I figured. There were a bunch of neighbors hanging around when we left the trailer park."

They had switched the conversation to chat about Jack and how he was doing with his recovery when Wayne came back into the bar, out of breath.

"Where did you go?" Mick asked.

"To see a golf buddy of mine at the Mel Fisher Maritime Museum. Hi, Jimmy! How are you doing?"

"Great, Wayne. What'll you have? The usual?"

"Sounds good. Thanks." Jimmy stepped away to pour him a Guinness.

"Why did you go to the museum?" Mick asked, now thoroughly confused.

"Let's finish our beer. We have an appointment in thirty minutes with my friend who's the head archaeologist there. I'll fill you in on the way over. It's only about a five-minute walk."

"That's it? Can you at least give me a clue?"

"No. It's easier if I show you."

Despite Wayne's cryptic message, he had no choice but to agree. They'd almost finished their drink when they overheard a man ask Jimmy where to find this *Mick guy*. Jimmy pointed in Mick's direction then resumed waiting on the other patrons at the bar.

"You're Mick?" the stranger asked as he approached.

"That's me."

"I'm a friend of Skiff's. Or I guess I was a friend of Skiff's. I still can't believe he's gone. Shit. Anyway, Andra told me where to find you and that you're paying for info."

"What's your name?" Mick asked.

"Let's say it's John." The stranger smirked at the use of an obvious fake name.

"Okay, John. What do you have for me? I'm trying to find out what Skiff's been doing lately. Where was he working? Was he having any kind of trouble? There's a hundred dollars in it for you if you can help me out."

"What's your angle? Why do you wanna know all that?"

"Skiff was at the marina a few nights ago when a friend of mine was hurt. I want to know if he saw anything that could help me out. Just looking to ask a few questions of anyone he may have talked to—nothing else."

"It'll cost you two hundred."

"One fifty but it needs to be useful."

"It is," John assured him. "I don't have any details about what kinda trouble Skiff was in, but he'd been running his mouth a lot the last two weeks about some big score. He planned to buy himself a dive boat with the money, setting himself up real good."

"Was he working for anyone in town?" Mick asked.

"No, he hasn't had a real job for months, but he'd been out diving lately. I only know that because it's the only time he'll turn down a beer. He has this ridiculous rule about not drinking the night before a big dive."

"Who's he been diving with? He doesn't have his own boat, does he?"

"Skiff doesn't even have a car. He never said who he was diving with, but it was someone in town, not out at Stock Island. He bummed a ride in with his dive bag."

"I've been told he was a talented diver. Wouldn't it be easy for him to get steady work?"

"You'd think so. He was my friend, but he could really be a pain in the ass sometimes—burned a lot of bridges. I doubt anyone enjoyed working with him."

"Did Skiff ever say when he expected to get this big pay out?"

"No, but if I had to guess, it was soon. He asked a mechanic buddy to take him for a sea trial on this boat that's up for sale. Skiff had been eyeing it for a while," John said. "That's all I got."

"What's the asking price on the boat?"

"Around a hundred thousand, but he thought he could negotiate a better price."

"Can you get in touch if you hear anything else about what he's been doing? I'll pay again." Mick reached for his wallet.

He nodded and held out his hand. "I'll check in with Andra if I need to find you."

John took the cash and left as quickly as he had arrived. Mick decided against giving him a business card, as the law enforcement angle might scare the guy away. It seemed the local bartender info network would be the easiest way to reach someone who was flying below the radar.

"That's interesting," Mick said. "If Skiff was about to get a big payday despite being unemployed, and he'd been out diving lately, it makes me wonder what he was up to when he was out diving with Abe." He turned to Wayne for input.

Wayne wore a wide grin, as if he was the only one in on the joke.

CHAPTER 20

"What's going on?"

"Let's settle up with Jimmy, and I'll tell you on the way. Have you ever been to the treasure museum off Front Street?" Wayne asked.

"No, but I've heard the stories about Mel Fisher and his Spanish galleon. He's legendary."

Mel Fisher, a famous American treasure hunter, discovered the *Nuestra Senora de Atocha*, a Spanish galleon filled with gold, silver, and jewels that sunk off the coast of Key West in the sixteenth century. Mel's salvage of the wreck had been valued at four hundred and fifty-million dollars. After a lengthy court battle with the State of Florida, he eventually gained full ownership of the rights to the treasure. The story of his twenty-year search for the *Atocha*, including many of its priceless artifacts, was on display at the Mel Fisher Museum in Key West, and Mick and Wayne were heading there next.

"My friend, Alex Balfour, is in charge of the Mel Fisher Maritime Heritage Society, a nonprofit division of the company that works to discover and preserve underwater antiquities. He's the head archaeologist, and when he's not on a dive site, he's usually in the working lab at the museum. They offer small behind-the-scene tours of the facility, and lucky for us, he's there today," Wayne said.

"Great, but why do you think we need to talk to him?"

"It was that picture of the weird tank in Skiff's trailer. I'd seen something like it before during my last visit to Alex's lab. He had some new artifacts from a dive site in the Bahamas they were working on preserving. Items retrieved from the ocean emerge covered in rock and coral. They use special equipment and techniques to clean off the junk while protecting the discovery. You'll see for yourself."

"Okay, but for the time being, don't mention the murder. I don't know what details the sheriff is holding back from the press, and if word gets out more than it already has, he'll have my head."

. . .

While Alex finished up with a private tour group, they checked out the museum exhibits. A short film chronicled the discovery of the *Atocha* followed by interactive displays showcasing silver bars, emeralds the size of golf balls, gold coins, and jewelry. Mick thought Mel's story would make a great movie. Alex eventually found them inspecting weapons recovered from the galleon.

"You must be Mick," he said, greeting them and shaking their hands.

"We appreciate you making the time," Wayne said.

"Follow me. I'll take you to the lab, and we can talk there."

The three of them went upstairs to the restricted working area of the museum. They entered a large room filled with diagrams, maps, and many tanks of varying sizes, similar in appearance to what Mick had seen in Skiff's trailer. Display cases contained pottery and the barrel from a large, iron cannon.

"This is where all the discoveries from our sites come to be cleaned, cataloged, and preserved," Alex said. "Wayne showed me the picture you took of the tank. I think you'll agree it looks like a few of our smaller ones over here."

"It looks the same. What's all the equipment attached to the tank used for?" Mick asked.

"Depending on the composition of the discovery, we employ different techniques. These tanks use a reverse electrolysis water bath method to remove all the coral and debris covering the items. This tank here contains small iron cannonballs. We can usually figure out what's under all that crust based on experience, then we confirm our theory with an X-ray."

Wayne leaned over to get a closer look. "How long does it take to clean something like this?" The item in the tank resembled a grapefruit-sized hunk of rock.

"Weeks to months. Even up to years for large items like those twelve-foot cannons we have in the far corner," Alex replied. "Other metals, like silver and gold, usually stay much more pristine in the salt water and can clean up in days. Gold is the most amazing of all, as it often looks brand new—even after being in the water for centuries."

Mick racked his brain trying to figure out how this connected to Jack's case and why Skiff had one in his trailer. "Do a lot of recreational divers have tanks like this?"

"No, I don't think the average diver would have one. Wayne said this guy you're looking for was a salvage diver in the area. Is that right?"

"Supposedly, but he wasn't working for anyone right now, as far as I can tell. His friend said he'd been talking about a big payday. What other types of things can someone clean quickly?" Mick asked.

"Likely just silver, gold, or some jewel stones. Anything else would take longer or be less valuable."

Mick pulled out his phone to locate the photo of the map from Skiff's trailer. "Does this mean anything to you?"

After zooming in and out of various sections of the image, Alex shook his head. "It's a chart of an area near here—Marquesas Keys and Rebecca Shoal. I can't decipher the handwritten notes, though. Sorry."

"Are there any archaeological dives going on around Key West right now?" Wayne asked.

"Always. The Mel Fisher family still have the dive rights for the other half of the *Atocha* they have yet to locate. It supposedly carried the mother lode of the treasure. There are a few companies diving for wrecks associated with Spanish treasure fleets from the 1600s and 1700s. These galleons loaded up on gold, silver, jewels, and artifacts from South America. Their route back to Spain took them from Cuba and up the coast of Florida before heading across the Atlantic to Europe. Hidden coral reefs, pirates, and hurricanes were hazards that made the voyage treacherous. That's why we have so many treasure hunters down here," Alex said. "Hundreds of millions of dollars are still sitting on the bottom of the ocean, yet to be discovered."

"Don't most of the big companies have exclusive rights to a specific shipwreck?" Wayne asked.

"Yes. Once we've been able to find some pieces to support the provenance of the ship. It's serious trouble for anyone who covertly takes antiquities from the ocean within a registered claim. When these ships broke apart and sank, their precious cargo would spread over extensive areas of the ocean floor. When you add in hundreds of years of storms and tidal changes, it explains why it can take decades to work through a staked-out search grid."

"Would there be any way to know if our guy, Skiff, had been working for any of these treasure hunters in his past?" Mick asked.

"I could probably find out for you. Give me his name, and I'll ask around a few of the larger companies working sites in the area. I'll get back to you if I hear anything."

Mick wrote Skiff's full name and physical description. Finally, he was on to something.

If Skiff had found an item of value on a dive, it would be one way to explain the large windfall he'd been banking on. And if he were stealing from an established dive site, it would also explain why he was keeping it secret. More than likely, dumb luck factored into it, and less likely, Skiff had orchestrated the discovery of a new wreck. From what Mick could make out, he wasn't a strategic mastermind.

The two of them enjoyed a guided tour of the discoveries Alex and his staff were currently working on until Mick got a call from the sheriff.

Not surprisingly, he avoided pleasantries and spoke in a curt tone. The crime scene techs would be at the marina in thirty minutes, and he expected Mick to be there. After hanging up his call, they thanked Alex for his help and promised to repay him with a round of golf.

CHAPTER 21

Wayne and Mick waited on the deck of *Bravo Zulu*, having kept the cabin door locked to preserve the illusion of a secure crime scene—even though Mick had already cleaned up the blood evidence. A sea of people filled the bustling waterfront, but they all paused when the sheriff and his team walked onto the dock. Curious onlookers craned their necks to get a glimpse at whatever grisly spectacle had brought such a show of force.

Without exchanging greetings, Mick escorted the sheriff inside the cabin, pointing out where he had found Jack the morning after the hurricane and describing everything as he remembered it, including his theory about the unsecured items that had remained upright and in place. The sheriff gave instructions to the technicians and signaled for the men to join him on deck.

"Thanks for bringing your team today. I get that you don't trust me, but I'm only acting in Jack's best interest. I'm not comfortable bringing him home from the hospital until we're sure it's safe," Mick said.

"I understand that, but to be clear, I won't tolerate you running a vigilante operation in my town. Let's reset and commit to full disclosure going forward."

"Done." Mick extended his hand to shake on it. The sheriff nodded before accepting his peace offering.

"Do you have any new leads on Skiff's murder?" Wayne asked.

"We won't know more until they finish processing the forensics and complete the autopsy. The security cameras mounted at the entrance to the park were installed over a decade ago based on the quality of the images, and none of them are directed at the trailer. With a constant flow of cars and people in and out of there, it'll take a while to sort through."

They updated the sheriff on what they'd learned at the Mel Fisher Museum regarding Skiff's tank. He didn't ask questions, apparently unsurprised by their discovery.

"So, tell me about Jack's neighbor—the one that had Bainbridge out on his boat," the sheriff asked.

Mick recounted his multiple interactions with Abe over the past week, including the day of the hurricane when he saw Skiff leaving with his dive bag. The sheriff listened without interrupting.

"I'm going to speak with Abe, but I need you to stay back. Understood?" The sheriff's directive was not open to debate.

"Sure. It's the trawler at the end on the right." He pointed toward Abe's boat then followed the sheriff halfway down the dock. Wheeler stopped and turned to look over his shoulder. His death stare clarified that was as far as Mick could go.

The sheriff called out Abe's name, and when Abe peered out of the cabin, his mouth gaped open before regaining his composure. Even from a distance, Mick could see the whites of his eyes as the color drained from his face. While maintaining his distance from the sheriff, Abe stepped on deck and closed the door behind him. He stood with his back against the wheelhouse. The two men talked, but Mick couldn't make out what they were saying. Abe disappeared out of view and returned carrying paperwork, which he handed to the sheriff. They spoke for about ten minutes until the sheriff gave him back the documents and walked toward *Zulu*. Abe continued to stare, not at the retreating law enforcement officer but at Mick, his uncontained rage visible on his face, then he turned around and disappeared inside.

"So?" Mick asked the sheriff as he stepped on deck.

"He wasn't exactly happy about volunteering information. He admitted to taking Bainbridge out for a dive but said it was a one time, private charter, and otherwise, he didn't know the guy."

"Do you believe him? There's something else going on here. I'm sure of it," Mick said. "Jack told me Abe almost never left port and had never taken out charters before."

"Stay away from him. You know how investigations proceed. We'll get to the truth, but we need to follow standard police protocols. Don't forget where you came from. I'm pretty sure you would have been less than hospitable if a rogue investigator messed around in one of your cases."

"Okay. I hear you loud and clear, but there's one more thing."

The sheriff crossed his arms over his chest, as if bracing himself for what came next.

"I still can't find Jack's cell phone. He had it on him the night of his injury because he texted Bea around eight o'clock. He would've kept that phone near in case she needed to reach him. It wasn't here when the paramedics arrived, and I've looked over every square inch of the boat, twice."

The sheriff shrugged. "Maybe it fell overboard in the storm."

"That's what everybody thinks, but that's not Jack. He's an experienced captain, and he doesn't make careless mistakes. I checked his laptop, and I couldn't locate it using his *Find My Phone* app. The battery is dead, or it's turned off."

"Ron, I have to agree with Mick," Wayne said. "That's not how Jack operates. He always grumbles about the foolish tourists that drop their phones overboard while taking selfies when they're out fishing."

"I have his cell number, and I'll see what I can do." The sheriff stood, moving toward the cabin door. "After I check with the evidence techs, I'm heading to the station. Can you wait here until they're finished?"

"Of course. Let us know as soon as you have everything back from the lab," Mick said, aware his request would more than likely be disregarded.

Without committing to further cooperation, the sheriff informed Mick he expected to see him in the morning to sign his official statement regarding Skiff's murder, then he wrapped up his business and departed the marina. Within the hour, the techs came on deck, confirming they had completed their evidence collection.

The crowd of spectators had disbanded, and Mick was thankful Earl and Betty had missed the entire event. He would have to tell them about Skiff's murder, even though it would only add to their worries. While he and Wayne contemplated what to do for dinner, Jo called.

"How are you feeling? Did you follow the doctor's orders today? Remember, I'll get the truth out of Wayne."

"Well, I can't say it was a restful day, but I'm fine. There's lots to tell you. Are you almost done at the hospital?"

After a brief pause, she said, "Yes, just finishing up. Tell Wayne I'll be there to relieve him in about fifteen minutes."

"Sure, but we're not at Jack's. We're at the marina. I can pick up some fish sandwiches for the three of us, and we'll meet you at the house soon."

"Uh, okay," she said, a hint of caution in her voice. "I spoke with Bea and Jack, and it's all good. I'll fill you in when I get there."

He could use some uplifting news right about now. They locked up *Bravo Zulu* then drove home after a quick stop at the local seafood shack. Jo arrived as they pulled into the driveway.

"Hi, guys. I missed lunch today, so let's eat before we catch up. It sounds like we both have updates to share."

They grabbed drinks and sat at the kitchen table to unpack their dinner. Mick caught Jo sizing him up out of the corner of her eye. At first, he thought she was flirting, but then he realized she was watching for any lingering medical concerns related to his concussion.

"How's your head? Any blurry vision or dizziness?" she asked.

"A dull headache—that's all."

She stood and walked behind him. "Let me take a peek at your stitches." She gently parted his hair to assess his wound and finished by trailing her fingers down his neck. Mick closed his eyes and inhaled, not from the pain, but from her intimate touch.

Wayne set down his sandwich and leaned back in his chair, watching the two of them with a widening grin.

Jo blushed. "Looks good," she said, trying to sound professional before returning to her chair.

"Let's start with your news. How's Jack doing today?" Wayne asked.

"Well, he really sounded like the old Jack when I talked with him on the phone. His voice was strong, and he joked about the hospital food."

Wayne laughed. "Sounds like him."

"He's improved by leaps and bounds at every physical and occupational therapy session. They're working on a treatment plan he can continue back in Key West—the doctors hope to discharge him from the hospital in the next couple of days. Bea told me he's still dealing with some physical weakness, but his therapists think he'll make a full recovery."

"That's such a relief," Wayne said.

Jo stopped talking and stared at Mick. The corners of his mouth had turned down and his jaw clenched, an unexpected reaction from anyone who'd just received positive news.

"Mick? What's wrong?" she asked.

"Well, knowing he may be coming home in a few days has me worried. It's not safe."

They told her everything that had happened since she left for work that morning. As the details of the story unfolded, shock and fear became etched on her face.

"A murder! Your attack last night was bad enough." The pitch of her voice climbed two octaves. "Do you really think this is all related to Jack?"

"I do, unfortunately. And after lots of arm-twisting, we finally convinced the sheriff to put the resources of his department behind the investigation. I have to go to his office tomorrow to sign my statement, and I'll tell him about Jack's imminent homecoming. Since we don't understand how, or if, this is all connected, Jack may need protection."

"Or we'll need to find a temporary place for him to stay near the hospital in Miami where he can continue his therapy until this is sorted out," Jo said. "I don't want him around here if there's even a tiny amount of risk."

"That would be a safer choice, but I think you'll have a hard time keeping him from returning home once he's out of the hospital," Wayne said.

"You're right," she said. "There's no way he'd stay away."

"Did you ask him again about his memories from that night?" Mick asked.

"Yes, I ask him every day." Jo's scratchy voice trailed off, her underlying exhaustion breaking through. "He vaguely remembers working with you to secure *Zulu* before the hurricane, but he draws a blank for any details later in the evening."

The weight of the situation closed in on all three of them as they finished their dinner in silence. Mick wondered if Jack's amnesia was keeping him safe for now. Of course, being away from Key West was a big part of that. If he had witnessed something dangerous that night, his return to town could make the wrong person jumpy. Even if word got out about his memory loss, it was too risky.

"Are you going to Miami tomorrow?" Mick asked her.

"That's my plan. I'll work until noon, then I'll drive straight there."

"If you want, I can drive you," Wayne offered. "You could take that time in the car to nap or catch up on hospital business. I'd also like to visit Jack, and I can drive back with Michelle so you'd have your car for the return trip."

"Thanks, Wayne. I'd love the company, but I'm not sure he should be left alone just yet." She motioned to Mick with her thumb.

Before he could object to their debate about his supervision, there was a knock at the door.

"Are you expecting someone?" Wayne asked.

"No. Everyone I know in town is already here. Unless it's the sheriff."

When he opened the door, he found Frank and Bryce standing on the front porch with luggage in hand and stood there, speechless.

CHAPTER 22

"Hey, Mick. Aren't you going to invite us in?"

He grabbed Frank and Bryce and dragged them to the kitchen for introductions. Jo smiled at the display of genuine friendship shared by the three men. Mick felt like an enormous weight had been lifted.

"What are you doing here?" he asked, even though he already knew the answer.

"Well, it looks like you've once again landed yourself in some trouble. We're here for backup. Wayne, Jo, I don't think you fully understand Mick's ability to wreak havoc everywhere he goes," Frank said with a twinkle in his eye.

"This time, trouble came looking for me—and Jack. I was on vacation, minding my own business." Mick feigned his innocence with an exaggerated shrug.

"Either way, we're here," Bryce said.

"How long can you stay? Wait—does the commissioner know you're helping me out?"

Frank nodded. "He does. Officially, we're taking a few days of vacation. There's been a bunch of stuff happening behind the scenes at work, and I think the commissioner is on the verge of handing in his resignation."

"I can't wait to hear those details." Mick grabbed a beer from the fridge for each of them.

"The three of you standing together could easily star in a recruitment poster for special agents," Wayne commented.

Bryce, the youngest of the team, had blond hair and stood an inch taller than Mick. His farm-boy good looks matched his Midwest accent. Frank could pass as Mick's cousin but with a stockier frame and more gray hair at his temples.

Jo insisted they stay at Jack's, and she excused herself to set up the bedding. When she returned, she and Wayne said good night, leaving the boys to catch up. They no longer had to worry about Mick getting into trouble on his own.

Frank and Bryce each raised an eyebrow when Jo hugged and kissed Mick good night. He ignored their stares.

"We actually have some information on that guy, Skiff, you asked us to look into." Bryce grabbed papers out of his bag. "Nothing too remarkable. Just background on his employment history and issues over suspected workplace theft."

"Thanks, but everything has changed since I talked to you last. Skiff's been murdered. Wayne and I found him in his trailer this morning. He was shot in the head."

Bryce dropped his papers on the table as Frank whipped his head around and stared at Mick. "What?"

"I've got lots to tell you, but first, have you eaten dinner?"

"No." Frank shook his head. "More importantly, what's going on here?"

"I've got a few theories, but food first. There's a great local restaurant around the corner. I just ate, but I can always make room for dessert." Mick was halfway to the door when he turned around. "Are you guys packing?"

They both lifted their shirts to reveal government issued Glocks secured in their waistband holsters.

"Good to know. Don't want a repeat of last night."

. . .

The welcoming courtyard and the free-roaming chickens mesmerized first-time visitors to Blue Heaven. A musician set up under the banyan tree played acoustic reggae tunes. While waiting for a table, the boys poked around the adjacent gift shop, each opting to purchase a baseball cap featuring the iconic blue rooster logo. Mick waited for them at the bar with a round of drinks. They laughed as they caught up on the latest news about their cases and coworkers back in Tallahassee. Frank shared his theory about the commissioner. It sounded like the political pressures that resulted in Mick's ouster were now bearing down on his former boss.

After being seated at their table, Mick pushed back on diving right into all the details about Jack's case. He wanted to take a minute to enjoy the comradery with old friends, so they ordered a bottle of wine and kept things light while they shared an appetizer. Mick skipped the main meal, and when Frank and Bryce's yellowtail snapper entrées arrived, he talked while they ate.

Hearing about his conflicted history with Sheriff Wheeler amused them. It definitely added another dimension to the investigation. They agreed with Mick—there had to be a connection between Abe, Skiff, and whatever Skiff had pulled out of the ocean. Between mouthfuls, they tossed around potential explanations for the lingering questions.

Was Skiff killed over some valuable find, or was it completely unrelated? Mick didn't believe in coincidences, so until proven otherwise, it was part of the puzzle. How did Jack figure into it all? Was he just in the wrong place at the wrong time? Anyone who knew Jack could be certain he would've acted on anything suspicious he had seen that night.

Their strategy was to work through the details in the same methodical way they would tackle a new case at work. Frank and Bryce wanted to check out the marina and planned to join Mick for his meeting with the sheriff. At a minimum, it would be a courtesy call to advise Sheriff Wheeler they were in town to support Mick, while assuring him they had no intention of interfering with the investigation.

Halfway through their second bottle of wine, Frank shifted the conversation. "So, Mick, tell us about, Jo."

"Yep, that's the real question." Bryce raised his eyebrows. Both men leaned in.

Mick laughed but couldn't hide his smile. "It's just friendship—I think. It's confusing. We've had to deal with a lot this past week, and it's brought us together. I have feelings for her, but I'm not sure I'm going to act on them. She's dealing with Jack's trauma and the stress of opening her hospital. The timing is terrible." He left it at that and tried to change the subject.

When his slice of key lime pie arrived, it drew applause from a neighboring table, prompting Frank and Bryce to order their own. The perfect distraction from a discussion about his romantic life.

Pursuing the leads by himself had weighed on him, but that all changed with his friends' arrival. He'd been doing a terrible job at keeping an open mind and staying objective, which increased his chances of overlooking key clues. The stakes were too high this time to be running a shoddy investigation.

Even though the attack in Jack's driveway hadn't scared him off, his friends' presence gave Mick the confidence to push forward without looking over his shoulder. They would start in the morning with fresh sets of eyes. Hopefully by then, the sheriff would have additional information about Skiff's murder and the forensic results from the cabin on *Zulu*.

It was like old times. For a few hours, Mick set aside his worries about Jack and recent events. They laughed, reminiscing over some of their favorite stories. Their evening lasted till long after the dishes had been cleared, and they realized the restaurant was trying to close up for the night.

When they arrived back home, Mick showed them the essentials then went straight to bed. After all, it had only been twenty-four hours since his ambulance ride to the hospital. His throbbing head reminded him he'd overdone it. It wasn't too bad, but the short-sighted decision to drink alcohol with dinner meant he couldn't safely take his pain meds. It was time to reset—a fresh start, and nothing would be more helpful than getting a good night's sleep. As he nodded off, he realized he'd forgotten to warn Frank and Bryce about the roosters. Oh, well. They'd figure it out soon enough.

CHAPTER 23

Mick woke up well past sunrise, shocked he'd slept through the roosters. He wondered if they had taken the morning off, sparing Frank and Bryce their usual jarring wake-up call. But that clearly wasn't the case. Frank and Bryce were already on their third cups of coffee, and Jack's kitchen wall was plastered with sticky notes.

"What's all this?" Mick asked.

"We've been up since dawn. And about those roosters," Frank said. "Does that happen every day?"

"Yup. I don't understand how the locals cope with it. It's strange—they didn't wake me this time. But I was pretty wiped out."

"We made a case board using all the info you've given us so far. Figured it'd help us map out the timeline, including any suspects or persons of interest. Improvised with the sticky notes we found in a drawer," Bryce said.

Mick took a few minutes to look it all over. A solid start. He definitely had a bunch more details to fill in, but that would have to wait until he had caught up with a few cups of coffee.

His head was the clearest it had been since before those early sleep-deprived days at the hospital. He expertly recounted the sequence of events that had occurred since he arrived in town, starting with his time prepping for the hurricane at the marina with Jack and ending with finding Skiff dead in his trailer. Finally, his razor-sharp focus allowed him to visualize the details as pieces of a puzzle. He added another dozen sticky notes to the makeshift crime board. Somehow, they all had to fit together, and it was his job to figure out how. Standing shoulder to shoulder with his partners as they worked through challenges motivated him to keep pushing.

During his last conversation with Sheriff Wheeler, he'd been reminded not to forget where he came from. Mick needed to hear that but not for the reasons the sheriff intended. He'd been too close to see everything clearly. Frank and Bryce helped him step back and follow the evidence using an investigator's eyes, without bias or prejudice. Just the facts, no more and no less. They'd start at the marina—the original scene of the crime.

"There's a great place on the way to grab breakfast. Let me check in with Jo, then we can drive over."

Frank and Bryce exchanged a look that Mick ignored. Trying to explain his relationship with Jo any further would be pointless, considering he couldn't even explain it to himself.

． ． ．

They cruised through town in the golf cart, heading toward the waterfront, when Frank pointed at a passing double-wide scooter. "I could get used to this lifestyle. It's so civilized."

Mick grinned. "If Jack was driving, he would've already waved at a dozen friends and acquaintances. He's like Key West royalty. Too bad you won't get to meet him. You guys would hit it off. I'm certain that once he's fully recovered, he'll want to roll out the red carpet and invite you down to do some fishing."

"We'll be here. And there's a chance we may still be in town when he gets home from the hospital." Bryce's comment was a stark reminder they needed to get this sorted out and fast.

Two Friends Patio sat on Front Street, a stone's throw from the marina. The restaurant combined the best elements of a bustling diner with a casual tiki-style atmosphere. Delicious, fast, and hearty.

After they had their fill, they moved on to their next stop—*Bravo Zulu*, where they planned to retrace Jack's steps. Mick needed to talk to Earl and Betty, as they had committed to surveilling the area for suspects, unaware that one of the bad guys was lying dead in the morgue. He led the way onto the dock and was relieved to find them sitting outside.

"I want you to meet Jack's neighbors. They've been providing overwatch duty when I'm not around. I haven't told them about Skiff's murder yet."

As they approached, Earl stood to greet them with a nod of his cap. "Hi, Mick. We haven't seen you in a couple of days, and we were getting worried."

"Sorry about that," Mick said. "It's been a little chaotic."

Betty removed her sunglasses as she scrutinized the newcomers. "Is everything okay with Jack?"

"Yes, he's good—great, actually. These are two of my best friends, Frank and Bryce."

Greetings were exchanged, then Mick jumped right in.

"I've got some news. The skinny guy from the surveillance photos I showed you was murdered yesterday on Stock Island."

Fear consumed both their faces. "Do the police know who killed him?" Earl asked.

"Not yet, but there are concerns it might be connected to what happened to Jack. The sheriff is now involved. You may have found out from others that he came to the marina yesterday. The cabin on *Zulu* is now being treated as a crime scene."

"Oh, no! Poor Jack!" Betty said. "It must have been when we walked over to talk with the dockmaster. We were only gone for a short while. I told you we should have waited." Betty turned to her husband. "I thought Key West was a relatively safe place to live."

"Should we be worried?" Earl wrapped a protective arm around her shoulder.

"I don't think so, but keep your eyes and ears open. If you notice the police around the marina, don't be alarmed. They're here to watch over things."

They both exhaled when they learned Frank and Bryce were also special agents in town to help Mick. That added layer of protection appeared to give them some comfort.

"Has anything unusual happened since we last talked? Has Abe been around?"

"I've seen him once or twice," Earl said. "He's grumpier than normal, but nothing else seems out of the ordinary."

Mick updated them on Jack's pending homecoming but omitted the part about his own assault and subsequent trip to the ER. They continued chatting about random topics, such as the weather and the fishing forecast, before Mick redirected his friends toward *Zulu*.

"Thank you, boys. And welcome to town. If you need anything at all, just ask." Betty took Earl's hand, and they retreated inside their cabin.

"Do they live on their sailboat full time?" Bryce asked once they'd moved across the dock.

"Yeah. Lots of people call the marina home, including Abe. They're the only ones in this section that live aboard. The other slips appear to be short-term stays—turning over every few days."

Mick stepped onto the deck. "So here she is."

Frank whistled. "My dream boat."

After the tour, they finished in the cabin where Mick pointed out all the pertinent details from the time of Jack's injury. Once they'd seen it for themselves, Frank and Bryce agreed it was unlikely the storm had knocked Jack over since all the other smaller, loose items had remained in their place and looked intact.

They grabbed chairs to sit out on the stern deck and brainstorm the rest of their day. There were still some loose ends to tug at—specifically Mick's grainy photo of the polo shirt tourist taken from Turtle Krawls.

His pursuit of Skiff had distracted him from following up on other leads.

Frank walked around to survey the areas of the marina within eyesight of the boat. "You said Abe returned to port just before the hurricane with Skiff on board. What if the polo dude had been with them? Abe could have picked him up at another dock, or he arrived to the marina by car earlier in the day. Are there any surveillance cameras in the parking lot or out on the street? Maybe there's one that captured a better image of the guy or a license plate number."

"Good question. After I saw him on my video, I rewound the footage a few hours to pinpoint his arrival at the marina. I couldn't find him, but with people coming and going along the Harborwalk—I might've missed him." He hadn't even thought to check for surveillance from the street in front of Turtle Krawls, and that made him angry. He'd been so focused on finding Skiff, he let the other lead go cold.

"What's that gigantic building over there?" Bryce pointed across the water. "There's a Coast Guard cutter docked on the gulf side."

"It's part of the Key West Naval Air Station," Mick said. "Why do you ask?"

"Well, I can see some huge radar equipment at the site. If it's a military base, I would assume they have high-tech security. Even though it's all the way across the port, there's a possibility they may have something we can use. Their image quality would be the best available."

"See, that's why I need you guys here. Apparently, it only takes a few weeks into retirement to lose a step." Mick shook his head in disgust.

"Go easy on yourself, buddy," Frank said. "You've been right in the middle of everything, and to top it off, you're exhausted and dealing with a head injury."

Mick didn't buy it, but he was grateful for the pep talk.

"The sheriff should be able to get access to any street-side security cameras near the marina." Mick reached for his phone. "And I still owe him my statement. Let me confirm he's at the station, and we can head that way now."

"While you call the sheriff, Frank and I are going to take a little walk down the dock to visit with Abe."

"Okay, but keep your distance. Saying he's territorial would be an understatement."

Mick watched as Frank and Bryce casually strolled past the neighboring boats. As they neared Abe's slip, he appeared on deck, carrying a five-gallon bucket. He didn't notice them at first then looked startled to find them standing there.

Bryce spoke first. Mick couldn't hear what he said, but the conversation didn't last long. Abe looked them up and down, his disdain smeared across his face when he turned toward town and spotted Mick staring at them from Jack's deck. He whipped his head around to face the two men. His eyebrows lifted and his jaw dropped open—that exact moment when he must have realized they were with Mick. He set the bucket down and retreated inside the cabin without saying a word.

Back on *Zulu*, Frank said, "No matter how hard we try, there's something about government agents that always look and sound the same. Criminals, or people with something to hide, can pick us off every time."

"I pretended to be a tourist looking for a recommendation for a fishing charter, but he didn't buy it," Bryce said.

Abe continued staring through his cabin window.

"I'm okay if he thinks he's being watched. He should be nervous. Just proves to me he's hiding something."

"He's a prickly bastard," Bryce said. "But that doesn't make him a murderer. We need more evidence."

"Let's go see the sheriff. If we're lucky, he'll be able to point us in the right direction."

CHAPTER 24

After arriving at the Monroe County Sheriff's Office, a deputy ushered them to meet with Sheriff Ron Wheeler, who lifted a brow when he saw three men standing in his doorway.

"Sheriff, I want to introduce you to my partners, Bryce Taylor and Frank De Lucca. They're in town for a few days of vacation."

"A vacation. Interesting." The sheriff turned off his computer screen and sat with his elbows resting on the desk, his hands clasped tightly in front of him. His facial muscles contracted, resulting in a squinting, pained expression. He obviously wasn't buying their story. "Don't you mean, former partners?"

Mick bristled then stepped into the office. The sheriff sure had a way of getting under his skin, but before he could reply, Frank spoke and put an end to their ruse.

"Sheriff Wheeler, I'm sure you've guessed we're staying with Mick, watching his back until this is all sorted out. We're not here in any official capacity, and we have no intention of interfering in your investigation."

"Well, I'm glad to hear you say that, Frank. It would be an uncomfortable phone call to your commissioner if that's not how things play out." He turned to Mick. "I need your written statement about Scott Bainbridge, aka Skiff." He handed over a clipboard and pen. "You know the drill."

"Sure, but can we ask you a couple of questions first?" Without waiting for a reply, he continued. "Are any of the results from the crime scene evidence collected on Jack's boat back from the lab?"

"They're still working on it. We've got your exclusion prints and the ones from the paramedics. We've contacted Bea to get her fingerprints taken at the Dade County Sheriff's office in Miami. Once we collect those, we'll see what's left."

"What about the polo shirt tourist—the guy in the photos I brought you a few days ago? Anything new on him? It's possible he arrived at the marina before the hurricane, and there might be a better image of him or his car captured on surveillance cameras in the parking lots along Margaret or Caroline Street."

"I can't share the details of an active investigation, but we're pursuing all leads, including the man you call the polo shirt tourist."

"What about the evidence from Skiff's trailer?"

"No comment."

"That's it? You can't share more?" he prodded.

"No, I can't. You'll have to trust me. In return, I'm going to trust you and your friends to stand down. Am I making myself clear, former Special Agent Mick Nassau?"

It was more of a command than a question. They weren't going to get any further with the sheriff, so they dropped their line of inquiry. Mick completed his statement before sharing the news about Jack's pending release from the hospital. He pushed the sheriff to ensure he understood the importance of finding out the motive behind these crimes. It would be the only way to manage any potential peril Jack could face when he returned home.

"I guess I can't blame him," Bryce said once they were outside the station. "We'd act exactly the same way if some outsider came messing around in one of our cases."

"I get it, but it's still frustrating." Mick stopped walking to take a call from Alex Balfour. He listened for a minute then said, "That's great. We'll be there in twenty."

"Who's that?" Frank asked.

"Alex, the marine archeologist at the Mel Fisher Museum—the one I told you about. He's got some news to share about Skiff."

. . .

Parking spots in Old Town Key West were hard to come by, even during the slow season. After a quick detour to leave the truck at Jack's, they drove to the museum in the golf cart and maneuvered into a tight space near the main entrance. Alex met them in the lobby gift shop.

"Hi, Mick." He extended his hand, introducing himself to Frank and Bryce. "Let's head up to the lab so we can talk."

As they stepped into the bright, lofted room, lab technicians huddled around a large encrusted blob turned to acknowledge their boss. Alex nodded at them then led his guests to a private office and closed the door.

"A new artifact arrived from our site in the Bahamas this morning." Alex pointed at his team.

"I told the guys about the special tanks used to clean items pulled from the ocean, like the one I photographed in Skiff's trailer," Mick said.

Alex nodded toward the lab. "The coral-covered artifact you saw them working on is likely an intact piece of pottery. Once it's clean, it may help us identify the wreck we're excavating. It could be an important breakthrough in establishing provenance."

The three men looked through the office window into the lab at the variety of equipment, charts, and tanks spread out across the room—an impressive operation.

"So, before you tell us what you learned about Skiff, you should know I found him yesterday on Stock Island—he'd been murdered."

"Geezus!" Alex took a step back. "What the hell's going on here?"

"We don't know yet, but whatever information you have is even more important now," Mick said.

Alex paced back and forth. "I tell you—this is a tough business."

The three men waited while he digested the news. "Okay, this is all I've got. Until recently, he worked as a diver for Deep Water Salvagers on a project based out of Key West. The company's headquarters are in Jupiter, Florida, and they've registered the rights to recover the Spanish Galleon *Santa Esperanza*. It's believed that she sank near Key West. They're still searching for the main wreckage."

"Any idea how long he worked for them?"

"No, but I found out they fired him—for a few reasons, including theft." He handed Mick a business card. "Here's the owner's contact information. He's expecting your call."

He took the card. "Thanks again, Alex. This is extremely helpful. And the sheriff hasn't released the details about the murder to the public yet, so I'd appreciate it if you kept it to yourself for now."

"Of course," he nodded. "Treasure salvagers are a unique group of people. We're competitive, but we also look out for each other. It's a small world. If this murder is linked to my industry, please let me know. I need to alert my friends and colleagues." He glanced at his phone. "I've got a private tour coming in, but you're welcome to look around."

All three men shook his hand and saw themselves out of the lab, but not before checking out the reverse electrolysis tanks stationed around the room.

Standing outside on the steps of the museum, facing Mallory Square and the Gulf, hordes of tourists wearing color-coded lanyards to identify their cruise ship spilled onto the sidewalk from nearby shops. The people-watching distraction gave Mick a moment to think.

"I'm going to drive up north today. I've been wanting to see Jack again, and I'm hoping I can meet with the owner of the salvage company. I should be back by late tomorrow. There's not much more we can do in town until the sheriff gets off his high horse and shares some case details."

"Our only other lead is Abe. Assuming your instincts are spot on, he's involved up to his eyeballs, so I think Frank and I should stay on *Bravo Zulu* and stake out the marina and his boat. We need to get a better handle on what he's up to. There's a cabin on board, and we can sleep in shifts."

"And we don't need to wait for the sheriff," Frank said. "I can check for any cameras mounted outside businesses near the parking lots off the harbor. Bryce mentioned trying to get access to the surveillance systems at the naval station. We can start making some calls."

"Thanks, guys. Earl and Betty will sleep better with you next door. Let me find out if Alex's contact is free to meet."

All the pieces began falling into place. Peter Harley, the owner of Deep Water Salvagers, would be in the Jupiter office the next day at ten o'clock. Mick immediately called Jo, hoping to catch her before she left for Miami, but she was already on the road. It would have been nice to drive together, but since he didn't know what his schedule would be, they might need two cars. She sounded happy that he'd be seeing Jack soon and thought Jack would be delighted.

Back at the cottage, the guys loaded any supplies they would need for a brief stay on *Zulu* and left for the marina in the golf cart. Mick packed his overnight bag after making a reservation at the same hotel near the hospital where Bea was staying. Thirty minutes later, he turned onto U.S. 1, heading north toward Miami. The three-and-a-half-hour drive would give him the time to rehash everything that had happened. Whenever Mick hit a wall during a case, it helped to get some distance. Time away from the minutiae of the investigation often allowed some overlooked clue or idea to float to the surface.

CHAPTER 25

Bea and Jo met Mick in the lounge when he arrived at Jackson Memorial Hospital. After spending the day with various specialists, Jack would soon be returning from physical therapy. The past week had taken its toll on Bea. She looked drawn and exhausted, but Mick could tell their presence bolstered her spirits. When Jo shared a funny anecdote about the vet hospital, the color returned to her cheeks. It felt good to laugh with friends.

"Mick!" Jack hollered from the hallway outside his hospital room. "You're a sorry sight!" He walked toward them with the help of a cane and his therapist.

Overwhelmed with emotion, Mick cleared his throat, a feeble attempt to hide the lump choking off his voice. That morning after the hurricane, when he found Jack unconscious on *Zulu*, he didn't think his friend would survive. Now, here he was—full of life. Despite needing some assistance to walk, he'd made a remarkable recovery.

Mick took a deep breath and followed Jack into his room. Before the therapist settled him in the chair next to his bed, he enveloped Mick in a Barton bear hug. There was strength in his arms, but when he stepped back, he accepted some help to get seated. That's when Mick noticed the shaved back of Jack's head, marked by a long row of staples. Thanks to Jo's warning, he contained his reaction in front of his friend.

"You have no idea how great it is to see you moving around. You scared the crap out of me." Mick patted his best friend on the shoulder. "It looks like you're plowing through your therapy, just as expected."

"Well, baby steps. Literally. This is Miss Lizzie, my drill sergeant for the day."

"Lizzie, you keep pushing him. He can take it," Mick said.

"Actually, Jack's the one pushing us," she said. "He asks for more than we have planned at each session. At this rate, he'll be running out of here." She grinned at her patient and excused herself from the room.

Mick had debated whether to share the past week's events with Jack, in case it jeopardized his recovery. He needed to see him with his own eyes to be certain. After chatting for a few minutes, he decided it was time to divulge all the details. Jack had a finely tuned bullshit meter and would have figured out Mick was hiding something. Jo and Bea had given him their approval since Jack would need to be on board with any plans they put in place after his release from the hospital.

"We're going to leave you boys alone to catch up," Bea said. "Jo and I will be at the hotel if you need anything."

"Sure thing, honey. Why don't you get some rest. We're all good here."

Jo squeezed Mick's arm then moved her hand down to his wrist before letting go. He hoped Jack hadn't noticed.

Once alone, Jack turned and looked him straight in the eye. "Isn't it about time you filled me in on whatever the hell's going on here? Those two have been sidestepping my questions for days now. I'm okay, Mick. You don't need to treat me with kid gloves."

"I know. But I had to see that for myself—to be certain. Last time I was here, it was touch and go. It's hard to believe it's only been a week."

"More like an eternity."

"I can't imagine what you've been through. We really thought we were going to lose you, you know." He exhaled through pursed lips. "Before I get started, I wondered if you've been able to remember anything new from your injury?"

"Not really. An image will flash in my mind, like I'm on the verge of recalling something, but then it fades away. It's frustrating."

"Well, a lot has happened. My buddies from the FDLE, Frank De Lucca and Bryce Taylor, are on *Bravo Zulu* right now, keeping watch."

"That doesn't sound very—" Jack rubbed his temple, apparently searching for the right word. "Promising. Why the reinforcements?"

Mick ran through all the events since the day of the hurricane. Jack didn't interrupt except to ask a few clarifying questions. He thoughtfully took it all in until Mick finished.

"First, are you okay?" Jack tapped his head, referring to Mick's recent injury.

"I'm fine. Just a few stitches is all."

He nodded. "Second, can you please tell Wayne, Earl and Betty, and Frank and Bryce how grateful I am to have them watching your back?"

"Absolutely. They'd do anything for you. You know that, right?"

"I do. And I'm definitely going to reach out to Alex and Little Jimmy when I get home."

Mick added more background info about his relationship with the sheriff. "I really hope our conflicted past isn't affecting his approach to the case."

"It won't. Ron's a stand-up guy. He'll do the right thing and won't stop until he's solved these crimes."

Jack's certainty about the sheriff came as a surprise but was reassuring to hear.

"So that's everything. My next step is to get more background on Skiff from this treasure salvager. I'm meeting him in the morning, then it's just a waiting game until the forensic reports are final."

"Could you show me those surveillance photos from Turtle Krawls again?"

Mick pulled them out of his bag and handed them over. Jack stared at the pictures of the two men then shut his eyes tight, as if to focus his concentration. He opened them suddenly and said, "I have it. I remember seeing Skiff on Abe's boat the day we were prepping for the hurricane. Maybe it's coming back to me. I don't remember seeing anyone else that day. The photo of the other guy is hard to make out, but I have this strange feeling I've seen him before. Probably wishful thinking."

Encouraged by this breakthrough, Mick said, "Don't force it. We can't be certain if you were even on deck when they passed by. One more question. Do you remember the last time you recall seeing your cell phone that night?"

"Not specifically, but I'll guarantee it was in my pocket if I wasn't using it. I never set it down. Never. A necessary habit you learn after spending time on a boat in rough weather."

Mick nodded. The missing phone had to be a key piece of the puzzle.

Jack said, "I wish I could go with you to talk to the owner of the salvage company."

"Your only job right now is to get better. I'll tell you if I learn anything helpful, and I'll make sure you stay up to date with the case every step of the way."

"No more holding back?"

"Absolutely not. You'll know everything I do."

CHAPTER 26

After Jo and Bea returned from the hotel, the four of them spent the rest of the day in relaxed conversation. Jo updated everyone on how things were going at the vet hospital, including the story of Bob the Dog, who still needed a forever home. Her lack of subtlety was not lost on Mick.

By late afternoon, Jack's contribution to the conversation dwindled. When he struggled to keep his eyes open, they left him to rest while they grabbed an early dinner at a nearby Italian restaurant. He pressured them to return with cannoli for his dessert. He'd grown sick of the hospital food, which they took as a sign of improvement.

Over dinner, Bea and Jo peppered Mick with questions about the investigation. They debated whether bringing Jack home to Key West would be safe. The recent attack on Mick and Skiff's murder obviously weighed on both of them.

"Things can change quickly in a murder case when all the resources of law enforcement focus on solving the crime," Mick said. "We may be forced to make a last-minute decision once they release Jack."

Bea agreed. "That's why we should look near the hospital for a potential short-term rental—so we have options."

"Jack will have something to say about all this. If we maintain a unified front, we might convince him to hold off on returning home," Jo said.

"I'm doubtful, since he made me promise not to insulate him from the facts of the case or hide the truth. Jack can be stubborn, but he's smart. He won't want anyone else to be in harm's way. We'll have to play up that angle if it comes to it."

They ordered the requested cannoli, and Jo put her leftover chicken parmesan in a to-go box in case he wanted a few bites. They paid the bill and walked the two blocks to the hospital. Outside the front entrance, Mick excused himself to make a call. "I'll meet you in Jack's room." He wanted to touch base with Frank and Bryce.

"Key West is quite the place," Frank said with a whistle after answering the phone. "This town is full of characters."

"For sure. It's what gives the place its charm," Mick said. "Anything new to report?"

"It's been mostly quiet at the marina. Earl and Betty brought us dinner from Turtle Krawls—amazing. Abe scowls at us from his deck all day, but that's about it. Have you heard anything from the sheriff?"

"No. I'll wait until tomorrow to follow up with him unless something urgent arises."

"Here's Bryce. He has a couple questions for you." Frank passed the phone.

"How are things there?"

"Better than I expected. Jack's plowing through his therapy like he's back in boot camp. I ended up telling him everything."

"We wouldn't want to be kept in the dark, so it's only fair to include him. I called over to the Key West Naval Air Station, and despite throwing around my FDLE credentials, I had trouble getting in touch with someone willing to help us access the surveillance footage. Would Jack have a contact on the base?"

"He likely does. I'll ask him and get back to you."

"Sounds good. It appears we're in store for a perfect Key West sunset. The plan is to sleep in shifts tonight, just in case. Are you still driving home tomorrow?"

"Yes, as of right now. I'll text you when I'm on the road. Jack asked me to thank you both for being there."

"You tell him we'll take repayment as a day out fishing once he's fully recovered. *Bravo Zulu* is no joke. Take care."

When Mick walked into the hospital room, Jack had finished the leftover parm and was halfway through his dessert. Seeing him act like his old self, appetite and all, encouraged Mick.

"Jack, do you have any local connections at the Key West Naval Air Station?" Mick asked.

"Lots. One of my closest friends is Base Commander Captain Phillips. Why?"

He shared Bryce's theory that surveillance footage from the naval station might include the marina near *Bravo Zulu*.

"It's possible. I'll call him first thing tomorrow."

Jack sat up and pushed his shoulders back. He'd never been on the sidelines of a skirmish—being part of the team appeared to invigorate him. Mick had made the right decision to bring him up to speed on the case.

"Jo told me you were thinking of adopting a dog." Jack winked at his sister.

"I didn't say that. Now you're just causing trouble," she chided her big brother with a nudge.

"I would love to have a dog, but I've never had a schedule that would allow it. Bob is the best." Mick turned to Jo. "I'm sure your team will find him a great home real soon."

"I guess this whole mess interrupted your retirement fact-finding trip to the Keys," Jack said. "Are you thinking of heading back to Tallahassee soon?"

"It's strange. I haven't even thought of home since I arrived in Key West. Of course, there's been a lot going on. My neighbor's taking care of my place, so I'm flexible. I'm not going anywhere until this mess is all cleared up."

"Thanks," Jo said.

Jack glanced at his sister and back to Mick, obviously trying to gauge her response to the news Mick might be sticking around town for a while. Jack was no fool.

"Mick, you can stay as long as you want. I still have that slow season to-do list you promised to help me with."

Relieved by the change in subject, Mick chuckled. Once Jack started to look and sound sleepy, Mick and Jo said goodnight, while Bea planned to stay a bit longer.

The walk back to the hotel gave Mick a private moment with Jo. He had nothing specific to discuss with her, but craved any opportunity where the two of them could be alone. Any reason to be close to her would do. As every swing of her arm brushed against him, the air between them pulsed with energy as they walked in silence.

Once they neared the hotel's front entrance, she said, "I have a few late day appointments at the hospital and have to be back by four. Jack gets his staples removed in the morning. It's hard to believe he's been in the hospital long enough to heal a surgical incision. I'll stick around until after that. What about you?"

"I'm meeting with the owner of the salvage company at ten, then I plan to relieve Frank and Bryce at the marina so they can get some rest. And I'll stop to see the sheriff on my way through town. The forensics from both crime scenes should be back, and if I catch him in a good mood, I hope he'll share the findings."

"Will we see you in the morning?"

"Not likely. My appointment in Jupiter is early, so I'll be on the road first thing in order to beat the traffic. I want to spend more time with Jack, but I think I need to focus all my attention on moving this case along."

"I totally understand, and so do Jack and Bea. But promise me you'll be careful." To stress her point, she took his hand and turned him to face her. "I don't know what I would do if anything happened to you?"

"I promise, Jo. But don't forget, I've been investigating crimes my entire career, and I'm still here. I don't take unnecessary risks."

They were now standing outside her room. Before it became awkward, she grabbed his belt buckle and pulled him close, leading the way in a slow and sensuous kiss good night. When Mick began tracing the side of her neck with his lips, she arched her body, pressing her hips into his. He slid an arm around her waist, lifting her onto her toes as his other hand moved up her side, brushing over her nipple. Her breath hitched, caught between a sharp inhale and a gasp, before she captured his lips in a passionate kiss.

When they eventually stepped apart, he whispered, "They're going to send hotel security if we keep this up."

She grinned. "We don't want that—or do we?" She kissed him again. "Bea will be back soon, otherwise I'd invite you in."

Mick breathed deep through his nose. "I get it. When things settle down, I'd really like to spend more time with you, just the two of us."

Jo smiled. "I'd like that." She opened her door with her key card, and said, "Night."

All he needed was a sign, something to tell him she felt the same way—and now, he had it. They both were dealing with a lot, which made the timing difficult. Jack's recovery and solving the crime had to remain the priority. Once life returned to normal, he planned to ask Jo on a proper first date and see where things might lead.

CHAPTER 27

Mick arrived early for his appointment with Peter Harley of Deep Water Salvagers. The office sat in an industrial complex along Dixie Highway. Framed photos of newspaper articles filled the lobby walls, telling the tales of treasures recovered from Florida waters. Peter poured Mick a cup of coffee and ushered him into his office.

"Alex, from the museum, said you're investigating a crime in Key West, and it might have something to do with a former employee of mine."

"Yes. I'm not sure about the connection between the two, but since Alex first contacted you, there's been a big development. Your ex-employee, Skiff Bainbridge, was murdered this week."

"Oh." Peter looked genuinely surprised by the news. "What happened?"

"He was found dead inside his trailer in Key West, and the investigation is ongoing." Mick held back details related to cause of death. "I'm the one who found him a few days ago."

"I'll tell you everything I know, but I'm not sure I can be of much help."

"I understand Bainbridge was an expert diver but hard to work with. Could you tell me why he left your employment?"

"Well, you're right about his dive skills. He is—was—one of the best, but he just couldn't keep his mouth shut and rubbed everyone around him the wrong way. It got so bad he affected the team's work. That's also when we had some expensive dive equipment go missing. We couldn't prove beyond a doubt it was Bainbridge, but enough questions surfaced about his innocence—we had to let him go."

"When was that?" Mick asked.

"About six months ago. He picked up his last paycheck, but I haven't seen or come across him since."

"What project had he been working on at the time?"

"We own the salvage rights to the Spanish galleon, *Santa Esperanza*. She's believed to have gone down during a hurricane in the waters near Key West. Some deep channels and treacherous reefs populate the area, and Bainbridge was the best diver we had. We've been running a small satellite operation out of Key West, but we had to move some resources away from there a few months ago to concentrate on a new shipwreck."

"A friend of his in town told me he'd been out diving lately. So far, I haven't been able to find anyone he was working for, but supposedly he'd been bragging about a big payday. Big enough to buy his own dive boat. When we found him this week, he had a reverse electrolysis tank in his trailer. I confirmed with Alex that it would clean objects brought up from the ocean."

Peter was about to sip his coffee then stopped and set the cup on the desk.

"Some amateur treasure hunters own similar kinds of tanks, but Bainbridge would be obligated to turn over anything he found on a dive to the company he worked for. Occasionally, an employee tries to steal from a site, but they're fully prosecuted if they get caught. We don't stand for any of that in our business."

"If he had found some valuable sunken treasure, where would he turn to sell it?"

"The sale of any salvaged antiquities from a staked claim would be illegal. We take our claims seriously. It's a small industry. Everyone knows everyone."

"The week before his death, I saw Skiff returning to the Key West marina, and he had his dive gear with him. He'd been out with a guy named Abe. My friend thought it was strange since Abe had never taken a charter before, or left the dock for that matter. They returned only hours before the hurricane came ashore—pretty risky."

Mick scrolled through the photos on his phone. "I found this map of Marquesas Keys and Rebecca Shoal in Skiff's trailer. It's marked up with some notes and symbols, but I don't understand what they mean."

Mick handed over his phone. Seconds later, Peter's eyes widened as he took in the details. He crossed the room and riffled through a storage rack of maps then unrolled a chart of the area around Key West on a large drafting table.

"I don't like what you're telling me. That area includes our staked claim. Our research and early surveys and discoveries led me to believe the galleon is located a little farther south of Rebecca Shoal, but we haven't started exploring the deep channels of the Shoal. The currents through there are notorious. It takes years, or even decades, to fully search an area—not for the faint of heart." He swiped and tapped on Mick's phone. "Let me send your photos to my printer. I can blow them up to a larger image." He walked into an outer office and returned with copies of Skiff's map, which he set down next to his charts for comparison, and returned Mick's phone.

"Do you recognize these notes on the map?" Mick asked.

"I think he's marked his dive sites, but I can't decipher this shorthand. My Key West project manager will investigate and see what he can find out. If Bainbridge stole artifacts from our claim and sold them on the black market, we may never find them. The antiquities market is full of shady characters, but there's a federal investigative branch in Miami working on these types of white-collar crimes. I can give you the name of my primary contact there."

"Thanks. That would be great. Likewise, if I find out anything relevant to your business, I'll contact you right away." Mick handed Peter his business card.

Peter consulted his own phone and sent Mick a text. "Here's the information on my FBI contact. The government gets a share of whatever we salvage, so they have a vested interest to ensure nothing goes off the books."

Mick recognized the name in the text message. Ruth Pender had been in the Miami FDLE field office while he was stationed there at the start of his career. Their paths had crossed on a few cases over the years. Ruth had a reputation as a brilliant investigator, and after transferring to the FBI's white-collar crimes division, she made a name for herself with her success in recovering valuable art and prosecuting cases of forgery and fraud. He would call her on his way back to Key West.

. . .

Mick had reached the southbound Florida Turnpike when he received the best news. Jack had been in touch with Captain Phillips at the Key West Naval Air Station. The captain hadn't been aware of Jack's injury, but when he learned about his friend's attack, he promised to handle it personally. All surveillance videos capturing the marina during the hurricane would be reviewed. The captain had Mick's contact info since he would become the point person for anything they turned up.

Once he exited the turnpike at Florida City, he pulled in for gas and a bite to eat. After a quick call to update Frank and Bryce about the captain's offer to help and his ETA into town, he phoned Ruth Pender at the Miami FBI field office. After charming his way past her assistant, she answered on the first ring.

"Mick Nassau. That's a name I haven't heard in a while. How are you? Where are you these days?

"Well, that's a really long story, Ruth. You'll probably find out—I'm no longer working at the FDLE. My retirement became official a few weeks ago."

"Retirement? You're younger than me. You must have a better financial planner," Ruth said.

"Not at all. It's a forced retirement, and that's the reason behind the long story. I'm actually calling you for a personal favor. I got your number from Peter Harley, owner of Deep Water Salvagers in Jupiter."

There was silence on Ruth's end of the phone. He assumed she was sorting through any possible connections between Mick and Harley, so he recapped an abbreviated version of the past two weeks.

"That's quite a tale. I would challenge you on your concept of retirement," she said with a laugh.

"Yes, you're not the first person to point that out. I'm looking for some help or guidance about the black market for underwater antiquities." He figured if there were any ongoing investigations about illegal sales, Ruth would be aware.

"I'll need to run this by a few people first to make sure I'm not stepping on any toes. I'll call you either way."

He expressed his gratitude and didn't push against her timeline for a follow-up. He believed she'd do her best to help him. Between Jack's connection with the naval commander and his contact with Ruth Pender, he felt close to a break in the case. Even without concrete information to act on, the wheels were turning.

During all his years as a special agent, he could sense a changing momentum in an investigation. He'd be slogging along in the weeds until, suddenly, things seemed to fall into place. It often took only one clue to lead him down a fresh path. For the first time in days, he had hope. Frank and Bryce wouldn't be able to stay in town forever, and the clock was ticking.

CHAPTER 28

Mick called ahead to confirm the sheriff was in his office. He dreaded the ongoing back-and-forth games they'd been playing and chose a different tone this time—more friendly and cooperative. Getting access to the forensic reports remained his priority, so he planned to hold his tongue, for Jack's sake. At least, that was the plan going in. Mick had many strengths, but diplomacy wasn't one of them.

"Hi, Sheriff." He sounded upbeat and friendly when he knocked on the door. "I'm back from visiting Jack in Miami and wanted to drop by with an update."

The sheriff's eyes softened when he asked, "How's he doing?"

"Better than I expected. He's pushing through his therapy sessions and is stronger every day. He still needs some help to walk longer distances, but the doctors expect him to make a full recovery. It wouldn't surprise me if he's released in the next few days."

"That's great news. Key West isn't the same without him."

"Agreed. I filled him in on everything happening in town—he needed to know," Mick said. "Unfortunately, he still can't remember anything from around the time of the hurricane."

The sheriff nodded and sat back in his chair. Mick proceeded to throw out the first white flag.

"I also wanted to tell you I met with Bainbridge's most recent employer, Deep Water Salvagers, up in Jupiter. I assume you're aware they fired Skiff over allegations of theft."

"I am," the sheriff said, his voice sounding tenuous.

"Good. Just making sure—full disclosure and all."

They locked eyes, neither saying a word, until the sheriff finally broke the uncomfortable silence. "Is there anything else?"

"No. That's it." He kept his tone pleasant, but his hands clenched into fists before he forced them to relax, attempting to ease the growing tension. "But I wondered if you've uncovered any new leads based on the forensics?"

"Again, I can't share that with you." The sheriff didn't sound open to a negotiation. "We're working to track down some prints. They're being run through the various databases, but you know how it goes," he said with a smug grin on his face. "One step at a time."

"No, I don't know how it goes, since you won't share anything with me." He couldn't hold back any longer, his composure slipping as his true feelings filled the room. "This is ridiculous. You have three special agents in town willing to help, and all you can say is, 'No, thank you.' Seems like a total waste of resources to me."

"I believe that would be two special agents and one retired government employee."

The sheriff's correction had intended to sting, and it did. But more than that, Mick was worried about his friend and guilt washed over him that his presence, given his combative history with the sheriff, might affect the management of Jack's case. There was no other way to explain this refusal to accept their help.

"Listen, things are very fluid right now. I can't have you getting caught in the middle and mucking everything up. I get that you have good intentions and are only looking out for Jack. As soon as the information is ready for public consumption, you'll be my first call."

Mick wondered why he bothered with the sheriff. Since there'd been no *quid pro quo*, he kept the information about his recent contact with Ruth Pender and Captain Phillips to himself. He stood and placed both hands on the sheriff's desk, as if drawing a line in the sand, shook his head, then walked out of the office, closing the door behind him. He was on his own again to work the case, except this time things were different. This time, he had Frank and Bryce on his team.

■ ■ ■

Mick couldn't get back to the marina fast enough and wasn't surprised to find both men out on deck giving *Zulu* a detailed cleaning.

"I guess it's been a while since we were on an old-fashioned stakeout together," Mick said as he climbed aboard. "Getting restless?"

"Sort of. We debated whether to mess with Jack's boat—it's obvious how particular he is with its maintenance. But we also realized it could be weeks or longer before he's up to this kind of work. Hope he doesn't mind if we don't do it quite his way," Bryce said.

"Jack is meticulous about *Zulu,* but it looks like you're doing a great job. He'd only be grateful for the help. I cleaned up after the storm, but that was almost a week ago. Thanks, guys."

"Nothing to report here," Frank said as he finished rinsing the port side hull. "Abe watches us as much as we watch him. I think he's getting jumpy with all this oversight."

"Good. If he becomes paranoid, he'll slip up and make a careless mistake. For the time being, he's still our only lead." Mick told them about his visit with the sheriff and his recent phone call with Ruth Pender. "Hopefully we'll catch a break, and soon, because the countdown is on for Jack's return."

They finished detailing the boat, then Mick grabbed a round of beer, which they drank while surveying their handiwork. His phone buzzed in his pocket.

"Hi, Jo."

"Are you back?"

"Yeah. I've been at the marina for about an hour. We just finished cleaning up the boat."

"I'm almost done with my day and can bring over some dinner for the four of us."

Mick voted for Cuban sandwiches and received enthusiastic nods from Frank and Bryce. Jo hung up, and before he could tell them the plan, another call came in.

"Is this Mick Nassau? I'm Captain Phillips, a friend of Jack Barton's."

"Yes, sir. Jack told me you might be calling. We're hoping you'll be able to help us."

"I'm working on it. Jack said you're a Florida Special Agent and you served as a JAG lawyer in Annapolis while he was stationed there."

"Yes, sir, but I left the Navy quite a while ago." Mick didn't correct him on his current employment status. Technically, he had negotiated a substantial severance package, so he was still on the payroll and receiving regular paychecks until his retirement kicked in. "I've also been working with the Monroe County Sheriff on this case." That last statement stretched the boundaries of a white lie, but he thought it would help the base commander navigate security protocols.

"Great. Avoids any paperwork getting you on station. Can you be here at zero seven hundred?"

"Yes, sir. Just tell me where to report. I have my Navy ID with me."

Captain Phillips provided the details about which base gate to enter. He also confirmed they had the requested surveillance and were working to clean up the images.

Mick ended the call and pumped his fist in the air, shouting a resounding, "Yes!"

"That sounds good," Bryce said. "Does he have something to show you?"

"It seems so. This is our first promising lead. I'm meeting him on the naval station tomorrow at seven o'clock."

Movement, finally. Now they could take a moment and enjoy the rest of the evening, relaxing under the Key West sky. Jo arrived at dinnertime with four Cuban sandwiches, guava pastries for dessert, and

Bob in tow. The moment the dog saw Mick, he pulled Jo on board *Zulu* in a mad dash to get to his new friend.

"He wanted to come along tonight. Hope you don't mind." She grinned. "Hi, guys." She waved at Frank and Bryce.

"Who's this?" asked Frank, the only one of the three with a dog at home. Of course, he was also the only one married with a family.

"Bob the Dog, or Bob for short. He found his way to the hospital right before our reopening, and we've been trying to find him a home ever since," she said. "He and Mick have become buddies."

"That's obvious. Look at the two of them." Focused entirely on Mick, Bob eventually lay next to his feet. He appeared relaxed on the boat and on the water.

"Seems to be a fairly simple solution," Bryce said. "You're retired now, Mick, and you've always said you'd like to have a dog."

"Can we first get through this crime drama we've found ourselves in the middle of before I make any big life decisions." He smiled as he scratched Bob under his chin.

"Okay, no pressure." Frank got a bowl of water for the dog.

Jo passed around dinner while Mick grabbed cold drinks from the cabin fridge. The next ten minutes were mostly silent as they concentrated on their meal.

"Thanks, Jo. Hands down the best Cuban sandwich I've ever had." Frank reached into the bag for his pastry.

"If all it takes is a sandwich and a cold beer to enlist your help, I'm getting off easy," she said.

Mick updated her on his conversations with Peter Harley, Ruth Pender, and his scheduled meeting with Captain Phillips.

"I get that this is all linked to a more serious crime of murder, but the most important thing to me is Jack's safety. Nothing else."

"Right," Mick said as they all nodded in agreement.

"So, what's the plan for tonight?" Bryce asked.

"I can take over here so you and Frank can head to Jack's and get some rest," Mick said.

"The whole point of coming down here was to watch your back. Leaving you alone in the same place where Jack might have been attacked doesn't seem like the smartest plan," Frank said.

"Exactly. We already worked it out," Bryce said. "I'll head to Jack's and get some shut-eye, and I'll be back before you need to leave in the morning. You and Frank can take turns resting in the berth."

"All right then." Mick trusted his friends with his life and happily relinquished control of the logistics.

Jo stayed on board through sunset then gathered her belongings while suppressing a yawn. "I've got an early day and lots of work to catch up on. Time to call it a night." She attached Bob's leash to lead him off the boat, but he tugged to stay next to Mick, forcing her to use dog cookies to lure him.

"I'll walk you out." Mick took the leash, and Bob fell in line beside him.

When they reached the top of the dock, she grabbed his hand, turning him to face her. "I wish I didn't have to say it, but please be careful."

"You don't need to worry. I've got the guys with me now. This is what we do best."

"What? Putting criminals behind bars."

"Exactly." He playfully swung her arm to lighten the mood.

Jo pulled his hand behind her back, forcing him to move closer. Mick wrapped his free arm around her waist and kissed her, gently at first, letting her lead the way. She responded with an intensity, catching him off guard. When they stepped apart, they looked down to see Bob staring up at them, tilting his head from side to side, his dog brain working to process the moment. They laughed and reached down to pet him.

Jo whispered, "Good night," into Mick's ear, then let her lips linger on his earlobe before leading Bob toward the parking lot.

CHAPTER 29

Frank and Bryce had wide grins as they watched Mick walk back to the boat. *Man, they never miss a thing,* he thought as he stepped on board. Knowing they were eager for details, he played it cool, taking a long drink from his bottle.

Bryce leaned over and flicked Mick's arm with the back of his hand. "So, what's that all about?"

"I'm not sure yet. It's unfolding all on its own."

"Well, she gets our endorsement." Frank pointed at him. "Don't screw it up."

"It's complicated. I think I should check with Jack first—out of respect." Before they could offer any more relationship advice, Mick changed the subject. "Bryce, here are the keys to the front door of the cottage. Go get some rest."

"You don't need to tell me twice," he said, and within minutes, he left the marina.

Frank retreated into the cabin to lie down, staying within earshot of Mick, who sat alone on deck listening to the island country music drifting over from Turtle Krawls. While Old Town's streets buzzed with nighttime energy, the marina grew quieter. He spotted people inside their cabins watching TV as the soft clanking of rigging against sailboat masts echoed like nautical wind chimes. Lost in the moment's serenity, he almost forgot the real reason he was sitting there.

Since Abe's boat had been dark all evening, the threat faded into the background. After a harrowing week, he looked forward to some peace and quiet. Around midnight, Frank took over surveillance duties on deck so Mick could recharge before his early morning meeting at the naval station.

When his alarm sounded at five-thirty, Mick woke, feeling encouraged about the day ahead. Voices on deck drew him from the cabin. Bryce had returned carrying breakfast and handed Mick a large coffee and a breakfast burrito.

"I didn't need to set an alarm," Bryce said. "Not with the damn roosters strutting around outside my window." He pointed to a clean shirt draped over a deck chair. "Can't show up to a meeting with the commander looking like that."

Mick raised his drink in salute. "Thanks." He wolfed down the burrito then washed up before leaving in the golf cart. There was zero chance he would be anything other than fifteen minutes early for his appointment.

■ ■ ■

Key West had a laid-back, tropical vacation vibe, especially first thing in the morning when all the Duval Street tourists were sleeping off their hangovers or just making their way home from an all-nighter. As Mick approached the guard gate for Naval Air Station Key West, it became all business and efficiency, a stark contrast to the rest of town. He showed his identification, signed in with security, and the guard directed him to wait in a nearby lot. Within minutes, a marine cadet arrived and parked next to him. After confirming his ID a second time, he escorted Mick to the communications center. Captain Phillips met him at the door, and after a quick update on Jack's condition, they got down to business.

"Mick, part of our station includes a marina at the outer edge of the Key West Seaport. Right now, there's a Coast Guard cutter docked there. It's visible from Jack's boat if you look northeast across the marina."

Mick nodded, aware of the location. "Do your surveillance cameras cover the entire port?"

"We have multiple monitoring systems, but the dock I referenced has cameras aimed toward the waterfront. Jack's section of the marina is directly beyond the main port of entry into Key West, in the same line of sight. We have the video keyed up. It's been cleaned to remove any sensitive data. What time should we start?"

"I have security photos from a nearby restaurant that picked up two different men on the dock near Jack's boat as the strongest rainbands from the hurricane came ashore. I'm trying to determine if these two men had any interaction with him as they left the marina. One of them was murdered in town this week, and the police are now investigating a connection between that crime and the attack on Jack."

Captain Phillips looked down at his feet, his lips pressed together while he processed this news.

"Mick, if we capture evidence of a crime, I'll have to pass it on to local law enforcement."

"Understood. I was with Jack at the marina until about 1800 that night." Mick quickly reverted to military time when speaking with the captain. "But please start a half hour earlier—it was during this time that a boat docked near Jack's returned to port with the future murder victim on board. Jack was unharmed at eight o'clock, I mean 2000— that's the time he contacted Bea, his girlfriend."

The camera image appeared exponentially clearer compared to the video from Turtle Krawls. It picked up the harbor entrance to the marina, including the end of the dock and Abe's boat. *Bravo Zulu* remained out of view since it was located closer to the harborfront. Just before six o'clock, Abe returned to port. Mick and Jack walked into the frame when they helped him tie off. Skiff then disembarked with his dive bag, heading toward town. No one else came into view until Mick and Jack left the marina about the time Jack dropped Mick at his place for the night. While Jack was gone, Skiff returned to Abe's boat, carrying a smaller duffle bag.

Over the next hour, no boat traffic entered or left the port. Earl and Betty and everyone else near Abe had already evacuated. But that's when Mick saw it. The polo tourist walked out of Abe's cabin, followed by Skiff and Abe. They stood huddled in conversation until all three turned toward Jack's boat. They hurried back inside, then minutes later, Skiff left the marina with the same smaller bag.

The remaining two men stayed indoors as the conditions deteriorated. The break between rainbands now offered only temporary relief from the approaching hurricane. Mick wished he could see what Jack was doing during this time but was grateful Abe's boat sat within view.

Had Jack been watching the three men on board that night? Is that why they turned and looked in his direction?

As the recording kept rolling, no activity was visible other than the worsening weather until closer to nine o'clock when the polo tourist appeared on deck, talking with Abe. The tourist turned, as if something had startled him. He grabbed a small bag out of the cabin and left the boat.

He moved outside the camera's range, but the tourist had to pass by *Bravo Zulu* and Jack to leave the dock. The time stamp on his departure coincided with the Turtle Krawls recording.

Abe stayed on deck watching something toward town, frenetically shifting his weight from foot to foot. Eventually, he scrambled back into his cabin and didn't reappear until the morning after the hurricane, around the time Mick returned to the marina. The morning he and Bea found Jack unconscious in his cabin.

What had captured the polo tourist's attention that caused him to leave in a hurry? Mick was pretty sure it had something to do with Jack.

With this additional confirmation that the polo guy had been out diving with Skiff, he asked the officer to rewind the video in order to pinpoint the exact time both men first arrived at the marina. They worked backward to sunrise on the day of the storm when they captured the tourist stepping onto Abe's boat, minutes before Skiff arrived. Fast forward half an hour later, the boat pulled away from the dock, headed for open water.

"Captain Phillips, this is the break we've been waiting for. Thank you for sharing this with me. I think it'll help us track down the men involved in both Jack's attack and the murder."

"Good. What do you need from us?"

"Can I get a copy of this video starting at 0600 on the morning before the hurricane until 1000 the next day. Also, is it possible to enlarge the best facial images of these three men and get a printed and digital copy of each?"

The captain nodded to the technician working on the video. "Done. Jack's one of my oldest and dearest friends. If you need anything, just call me. Here's my personal cell number." He handed Mick a business card. "And we'll be forwarding the video over to the local police."

"I understand. As I mentioned, I'm working with Sheriff Ron Wheeler on this, and I also plan to show him my copy as soon as I leave the station. He might contact you if he needs more information, if that's okay?"

"Sure, Mick. If I don't hear from him by midday, I'll call him direct. It's important to keep a good working relationship, and I don't want him to think I've gone around him."

Captain Phillips left for another meeting, but his staff ensured Mick had everything he needed. He hustled back to his golf cart and waited until exiting the naval station before turning on his cell phone. A message from Jo popped up, as well as three additional missed calls from her number. Mick's elation quickly turned to dread when he saw the urgency in which she had tried to reach him.

CHAPTER 30

Mick's heart rate skyrocketed as his mind filled with concerns for Jack's health. He pulled to the curb, bypassed Jo's message, and called her directly instead.

"Sorry, I was at the naval station and had to turn over my cell phone at security. What's happening?

"Oh, I didn't mean to alarm you. Everything's fine—excellent, actually. Jack's being released from the hospital tomorrow. It's what we've been hoping for, but I can't help feeling scared about bringing him home. What're we going to do?"

Mick placed a hand over his heart, took a deep breath, and exhaled loudly. "We'll figure it out. Jack is okay, and that's all that matters. I have a new lead, and I'm on my way to meet with Frank and Bryce right now."

"Anything to share?"

"Not sure yet, but I'll keep you posted."

Jo didn't push for more details, which led him to believe she already had enough occupying her mind.

"I'm leaving for Miami when the vet hospital closes so I can be there first thing. Bea thought one option would be to move Jack to the hotel where we've been staying so he could continue his therapy, at least for a day or two. There's no way we'll be able to keep him away any longer than that. He made that perfectly clear to me on the phone this morning. I think the only reason he agreed to a delay was to avoid worrying Bea."

"A couple days might buy us enough time to be certain it's safe to come home. And Jo—tell Jack how happy I am for him."

Mick deliberated on his next destination. Now that he had a thumb drive with the video and images, his first stop would be Jack's place to upload the file to his laptop, and he was long overdue for a shower. He called the guys to fill them in.

"Send me the head shots you have of the men, including Abe," Frank said. "I'll pass them on to our crime techs in Tallahassee. They can run the unknown guy through the databases. Maybe we'll get a match for the tourist."

"Will do. I'm also going to forward them to Ruth Pender. If we get a hit, we can loop her in on the ID."

"What about the sheriff?"

"I'm not going to make it easy for him. This time, he can come to us at the marina, and we can negotiate an information swap. I'm hoping to get to him before the base commander sends him the video."

Mick left Ruth Pender a message telling her to check her email for the pictures of the three men. The sheriff's phone went to voicemail.

"Hey, Sheriff. It's Mick. I have fresh evidence connecting Skiff and Abe to the polo shirt tourist. I'll be on Jack's boat if you want to stop by." He smirked as he ended the call. He enjoyed regaining some power in their relationship.

. . .

Mick turned into the marina parking lot when the sheriff called to express his disdain for the cryptic message. He warned against withholding pertinent information in a murder investigation. Mick assured him that was not the case and invited the sheriff to join him at the marina before hanging up.

When he stepped onto the gangway, Frank and Bryce met him, talking over each other. They'd already heard from their contact in Tallahassee. Abe's full name was Abraham Levin, and he had a criminal record dating back thirty years. He did time for running guns in the late nineties and was arrested, but not charged, for possession with intent to sell narcotics. Ever since his release, he dropped off the radar, and his record had been clean. They had nothing new on Skiff's background search, and the team was running the polo tourist's picture through the system. It might take a while.

"Oh boy," Frank said, looking over Mick's shoulder. Sheriff Wheeler was marching down the marina dock. He looked ready for battle.

"What's so important that you needed to drag my ass down here?" The sheriff's anger was on full display.

"First off, this information I'm about to share with you directly results from Jack's friendship with the Key West Naval Air Station Base Commander, Captain Phillips. We wouldn't have it otherwise." Mick pulled the laptop from his bag, set it on the seat of the fighting chair and swiveled the chair to face the three men. He paused before pressing play and turned to look at the sheriff. "We're an asset to your investigation, and I hope you'll show us the respect and courtesy of sharing information in return." He didn't wait for a reply.

"This is from the night of the hurricane. You'll see Abe returning to port, Jack and I helped him tie off, then Skiff exits the marina with his dive bag. Nothing new here." They all watched the recording. "It's not long after when Jack and I leave—he drops me off at the cottage, and while we're gone, Skiff returns."

Mick fast forwarded the footage until the polo tourist walked into view on Abe's deck. He froze the screen so they could see a clear picture of the guy, then played the remaining video without commentary. Mick watched their faces closely, trying to gauge an unbiased reaction as the images flickered across the screen. When the polo tourist eventually departed the marina, he pressed pause.

"As far as I know, Jack was the only other person remaining at this section of the marina. We can't see his boat to determine if Skiff or the tourist stopped to talk to him or boarded *Zulu*."

"But something caught their attention," Bryce said. "And what was Abe freaking out about after the tourist left the boat?"

"Exactly," Mick said. "Now that we have a quality image to work with, I hope we can identify this guy. Oh, and this recording also captures Skiff and the tourist arriving at the marina on Abe's boat earlier that day, right after sunrise. They left the dock minutes later."

They watched the footage one more time before the sheriff spoke. "You win." He stepped back and removed his sunglasses. "I'll let you in on a key piece of evidence, assuming you'll keep it confidential."

They nodded their agreement.

"Surveillance cameras captured this same guy, your polo tourist, entering and exiting Skiff's trailer park around the time of his death. We tracked him through a rental car he picked up at the Miami airport using a fake ID—the name doesn't show up in the system. Clearly, he's a suspect in Skiff's murder, and we now have further evidence of his proximity to Jack."

The sheriff's capitulation surprised them.

"Any tracking on the car since then?" Frank asked.

"Someone dropped the car off after-hours at the rental agency here in Key West four days ago, on the morning after Skiff's murder. The crime lab collected a partial fingerprint that matched a print we collected from Jack's cabin. I just received that report on my way over here. Unfortunately, we have no usable prints from Skiff's trailer— someone wiped it clean. But we do have DNA evidence that's being processed."

"Thanks, Sheriff. I know that was hard for you." Mick struggled to contain a smirk. "We'll do you one better. We already have this clearer image of the tourist running through facial recognition in Tallahassee."

The sheriff lifted his eyebrows. "I'm sure you'll tell me if you get a name."

"You'll be our first call," Frank said. "What's the alias the tourist used to rent the car? I can forward that to our analysts."

"It's Juan Herrero, which is essentially equivalent to John Smith, obviously a fake name."

"I'll send you a copy of this video file. Captain Phillips will be contacting you this afternoon, and I'll forward his number to your phone—in case you need anything," Mick said.

Wheeler nodded. "Are you planning to stay on board?"

"We are. Abe is our only lead, so we're not letting him out of our sight," Mick said. "More importantly, when are you going to haul him in for questioning?"

"I'm headed to the station to work on a warrant—we need to get on that boat. Until I return, do me a favor—stay away from Abe and stay out of trouble." The sheriff tapped his forehead and saluted before leaving the dock. Mick interpreted that subtle gesture as his acceptance of their role in the case.

CHAPTER 31

"Well, that turned out better than I thought," Mick muttered as he grabbed the laptop. He sank into the chair and forwarded the file to the sheriff. "Either he's out of leads and desperate for our help, or he's actually trusting us."

"It's tearing me up not to storm down the dock and confront Abe with this new evidence," Bryce said. "But if we back him into a corner, he could turn dangerous. That's my take on him, anyway."

"You're right. It's not officially our case. We'll keep our distance and stick to surveillance until we hear from the sheriff or our contacts." Frank opened the cabin door. "I'll have the office add the tourist's alias to the search," then he stepped inside.

Bryce positioned himself in front of Mick, forcing him to glance up from the keyboard. "So, what's your plan for when Jack gets back in town?"

"I haven't really thought about it. I don't have anywhere else to be, so I guess I'll take it day by day for now. I told Jo and Bea that I'd stay to help Jack at home for as long as he needs me."

"It seems like you and Jo are getting pretty close through all of this. Am I right?" Bryce asked.

Mick smiled. "You've met her. She's incredible. Smart, funny—"

"And hot," Bryce added.

"Yeah, she's gorgeous. But for now, Jack has to come first."

"Yes, but eventually he'll be back to full strength, and the bad guys will get caught—they almost always do. Then what? Have you thought about that?"

"No. That time will come, but I'm trying not to get ahead of myself."

"For what it's worth, I'm going to offer you my two cents. This town looks good on you, Mick. You seem settled here, despite all the trauma and chaos."

"Yeah, it's strange. I can't imagine going home to Tallahassee right now. Obviously, being close to you and Frank is a big draw for me, but it might be time for a change."

Frank came storming out of the cabin. "Guys! The techs got a hit on the tourist."

Mick jumped to his feet. "Who is he?"

"A Venezuelan national, name of Alejandro Morena. He's on the Interpol watch list for dealing in stolen antiquities, including the illegal sale of artifacts raided from museums during the fall of Iraq and for handling the sale of stolen art. He facilitates the transfer between unscrupulous private collectors. He's stealthy and has a bunch of aliases, but the name used to rent the car was a new one."

Bryce furrowed his brow and shook his head. "How did a guy like Skiff get connected with an international art thief? He must have found something of high value to warrant Morena's personal involvement. Of course, the dark web has no borders—making it an easy platform for them to connect."

"I've got to get this info to Ruth Pender. Combined with the evidence collected by the sheriff, the FBI should be able to expedite a federal arrest warrant, assuming he's still in the country."

"Why would he stick around after returning to port that night?" Frank asked.

"He likely needed Skiff to clean whatever he salvaged from the ocean," Mick said. "That must be why Skiff had an electrolysis tank. Clearly, something went wrong with their partnership."

"Skiff was out of his league with this guy. He probably got greedy, or his big mouth became a liability. Either scenario would've put his life in danger," Bryce said.

Frank pointed to the trawler at the end of the dock. "Abe needs to be hauled in for questioning. His hands aren't clean in all of this."

"If you guys are okay here, after I reach Ruth, I'll drive to the sheriff's office to talk to him in person." Mick looked across the dock. "And I better give Earl and Betty a heads-up."

"We've got this end covered. Abe's not going anywhere."

Mick stored the laptop in the cabin then walked over to Earl and Betty's boat. After calling out their names without a reply, he texted them, asking them to get in touch. He would try to persuade them to leave town for a day or two. He didn't want them getting caught up in the middle of anything that might go sideways with Abe. Before pulling out of the marina, he phoned Ruth Pender, and once again, she picked up on the first ring.

"Mick, I got your email—"

"That's why I'm calling. We just found out the unidentified tourist's name is Alejandro Morena—from Venezuela."

"Give me a sec." Mick could hear her tapping on a keyboard. "Oh yeah. Now I know why that name's familiar. He's been linked to many crimes involving stolen artifacts, but we've only ever had circumstantial evidence on the guy. Interpol's been investigating him for years and issued a Red Notice for his arrest. He's a nasty one, too—known for using intimidation and extortion as a means to an end, but this is the only time anyone has linked him to a murder."

"What would he be doing with a washed-up salvage diver in Key West?"

"Gold. I'm pretty sure, anyway. There's been some chatter about a wealthy South American with ties to the drug cartels trying to buy up gold bars and coins salvaged from sunken sixteen and seventeenth century treasure ships. The Spanish Armadas stripped his people of their wealth and freedoms, and it's his goal to repatriate the stolen items, for his own private collection of course."

"Is there any current intel on Morena's whereabouts?"

"No, he last turned up in Argentina, but that was almost a year ago."

"Well, you'll want to speak with the Monroe County Sheriff because Morena is the prime suspect in the salvage diver's murder here in Key West. The diver's name was Scott Bainbridge, the skinny guy in the picture I sent you. I'm texting you Sheriff Ron Wheeler's info as we speak."

"I'll call him. Sounds like there's enough probable cause to issue an arrest warrant. But don't get your hopes up. He's probably in the wind since he has half a dozen aliases he can use."

"You'll have to add another name to the warrant—Juan Herrero."

Ruth snorted—clearly amused by the irony in the name equivalent of John Smith.

"But could you give me an hour? I've been on the sheriff's bad side for a while, and I want him to hear the information from me first. I'm on my way to see him right now, and I'll let him know you'll be reaching out ASAP."

"Okay. I'll get the Herrero alias added to the No Fly List. Mick, you've got thirty minutes. This guy's been outside our reach for too long to let him slip through the cracks."

"Thanks, Ruth. I owe you one."

CHAPTER 32

As Mick raced across Old Town to Stock Island, he called Frank and Bryce to give them a one-minute update on Morena. When he pulled into the station parking lot, he saw the sheriff walking toward his car.

"Sheriff!" he shouted. "Wait up."

"What now, Mick?" The sheriff kept walking.

"It's important." He ran to catch up with him. "We identified the polo tourist from facial recognition—Alejandro Morena, a Venezuelan. His extensive career brokering illegal artifact and art sales resulted in an Interpol Red Notice and landed him on the FBI watch list."

The sheriff abruptly turned back toward the station. "Come with me." He led Mick into his office and closed the door. "So, tell me everything you've got."

He filled in all the details on the background information he'd received from Ruth Pender, including her suspicion that he had brokered the sale of recovered gold from sunken galleons. He assured the sheriff she'd be calling any minute now. The sheriff excused himself from the room, and Mick watched him confer with a deputy through the office window.

When he returned, Mick said, "It's time you pushed Abe on his role in all this. You know he has a record."

"Of course, I do. Contrary to what you think, the wheels of justice have been turning without you. If you don't mind seeing yourself out, I need to make a few calls."

Left with no choice but to trust Jack's assessment of the sheriff—Mick had to believe he'd do the right thing. "Will you keep me apprised of any operation planned at the marina? Some of Jack's neighbors and good friends need to stay clear. I don't want them to get caught up in anything dangerous."

"I will. Things are happening fast. I'll be in touch. And thank you—to you, Frank, and Bryce. I appreciate your help."

Before he could reply, the sheriff picked up the phone to make a call. Mick left the office encouraged he and the sheriff were now on the same team. Plus, he had Ruth as another source of information. None of that eased his frustration at not being able to work the case directly.

He stood in the parking lot and planned his next move—a quick visit with Jo at the hospital before grabbing lunch for Frank and Bryce. Keeping track of Abe was the priority, as the sheriff had provided no insight into the timing of Abe's questioning.

Mick walked through the back door into the treatment area of the hospital and found Jo sitting in her office. He lucked out with his timing since she had a break in appointments for lunch.

"Mick!" She jumped to her feet. "Is everything okay?"

"It's all good. I have lots of news to share and thought I'd do it in person, but from your reaction, I should've told you I was going to drop by."

"No, I'm glad you're here. I'm just a little on edge is all. Why don't you grab Bob and come sit with me."

Bob's wagging tail banged the sides of his run when Mick walked into the kennel. After a quick trip outside, he led Bob into her office, but not before snagging him a few treats.

"So, what brought you all the way over here?" She placed a towel on the floor for Bob next to Mick's feet.

He wanted to tell her he didn't need a reason to see her, but he said, "I just left the sheriff's office. We have an ID on the second guy from the photos."

She listened intently until he got to the part about the FBI and Interpol.

"This sounds like some international spy thriller." She leaned over to pet Bob, stroking his fur. "How is it that this Morena guy isn't already behind bars?"

"No idea, but that's why everyone is scrambling to find him right now."

"What if he's still in town when Jack returns? What if Jack saw something that night—something that could put him in danger? If only he could remember."

"Odds are he's already fled the country. He'll want to get the gold, or whatever was salvaged by Skiff, to the buyer as soon as possible. The longer he holds on to it, the riskier it gets."

"I hope he's not motivated to get rid of any eyewitnesses. That leaves only Jack and Abe as loose ends," she said.

"The sheriff will be questioning Abe soon. If he realizes how much trouble he's in, he might come clean. I wouldn't count on it though."

"I'm ending my day early so I can be at the hospital in Miami to meet with Jack's doctors and get a firsthand update on his planned therapy and follow-up visits. He always glosses over everything, and Bea is still so overwhelmed."

"Jack told me how much it meant to him when you returned home to Key West. Who would have known how important that decision ended up being? With you and Bea advocating for him and making sure he follows doctors' orders."

"He can sometimes be too tough for his own good, but he's actually been a cooperative patient." Jo's technician stood at the office door, signaling the next appointment was in the exam room.

"I've got to go, Mick. I'll wait for your update about whether we should stay in Miami after Jack's discharge. Let me know if anything happens, please," Jo asked.

"I will. Either way, I'll call later tonight. Tell Jack I'll see him soon."

"Be safe." Jo squeezed his hand to stress the point before slipping into her doctor's white lab coat and wrapping her stethoscope around her neck.

Bob enjoyed two more cookies. It was harder leaving him behind at the kennel after each visit.

Mick called ahead to order three grilled grouper sandwiches and three iced teas. He was eager to get back onboard *Zulu*.

. . .

When Mick pulled up to B.O. Fish Wagon, people enjoying various house specialties filled the picnic tables outside the seafood shack. He collected his order from the pickup window, set the food and drinks on the passenger side floor, then Frank called.

"Hey. I got our lunch. I'll be there—"

"Mick. It's Abe. We left for a minute to help Betty carry down her provisions. He just untied his dock lines and is pulling away from the marina. He's sure in a hurry to get somewhere, or should I say, get away from somewhere.

"Shit," Mick said under his breath. "I'll be right there." He hung up and called the sheriff about Abe's attempt to skip town. The sheriff instructed him to stay on the dock. He'd handle it.

Mick raced to the marina parking lot. He wasn't comfortable captaining *Zulu* off the dock, but he'd consider it if it was the only way to keep Abe in his sights. With Jack on the mend, he'd never forgive himself if he damaged his prized vessel.

While contemplating the risks involved with piloting a large boat in a busy marina, police cruisers sped past. The calvary to the rescue! He wasn't sure what they could do from land when Abe was already nearing open water. He hoped the sheriff had a well thought out plan, and as he sprinted down the dock, he could see Frank and Bryce standing on the deck of *Zulu*, cheering.

CHAPTER 33

Before Abe reached the Gulf of Mexico, a Coast Guard vessel pulled alongside and boarded his boat. A Guardsman took over the helm and piloted the trawler back to the marina. Abe sat on his stern deck with his hands cuffed behind his back while an officer stood guard. Mick and his friends moved down the dock and were so focused on watching Abe's arrest they failed to notice the sheriff's arrival.

"I told you to trust me," the sheriff said.

"I actually think you told me to piss off, but none of that matters now. I'm glad you're here."

The sheriff's laughter surprised Mick, especially since he had never seen the man smile.

"You three are welcome to observe his interrogation. I'll call you later about the timing." The sheriff joined his deputies at the end of the dock to coordinate the handoff from the Coast Guard and the subsequent arrest of Abe Levin.

Stunned by his conciliatory offer, Mick stood silent.

Bryce elbowed his ribs to get his attention. "You don't get to see that every day. The Coast Guard coming to the rescue."

"The sheriff came through in the end," Frank said.

Mick nodded. "That he did. Just like Jack said he would. Let's move back on deck to take in the show."

Two officers secured Abe's boat and helped him step onto the dock. He moved awkwardly with his hands zip-tied behind his back. The usually wiry and surly Abe now had slumped shoulders and a dejected expression.

Mick wanted to look him in the eye, but Abe kept his head down as a deputy led him away—not once did he glance in their direction. Earl and Betty were outside to take in all the drama. They weren't the only ones breathing a sigh of relief—Mick had to admit Abe's hostile attitude had been a constant burden.

"They'll want to get a handle on any evidence on that boat before his interview," Bryce said. "Let's hope the deep shit he's in makes him more cooperative."

"I hope so, for Jack's sake. Let me grab our food. I'll be right back."

After he returned with lunch, Earl and Betty joined the three men on the deck of *Zulu* while they ate. None of them were sure about Abe's full involvement in Jack's attack, but his arrest was certainly something to celebrate.

Mick updated Jo about the recent turn of events. It didn't mean Jack should return home, but they were one step closer to getting some answers. Jo was already driving north to Miami and would pass along the good news.

The Coast Guard vessel departed from the dock, leaving the crime scene techs to search Abe's boat. The sheriff, taking a hands-on approach, managed the process from start to finish. After they carted away the last bag of evidence, an officer locked up then draped crime scene tape across the dock in front of Abe's boat to deter nosy neighbors from snooping around.

The sheriff, in the middle of what looked to be a serious phone conversation, didn't stop to talk on his way out. He gave them a nod as he passed by. When all the excitement had died down, Earl and Betty returned to their sailboat to enjoy a peaceful afternoon.

"I can't believe he invited us to Abe's interrogation," Mick said.

"Impressive. You must be growing on him," Frank said.

"There are still lots of unanswered questions. Maybe Abe will say something that explains how Jack got wrapped up in all of this. Until then, I don't think he should return home."

"We'll know more soon enough." Frank sounded confident.

"We haven't really talked about it, but how much longer can you guys stay in town?" Mick asked. "When you showed up, it was the shot in the arm I needed, but you've got work and your own lives to get back to."

"We're good for a couple more days," Bryce said with a nod from Frank.

"I spoke with the commissioner—before I had the techs run Morena through facial recognition. He must be feeling guilty about how things ended with you," Frank said, "because he officially sanctioned our role here as *assisting in the investigation*."

"I'm also sure he'll appreciate any credit the FDLE can take in apprehending an international criminal," Mick said. "I can't help being skeptical about his good intentions—my experience justifies my jaded outlook."

"True," Bryce agreed.

"There's nothing left for us to do here, so how about we head back to Jack's place until we hear from the sheriff? I want to get things cleaned up and the fridge restocked."

"We can give you a hand, and we need to pack so we're ready to leave before he gets home," Frank said.

Frank and Bryce drove the truck to the grocery store while Mick started some laundry and did a quick clean of the house. He wasn't sure if Jack would be coming to his own place or staying with Bea, but he wanted to be prepared either way.

Mick received a call from the sheriff midafternoon. Abe's interview would begin within the hour. Mick confirmed they would be there soon and told the sheriff how much they appreciated being included.

. . .

After arriving at the sheriff's office, a deputy led them into an interrogation room. Through the two-way mirror, they could see Abe sitting alone, his cuffed hands resting on the table. Every few seconds, he moved his arms, as if trying to find a comfortable position.

"They're probably leaving him to stew for a bit. Look at him. His anxiety is building every minute he sits there, wondering what will happen next," Bryce said.

"Well, he *does* have first-hand experience in a police station, even though it was decades ago," Frank said. "I'm sure all those memories from his months behind bars are coming back to him right about now."

A young woman entered the room and sat next to Abe. They spoke in hushed tones.

"Must be his lawyer," Mick said. "Likely court-appointed."

A moment later, the sheriff and a plainclothes deputy walked in, just as a man dressed in a classic, government-regulation black suit entered the observation area.

"Gentlemen." He closed the door behind him. "My name's Agent Jeffrey Bellinger with the FBI. I'm a colleague of Ruth Pender's. She told me I might meet up with you today. Which one of you is Mick Nassau?"

Mick extended his hand and introduced Special Agents Frank De Lucca and Bryce Taylor.

"Is there any word on Alejandro Morena?" Mick asked.

"Not yet. If he's still in the country and attempts to leave through any of the ports or airports, we'll catch him."

"You seem awfully confident, considering this guy evaded arrest for over a decade," Frank said.

"Maybe, but this time is different. He's made mistakes."

They turned their attention back to the interview. Abe sounded predictably combative as he resisted answering the sheriff's questions. "What's the crime? Taking out a couple of tourists on a diving charter?" He sat slumped in the chair with his arms crossed.

His body language and tone shifted when the sheriff presented him with the evidence linking Morena to the murder of Skiff and his own connection to both men. Almost as if a lightbulb went off over Abe's head, he started talking rapid fire. His lawyer tried to shut him up, but he ignored her advice. He then attempted to negotiate on his own behalf for some consideration in exchange for his cooperation.

He balked when the sheriff tried to implicate him in Skiff's murder, adamantly denying any wrongdoing. Common sense seemed to prevail when his lawyer seized his arm and firmly advised him *not to say another word.* She suggested a plea deal for Abe's testimony against Morena, putting an end to the interview while all the parties involved evaluated the offer. The sheriff left the interrogation room and joined the men on the other side of the mirror.

"Well, that was to be expected," the sheriff said. "He'll be taken down to booking. We're charging him as an accessory after the fact for Bainbridge's murder. Right now, it's iffy if we can make it stick, but if we shake the trees hard enough, something will fall out."

"He knows more than he's letting on," Mick said.

The sheriff nodded. "Nothing else will be happening here for a while, but I'll update you if anything changes. And by the way, you owe your former commissioner a thanks. He called earlier to offer Frank and Bryce's help with the investigation, along with the resources of the FDLE. Seems he was worried about you."

Mick's lower jaw dropped, surprised by the news. The sheriff's willingness to let them in on the case now made sense.

"Mick always was his favorite." Frank's sarcastic comment made them laugh.

The sheriff escorted the men to the lobby and excused himself before returning to the station with Agent Bellinger. Since arriving in town, this was the first moment Mick didn't have anywhere he needed to be. Federal, state, and local agencies were looking for Morena, and Abe would be silent until he'd been processed and conferred with his attorney. The sheriff hoped to get another crack at interviewing him later in the day, but until then, Mick planned to show Frank and Bryce around Key West.

CHAPTER 34

Mick invited Wayne to join them at the Green Parrot—the first stop on the tour. He owed him an update and hoped to catch Little Jimmy at work. Wayne confirmed he'd be there shortly.

"That's him." Mick gestured to the rather tall bartender busily tending to a raucous happy hour crowd.

"Hey, Jimmy. These are my friends, Frank and Bryce. They're in town helping me look into Jack's injury."

Jimmy raised his brows, eye wide open. After giving them a once over, he asked, "Special Agents, like Mick?"

They nodded.

"Nice to meet ya. Welcome to Key West." He placed a cold beer in front of each of them. "First round is on me. Any friend of Jack's is a friend of mine."

More than once, Mick had heard that saying. Jack's friends were fiercely loyal.

"Thanks. I'm glad we caught you. I've got good news. Jack's being discharged tomorrow. He'll have to continue his physical therapy here in town, but he's doing great."

"I never doubted it for a minute. He's tough as nails."

"And thanks for all your help in finding Skiff. We've identified his murderer and Jack's likely attacker, but so far, he's in the wind."

"Was it a local?"

"No, and he may have already fled the country. I can't say more since it's an active investigation."

"Word'll get out. Always does. If he's smart, he'll be far away from here." Jimmy wielded a long, sharp knife, making quick work sectioning some lemons. "I'd give anything for a few minutes alone with the guy in a locked room." He looked up at the law enforcement officers watching him and softened his tone. "But the only thing that matters is Jack's okay."

Jimmy was sharing his list of must-see spots with Frank and Bryce when he glanced over their heads toward the entrance. "Hey, Wayne."

Wayne and Alex, from the Mel Fisher Museum, walked into the bar dressed in golf attire.

"We were on the 18th when you called," Wayne said.

"And I'm curious if you've learned anything about a treasure, so I tagged along," Alex said. "Hope that's okay?"

"Absolutely." Mick gave the newcomers the rundown on the potential link between Skiff and Spanish gold.

"I'm amazed he kept his search quiet," Alex said. "Key West is a small town, and the underwater antiquities world is even smaller. Someone would eventually figure it out."

"That's likely why he worked with Abe. He's a loner with no connections to the salvage industry, and he had a history of operating outside the law," Mick said.

"Well, that stupidity cost Skiff his life," Wayne said as Jimmy set down two more drinks.

For the next hour, they left their current worries behind. Alex shared entertaining stories about pirates on the high seas and the modern-day search for sunken treasures. Billions of dollars in valuables remained buried on the ocean floor. Lives and fortunes had been lost throughout the ages when dreamers believed their next dive would be the one that uncovered sunken wealth. Mel Fisher had famously said, "Today's the day!" every time he left the dock during his decades-long search for his Spanish galleon, the *Atocha*.

Looking for a distraction until the sheriff called, Mick offered to buy dinner for everyone at Louie's Backyard. Still early, he hoped the wait for a table would be short at the popular waterfront restaurant. A delicious meal would be a fitting reward after a successful day. Wayne and Alex politely declined because of previous commitments, leaving the three friends to dine alfresco.

. . .

After being seated on the oceanfront deck, Mick ordered a round of rumrunners and a variety of appetizers. They were there to celebrate. In between courses, he excused himself from the table to answer a call from Jo.

"Hi. Jack must be itching to get out of there," Mick said.

"That's an understatement. He's counting the hours until he's discharged, but that's not why I called. I picked up a new cell phone for him today to replace the one that's gone missing. It's remarkable, Mick, but I'm going to let Jack tell you."

"It's all back," Jack shouted into the phone. "My memory—it's crystal clear now."

"What? You remember everything?"

"All of it. But first, let me tell you what happened. Jo bought me a new phone, and as I was going through all the startup prompts, it asked me to log in to my cloud account. I entered my password without even thinking about it—on muscle memory. My old data, including my photos, loaded onto the new phone. That was the key. The last pictures I took were from my deck the night of the hurricane, and when I saw them, everything came flooding back."

"All at once or little bits at a time?"

"It sort of played like a movie in my head, scene by scene as it came into focus. When I got back to the marina after dropping you off at home, I saw people moving around on Abe's boat. I thought the marina had already emptied, so I stayed on deck to watch. I recognized Skiff right away, but I also recognized the other guy, the polo tourist. Do you remember me telling you about that strange fishing charter—the guy that had no interest in fishing?"

"The same person who wanted you to take him out again right after the hurricane?"

"That's the one. It was the same guy, this Alejandro Morena. My alarm bells went off, so I snapped some pictures with my phone, but they saw me. I tried to play it cool and moved back into the cabin. Not long after, Morena boarded *Zulu* unannounced. He started out by making small talk about the hurricane and our last charter trip. Then, without warning, he lunged at me, grabbing for the phone in my hand. I wasn't expecting it and lost my balance. He took advantage of my surprise and shoved me hard against the table. That's when I must've hit my head and blacked out."

Jack seemed out of breath, prompting Mick to say, "Take your time."

"I'm good. Really. Anyway, I assumed he wanted my phone so he could erase any evidence placing him at the marina. What he didn't know was those photos also automatically loaded onto my cloud account, and he would have needed the password to access them. I use a special app to save pictures of my charter guests on their trip. It's a service I offer."

Now everything made sense to Mick. His hunch had been right all along—the missing phone was an important clue.

"Are you sure about all this? I mean, it's a lot for anyone to process." Mick wondered if Jack's head trauma could affect his recall of the facts.

"You kidding me? I'm positive. There's no doubt in my mind—this happened. You know me. If I wasn't sure, I'd say so. It's been so frustrating trying to force these missing memories. This is another step in my recovery, but more importantly, it'll help with the investigation. I'm just pissed this guy got the jump on me, on *my* boat."

"You had no reason to suspect you were in danger, Jack."

"Yeah, but I knew something was off. Those first instincts are never wrong."

"This is direct evidence tying Alejandro Morena to your attack and Skiff's murder. It also explains why Abe was so agitated after Morena left his boat that night. He must have seen him go into your cabin. I don't understand why Abe risked everything by sticking around town unless he was waiting to get his hands on his promised share of the treasure. He's been jumpy, likely living in fear you would wake up and place him at the scene of the crime."

"Did he know about my memory loss?"

"When I first told Earl and Betty about your injury and coma, he was standing nearby. And during one of our altercations, I sort of mentioned you were struggling to recall details from that day. I should've kept my mouth shut."

"This is not on you. Abe is a son of a bitch. He left me on board not knowing if I was dead or alive. I hope he rots in jail."

"He's being booked as an accessory to Skiff's murder, but he's hoping for a cooperation deal from the sheriff."

"Sheriff Ron better not let him off the hook. I don't give a shit how much information he has to share."

Mick agreed with Jack but also understood how these deals worked when there were bigger fish to fry and a murder to solve. On top of all that, a treasure of Spanish gold was at stake.

"Why would Morena charter *Zulu* to go out with you if he was working with Abe?" Mick asked.

"He probably wanted to survey the area where Skiff had reported the treasure to be located. You said Skiff was a lowlife, so maybe he didn't trust him. We were all around Rebecca Shoal that day, allowing Morena to see for himself if there was any other commercial salvage activity going on at the dive site. If they hadn't met in person yet, he could get a look at Abe and his boat—a way to verify if the deal he made with Skiff was legit."

"Makes sense. This guy's been able to avoid arrest all these years by being shrewd and careful."

"Mick, you're not going to like this, but I'm coming home. Nothing you can say will change my mind. Abe's in jail, and Morena is likely long gone. If you're at the house with me, I'm certain we'll both be safe."

"I wouldn't even try to convince you otherwise. Is Bea okay with this plan?"

"She is, and she'll stay at her own place until we sort this out. I don't want her in harm's way. Besides, she needs to get caught up on work at the gallery. She only agreed because you've got my back."

"You bet—just like you always have mine. Send me those photos, and I'll get them to the sheriff. He can use them as leverage when he interrogates Abe."

"Sending now. And thanks, Mick." Jack paused, and when he spoke, his voice broke. "I owe you—for everything."

"Stop right there. We don't keep score."

"Well, I disagree this time. Listen, I've got to go, but I'll see you tomorrow, buddy. We'll let you know once we're on the road."

Mick hung up, eager to share the latest break in the case.

CHAPTER 35

Mick left the sheriff a voicemail. He informed him about Jack's memory returning and told him to check his email for the new evidence. It was essential he saw the photos before he made any deals with Abe. For now, there was nothing else to do except enjoy a delicious meal with his friends.

He returned to the table to share the news about Jack's remarkable breakthrough.

"You were right all along," Bryce said. "You knew it wasn't an accident because you knew Jack. How he operates. How he lives his life."

Frank nodded. "The untied lines and missing phone stood out because it was so out of character. That suspicious mind of yours picked up on things inside his cabin that ruled out an accident."

The discussion about the ramifications of Jack's memories from that night continued until their main course arrived. They savored their meal and settled the bill by the time the sheriff called.

Abe had met with his attorney and agreed to cooperate with the investigation in consideration for leniency at his sentencing. After consulting with the FBI, the sheriff approved his terms but still wanted to hear more about Abe's role and connection to the crime before signing the deal.

Mick accepted his invitation to watch the second interview and confirmed they would be at the station shortly. They were also interested in hearing what Abe had to say, given Jack's recent revelations. It's possible this whole thing could be wrapped up by morning. That had always been Mick's priority, and he owed Frank and Bryce for helping ensure Jack's safe return.

. . .

After being escorted to the observation side of the interrogation room, they found Agent Jeffrey Bellinger already seated behind the two-way mirror. This time around, Abe's attorney did all the talking. Abe stayed quiet while they hashed out the details of his plea agreement, and only after the sheriff signed the document would he agree to answer questions. The terms required Abe's complete and honest disclosure of all the facts, or it would become null and void. He may have been able to make a deal for leniency, but no matter how you sliced it, Abe faced jail time.

The interview lasted a few hours as the sheriff cycled back through the same details, ensuring Abe was consistent with his facts. The biggest revelation came when he admitted to hitting Mick over the head in Jack's driveway.

"Damn! I'm not surprised it was him. But it still makes me angry he was hiding in plain sight. Obviously, I asked him one too many questions, and he got desperate."

"I told you he could be dangerous if he felt cornered," Bryce said. "The sheriff did some fancy footwork to get Abe to cop to your assault. It's possible there's evidence we're unaware of."

"That will be an additional felony charge he'll have to answer for," Frank said.

As they listened, Abe brought clarity to the chain of events leading up to Jack's attack and Skiff's murder, but he was light on any details about the Venezuelan. Skiff had approached Abe about fronting him for the costs involved in searching the dive site on Rebecca Shoal in exchange for a big payout if the site panned out. Skiff showed off a single gold coin he had found when diving the Shoal as proof of the potential windfall. At first, Abe didn't trust him but considered the risk to be minimal. He checked around town and confirmed Skiff had worked on other marine salvage operations, so he agreed to take him out for a dive. That's when Skiff discovered a stash of Spanish gold and silver coins tucked away in a deep reef wall.

Abe relied on Skiff's estimation of their value to be over a million dollars, and that's before they factored in the historical significance of the find. He didn't know they were part of a legally staked claim held by Deep Water Salvagers, but he also didn't ask.

It wasn't until after they discovered more coins on a second dive that Skiff told Abe about the involvement of Alejandro Morena—the key linchpin in facilitating their sale on the black market. Abe, a recluse and suspicious by nature, didn't like being tricked. He understood the risks went up exponentially by adding a third person to the deal, so he renegotiated his share with Skiff. After that, Abe agreed to one final dive on the Shoal with the Venezuelan on board since Skiff was certain there were more coins to be recovered. Unfortunately for them, Skiff ran out of bottom time on his oxygen tanks during their last dive trip, forcing him to abandon his search prematurely.

Abe tried to talk both of them out of doing the last dive as the hurricane approached, but the Venezuelan, who had no boat sense, insisted. They were concerned the storm would move the coins from their current location and be lost forever. So, Abe negotiated an extra fee as hazard pay for going out in rough conditions. In Morena's mind, the storm would provide cover from the prying eyes of the locals at the marina and allow them to avoid any boat traffic at the dive site.

Despite his other admissions, Abe was adamant he had no idea what happened between Jack and Morena, but he struggled to explain his nervous behavior during that time as he watched from his deck. He'd been told to mind his own business and to keep his mouth shut. Though the Venezuelan had a polished exterior, Abe said he knew he was a dangerous man. He'd had enough life experience on the wrong side of the law to recognize a ruthless killer when he saw one.

More than once, Morena threatened Abe's life if he interfered with the operation and warned Skiff against holding back any of the gold. They weren't idle threats. Abe's powerful instincts of self-preservation meant he didn't need to be told more than once.

According to Abe, Skiff ended up being a disaster to work with. He wouldn't shut up and kept boasting about his discovery. He assumed Morena killed Skiff, but he didn't have any first-hand knowledge of that fact. When they were still out on the boat, Skiff hinted at renegotiating his deal with the Venezuelan. While Morena agreed to consider it, Abe thought he was placating Skiff. This wasn't someone to mess with, but Skiff was too stupid—or too arrogant—to recognize the risk. Abe didn't know whether Skiff had skimmed any coins during the cleaning process, but he admitted it wouldn't be a surprise if he had and got caught.

After Morena left the dock the night of Jack's attack, Abe had no further contact with him. Lastly, Abe confirmed Skiff's deal included cleaning the coins in his special tank before handing them over to Morena a few days later in exchange for the payout. He didn't know what Morena had planned for the coins, and he didn't care. He wanted to distance himself from the two of them and told Skiff after they settled, he never wanted to see him again. That wasn't a big deal for Skiff who already had his eyes on a dive boat he planned to buy with his profits.

After Abe told his story, the sheriff pushed back, trying to catch him in a lie, but his testimony remained unchanged. He had no information about Morena or where he was staying and swore up and down he had nothing to do with Skiff's murder. He had already admitted responsibility for Mick's assault but would plea down for his role in Skiff's murder as an accessory after the fact. Additional charges would be added at a later date related to his failure to report the sunken treasure, as required by law.

In the end, a new spot would be opening at the end of the dock near *Zulu*—Abe wouldn't be getting out of jail anytime soon.

When the interview finished, an officer escorted him back to his cell, and the sheriff invited the four men to join him in the conference room.

"Nice trick getting him to admit to assaulting me."

"That was easy," the sheriff said. "When I told him we had evidence against him, and delayed his arrest to keep him under surveillance in case he led us to Morena, he fell for it. A Hail Mary pass but it worked."

"It seems like most of the pieces of the puzzle are coming together," Frank said. "Any word on Morena's whereabouts?"

"No, but we're monitoring all the ports. We believe he's still in the country," Agent Bellinger said. "He'll need to offload those coins to the buyer and collect his payment. This time, he made some uncharacteristic mistakes after being forced to work with an unpredictable, small-time crook. Skiff's murder probably wasn't part of the plan, so he appears to be lying low."

"Do you think he'll head to Venezuela?" Bryce asked.

"It's possible, but he has many international connections and could disappear anywhere. If he's smart, which he is, he'll make his way to a country without an extradition treaty with the U.S.," Bellinger said.

"Venezuela has an official agreement with the States, but they aren't honoring it these days since relations between our two countries are at an all-time low," Frank said. "Once he gets back to Caracas, he can move anywhere in South or Central America and transport the coins to the buyer. We'll never see them again."

"And that's why we have all our resources focused on finding him. We need to catch him before he leaves the country." They all agreed that would be an ideal outcome, but Mick remained skeptical.

Even though Jack had witnessed Morena and Skiff on Abe's boat that night, Mick thought the chances were low that Morena would stick around to silence him. Not after stealing Jack's phone. And with the gold in his possession, he'd want to leave the area as soon as possible. But low didn't mean nonexistent. Now was not the time for them to get complacent. The other men agreed with his assessment that Jack faced little risk in returning home, but Mick planned to stay close, just in case.

"Gentlemen, a pleasure, but I need to get back to Miami. Sheriff, thanks for your cooperation and support. I'll keep you updated if we find out anything on Morena." Agent Bellinger shook the sheriff's hand. "Mick, Ruth Pender wanted me to tell you she owes you a dinner."

He laughed. "You tell Ruth it's a deal." The agent quickly departed the conference room.

"It's been a very, long day," the sheriff said. "After I wrap up here, I'm heading home. Mick, I'll follow up with you if anything changes. Are you planning to stay in town, or are you going back with Frank and Bryce?"

"I'll be around until Jack kicks me out. I want to ensure he's settled before I consider my next move."

The sheriff nodded. "I doubt Abe's case will go to trial, but we'll contact you if we need your testimony. Thanks again for all your help. I realize I gave you a hard time, but I hope you understand I was only doing my job. I remember a young Agent Nassau telling me the same thing years ago when we first met."

"I get it. My only motivation was to look out for my friend." The two men shook hands. "It was nothing personal."

CHAPTER 36

Before leaving the sheriff's office, Mick sent Jo a brief email updating her on recent developments with Abe. It was too late to call, but he wanted to reassure her everything was set for tomorrow. Exhausted by the time they returned to Jack's cottage, all three men dropped into a deep sleep.

. . .

Mick woke the next morning, barely able to pull himself out of bed. With less adrenalin pumping through his veins, the stress from the past two weeks left him depleted of energy. The sun had cleared the horizon, and for the second time in as many days, he hadn't heard the rooster wake-up call. When he joined Frank and Bryce in the kitchen, they were complaining about the birds over their cup of coffee. He wondered if he'd developed an essential Key West survival skill—the ability to tune out the crowing in order to get a full night's rest.

"Morning." Mick grabbed a mug from the cupboard.

"How do you do it?" Bryce asked.

"What?"

"Sleep with those roosters crowing outside your window."

"Not sure, really. I guess I finally figured out how to turn them into white noise."

Frank filled everyone's cups. "We've booked our flight home, leaving this afternoon. With Abe in custody and the Feds taking the lead, things seem mostly settled here. And with Jack coming home today, it's time to clear out."

"I'm just grateful you've been able to stay this long. I might even reach out to the commissioner to tell him I appreciate his support. One thing I've learned over the past couple of weeks—it's wise not to burn bridges. My relationship with Sheriff Wheeler is a prime example."

Bryce agreed. "The commissioner paved the way for us to be down here without getting into any official trouble."

"What time is your flight?"

"At two," Frank said. "We have just enough time for a big Key West brunch. Your treat, Mick."

"Least I can do."

The three men rehashed the last few intense days while they cleaned up and packed for their trip home. Breakfast at Turtle Krawls included a few dozen oysters and a couple pounds of peel-and-eat Key West shrimp. Thinking of Jack, Mick added an entire key lime pie to go, picked up the tab, and suggested they make a quick stop by *Zulu*. When they arrived at the marina, Earl and Betty were sitting on deck.

"Hi, boys." Earl pointed toward Abe's slip. "Check that out. They towed his boat away early this morning." All evidence of Abe had been removed from their section of the marina, including the crime scene tape draped across the dock.

"We're glad to get rid of him," Betty said. "What're you up to today?"

"Frank and Bryce are leaving soon, but we wanted to drop by one last time."

"Will you be staying longer, Mick?"

He nodded. "Jack's coming home this afternoon, and I plan to stick around to help."

"We can't wait to see him. You three made it possible for Betty and me to get some sleep these last few nights. We were safe with you here, and we'd like to show our appreciation—maybe take you out for a sail?"

"Thank you. Jack and Mick also promised us a day on *Zulu*, and I think a round of golf is on the list as well. We'll be back," Frank said.

"Well, don't be strangers." Betty stepped onto the dock to give them all a hug goodbye.

While they chatted, Mick excused himself to answer a call from Jo.

"Morning. Any word on the timing of Jack's discharge?"

"That's actually why I called. We're getting ready to leave the hospital right now. You should see him. He's so happy. How are things on your end? Your email about Abe admitting to your attack was a shocker."

"He can't hurt anyone else now that he's behind bars." It felt good to say the words out loud, to reassure her. "On a more practical note, we cleaned up the house and replenished the fridge with the basics. What time do you think you'll be home?"

"Likely midafternoon."

"Frank and Bryce won't be here when you get back. They wanted to meet Jack, but they've promised to return for a real vacation."

"He keeps talking about taking them out fishing and diving."

"I think they're counting on it. Drive safe, Jo. I'll be at the house when you get there, and I'll arrange dinner for all of us. Ask Jack if he has any special requests."

After a minute, Jo came back on the phone. "He wants a homemade grilled cheeseburger."

"Tell him it's taken care of."

■ ■ ■

They dropped the pie off at the house, grabbed their luggage, then drove to the Key West International Airport. The tiny terminal meant checking in an hour before departure provided ample time to clear security and get to their gate.

Saying goodbye to Frank and Bryce was a stark reminder of how far their lives had diverged. Mick missed seeing them every day at work. Though he would have been there for them without a second thought, he deeply appreciated how they showed up for him this week. Friendships like that didn't come along every day.

Mick promised to call with regular updates while trying not to think about the fact his friends were returning to their careers as special agents. A couple weeks prior, he'd have given anything to have his old life back, but as he pulled out of the airport, he couldn't imagine leaving Key West.

It might have been the unfinished business surrounding Morena or his commitment to support Jack during his recovery, but either way, it surprised him. He stopped to pick up burger-making supplies, and before he pulled onto the road outside the grocery store, Ruth Pender called.

"Mick, how are things down there in paradise?"

"Better now. I'm sure you heard from Agent Bellinger about our local murder case and Morena's involvement."

"Yes, and we have a lead. A plane ticket booked using Morena's alias departs two days from now out of Miami for Quito, Ecuador. He used one of his lesser-known identities, and I can only assume he thought it was secure. We'll have undercover agents posted all over the airport, at security checkpoints and the gate. With this level of law enforcement presence, I'm hoping we can apprehend him without making a scene. We plan to wait until he's cleared security to eliminate any risk of a weapon. I pulled a few strings and cleared it so you can join the operation at the airport—as my consultant.

"Oh." He was surprised by the offer. "How did you manage that?"

"Well, I checked out your story about an early retirement. Not a shock to find out you got in between the governor and his campaign coffers. But since your retirement doesn't kick in until you use up your vacation days and severance, you're still officially employed. Seriously Mick—eight weeks of backlogged PTO—did you ever take a break?"

"Obviously not." He paused while he contemplated Ruth's offer. "So, this has been cleared with my commissioner?"

"Uh, huh. Just this one time, and you'll be far away from the prying eyes in Tallahassee."

Mick shook his head, somewhat disappointed. "I'd give anything to be the one to put cuffs on that guy, but my friend is coming home from the hospital this afternoon. He's an eyewitness linking Morena to the entire scheme and will be testifying in his own assault case. Until you get Morena in custody, I'm not going anywhere. There's no way I can leave now."

"I understand, but if you change your mind, you know where I'll be."

"We're so close. This guy has evaded arrest for years, but it sounds like his time may be up."

"Thanks to you and the great work of Sheriff Wheeler. We wouldn't be having this conversation without all your input in this case."

"Well, you know how it goes—wrong place, right time. Is the sheriff aware of the operation?" Mick asked.

"He'll be working with the team at the airport. The FBI will handle Morena's arrest and hold him in federal custody, but the sheriff insisted on seeing this case through to the end. He's a good man."

"Yeah, he's growing on me." Mick smiled into the phone. "Thanks again, Ruth. I appreciate you going to bat for me. If circumstances were different, I'd be there, but it's not my fight anymore. Be safe."

"Will do. Talk soon."

Ruth's call brightened his mood, erasing the lingering melancholy from saying goodbye to his friends. Deep down, he had to admit he had mixed emotions about declining Ruth's invitation to join the airport operation. While witnessing Morena's arrest would have been satisfying, it paled compared to the importance of being there for his friend. This promising break in the case likely had as much to do with all the good karma Jack Barton had put out into the world during his lifetime as it did with Mick's skills as an investigator.

He couldn't wait to share the latest news with his friends but decided to keep Ruth's offer to himself. It was time to move on—time to let go of Special Agent Mick Nassau. He needed to step aside and let others lead while he focused on celebrating Jack's homecoming.

CHAPTER 37

Mick prepped for dinner and still had enough time to catch the baseball scores while enjoying a cold beer. It seemed strange to be occupied with normal, everyday things, especially after the past week. A nagging feeling that he had something else to do persisted, but after surveying the room, he realized there was nothing. Once Jack arrived home, they'd work on a plan to protect against any possible remaining threat if Morena returned to town.

A text from Jo alerted him that Jack insisted on going straight to the marina, even before dropping by the house. He wanted to check on *Zulu* and refused to consider resting first. Jack was Jack, and a head injury wasn't going to change that. She reported he compromised by agreeing to keep his visit short, and he promised to follow doctor's orders. They had just passed Lower Sugarloaf Key and would meet Mick at the dock.

There had been a few days he wondered if Jack would ever be coming home. To be back in Key West, surrounded by friends and family that loved him, would be the catalyst he needed to achieve a full recovery. Mick updated Wayne and Michelle on Jack's ETA, since they all planned to meet at Jack's for a barbecue. But not wanting his first night at home to be overwhelming, they kept the guest list short.

Mick arrived at the marina as Earl and Betty returned from a rare sail. He helped them tie off their dock lines and told them about Jack's imminent arrival.

"Jack!" Betty shouted, waving her arms wildly.

Mick turned and looked over his shoulder toward Turtle Krawls, spotting Jack standing at the top of the dock with the widest smile, stretching from ear to ear. Despite using a cane to walk down the ramp, Jack appeared strong and infused with energy. He wore a baseball cap which hid the shaved back of his head and any evidence of his trauma.

Earl and Betty embraced him before he made it to the boat. A few of his neighbors, unofficial members of the welcoming committee, joined in. They looked surprised to see their friend needing support to walk, but once they heard him speak, his voice strong and animated, they stopped staring at the cane and moved on to telling stories about what had transpired since the hurricane.

"He looks so happy." Mick whispered to Jo. "He's much stronger than when I saw him only a couple days ago."

"He's definitely bolstered by being back home. I don't want him to overdo it though. Can you help me get him on *Zulu*. If I leave it up to Jack, he'll be here for hours."

Mick politely intervened with the group on the dock, reminding them there would be lots of time to reconnect over the coming days, but Jack needed to rest.

"Thanks, buddy, for looking out for me," he said.

"I'm following Jo's orders."

Jack snorted a laugh. "She sure can be bossy but in the best possible way. I only want to do a quick check on board, then I'm looking forward to going home. I promise. And I can already tell you've taken good care of her. She's spotless."

"That was all Frank and Bryce. They wished they could've been here to meet you, but they had to head back. They said they'll return whenever you're ready to take them fishing."

"I hope it will be sooner than later. I'm feeling more like my old self every day that goes by."

"I can tell."

Mick helped Jack safely step aboard. He sat down on the stern deck for a few minutes, taking it all in. He shut his eyes and took a deep breath. When he opened them, Jo and Bea were standing next to him.

"I needed this," Jack said. "After I check out the cabin and engine room, I'll be ready for that burger."

This was the first time Bea had returned to the boat since finding Jack on that fateful morning after the hurricane. She appeared pale, the creases on her forehead revealing her struggle as she confronted that memory. Jack reached for her hand, and the two of them entered the cabin alone.

"I wish I could take away those terrible memories for both of them," Jo said.

"They're strong and have each other for support. This may be a necessary part of the healing, so they can let go of the trauma."

"I get it, but I want their pain to be gone." Jo eyes welled up.

"I think we all have some healing to do." Mick put his arm around her, and she melted into his embrace, leaning on him to keep from crumbling.

Ten minutes later, Jack and Bea emerged from the cabin. It looked like they both had been crying, but their faces were also bright and smiling. *Facing their demons had been cathartic, after all*, Mick thought.

"Okay, you two. Let's get this show on the road." Bea signaled with a wave of her hand.

"You've got it. I'll run ahead to get the grill started for the burgers. Everything else is ready to go, and Wayne and Michelle should be there by now." Mick left first, after ensuring Jack didn't need any help to disembark from *Zulu*.

. . .

They had an amazing night. Jack sat in his recliner in the living room and appeared relaxed and at peace in his own home. Wayne and Michelle chatted with him as the rest of them worked on dinner. Everyone agreed Mick had some serious grilling skills as they enthusiastically devoured their burgers.

Before dessert, Jack tapped Mick on the shoulder. "Come with me." He led him through a door at the back of his walk-in closet, revealing a gun safe with a biometric fingerprint lock. Jack pressed his digit against the reader, and the safe opened revealing a Sig Sauer P365.

"I didn't want to talk about this in front of the others, but until the threat has been eliminated, we need to be smart. Thought you'd like to have some back up now that Frank and Bryce are gone."

Mick accepted the weapon and checked the slide.

Jack handed him a full magazine. "I don't trust my shaky hands, but I trust you."

Mick chambered the first round and secured the gun in his rear side waistband. "I look forward to giving this back to you. I'm supposed to be retired, you know."

"I hear you, brother. We need to move on to more important tasks like catching tuna and spearing grouper." He slapped Mick on the back and locked the gun safe before rejoining the others in time for dessert.

Jack took one bite of his key lime pie, smiled, and inhaled deeply. "A perfect welcome home dinner. Thanks, Mick," he said.

Bea stood to clear their plates. "Yes, thank you. For everything."

Mick wondered whether it was an appropriate time to steer the topic of conversation back to the murder case and Morena's impending arrest. They had avoided talking about it, instead focusing on Jack. But it had to be on their minds, even if they didn't say it out loud. He ended up sharing Ruth Pender's prediction that they would soon have more news to celebrate.

Based on the look of relief on their faces, he'd made the right decision to disclose the details. They all agreed Jack's attacker had likely fled town, and knowing he'd booked a ticket to leave the U.S. meant everyone would sleep better tonight—everyone except Mick. He anticipated lying awake all night, mulling over all aspects of the case. He couldn't shake the possibility the ticket had been booked as a decoy, but he kept that suspicion to himself. Until Morena was apprehended, he had to assume Ruth and the team would have all their bases covered.

Letting go and sitting on the sidelines didn't feel good, but this wasn't his direct fight anymore. The abrupt end of his career had weighed him down. He now realized he'd been mourning his loss of purpose. Now that Jack was home safe and sound, he'd have to get back to redefining his place in the world. After all, that had been the original motivation for visiting Key West.

The person who had showed up in town on the eve of a hurricane felt like a stranger to him now. He'd since been reminded of all the things he had to be thankful for. There was no room in his life to continue wallowing in his own self-pity.

Conscious of Jack's need to rest, they ended their evening early. Jo had a big day scheduled at the hospital and left with Wayne and Michelle. Bea helped get Jack settled but planned to sleep in her own home. With Morena still at large, she agreed to stay away and needed time to regroup after being gone for almost two weeks.

Bea motioned for Mick to walk her to the door. "Promise me you'll call for anything."

"I will. I'll give you an update after breakfast tomorrow."

She squeezed his hand and smiled. "I hope you know how much you mean to us. You were there for Jack and risked your own life—thank you sounds so inadequate."

"I don't need any thanks. Jack's done the same for me over the years. Case in point—the way he opened his home to me when I was struggling."

Bea hugged him, and when she stepped back, tears streamed down her face.

"What's wrong?"

"Nothing's wrong. I think these are tears of relief. I've been keeping it together for Jack's sake, but it's been a lot to deal with."

"You and Jo need to focus on your businesses and take care of yourselves. If it would help, I'd like to take him to his first few therapy sessions. This investigation has occupied all my attention, leaving me disconnected from the details of his recovery and how I can best help him at home."

"I think that would be great. His first appointment is tomorrow afternoon. I'll talk with Jo, but I'm sure she'd also be grateful if you took the lead. He's fully committed to doing the work, so the hardest part will be keeping him from pushing himself too hard."

"I'll watch out for that. It'll likely take us the rest of the week to find a new rhythm to our days."

Bea said good night and left Mick alone with his thoughts. Until everything was resolved with Morena, he couldn't keep himself from mentally reviewing all the steps involved with planning the airport operation. He checked his phone one last time for any updates from Ruth but saw nothing. He decided against calling her, but sent Frank and Bryce a text to update them on the Feds' plans, omitting the part about his invitation to participate.

Mick climbed into bed and tapped the gun under the pillow next to his head. With so much on his mind, it would be an uphill battle to get any sleep.

■ ■ ■

The next morning, the roosters began crowing at the same time Mick's phone rang. He was lying in bed wide awake and answered on the first ring.

"I hope it's not too early," Ruth said.

"Not at all. Especially if you have good news."

"Not really. Plans have changed."

CHAPTER 38

Mick bolted upright. "What happened?"

"Two more plane tickets departing tomorrow have been booked on different airlines under the name of Juan Herrero. One is a flight from JFK to Bogota, and the second is from Fort Lauderdale to Sao Paulo, Brazil. And a cruise ticket was booked departing from Miami with stops in Cozumel and Roatan, Honduras."

"Shit. Do you think he's on to us?"

"Not sure. I'm hoping he's just being cautious—it's smart trade craft. He's forced us to spread around our resources."

"Are you able to get a team in place at all the ports?"

"We're scrambling right now—he's not going to get away. Not on my watch. Listen, Mick. I have to go. Let me know if you reconsider my offer."

After hanging up from Ruth, he felt the need to vent but sat alone in the kitchen, sipping his first cup of coffee. Since Frank was an early riser, he took a chance and called him.

"What's up?" Frank bypassed the usual greetings.

"Ruth called to tell me Morena has now booked three flights using aliases, all departing from different airports and a cruise ticket in the name of Juan Herrero leaving from Miami."

"Hmm. And there's a chance he's not planning to take any of them. He could be driving over the southern border as we speak."

"There's more I didn't tell you. Ruth asked if I wanted to join the op. A onetime deal and supposedly with the blessing of the commissioner. I declined, of course, since Jack just came home. But it's tearing me up."

"Did you tell Jack?"

"No, he's dealing with enough right now. I'd put it out of my mind—or tried to, anyway."

"Did everything go okay with his homecoming?"

"It was amazing. I could see it in his eyes—being back on his own turf gave him a jolt of energy. Our only problem was getting him off *Zulu* and away from the marina before he overdid it."

"That sounds like a nice problem to have."

"For sure. Listen, I hear him getting up. I'll call you once I get more info. Can you fill Bryce in for me?"

"Sure thing. And, Mick, think about Ruth's offer. I know you. It'll eat you up if things don't work out the way you want and you weren't there. This one is personal."

"We'll see."

Jack walked into the kitchen, resembling a bear waking up from hibernation. The front half of his thick crew cut had missed a regularly scheduled trip to the barbershop and now stood pointing in a variety of directions.

"How was your night?" Mick asked.

"Great. Nothing beats sleeping in your own bed. I woke up thinking it was like any other normal day until I saw my cane and remembered— nothing about the last two weeks has been normal."

"Well, you're doing amazing. I know you're impatient, wanting to get back to a hundred percent. It'll happen."

Jack nodded. "Damn straight." He walked to the living room, leaving the cane behind. "Can you pour me a cup?"

Mick filled two mugs then took a seat in the chair opposite him. "Frank and Bryce stocked the fridge with staples, but I wasn't sure if you had any special requests or diet restrictions now that you're out of the hospital. Take a look, and I can pick up whatever else you need."

"I can have what I want—but no more bland and mushy hospital food."

"I'm sure you're accustomed to the freshest catch of the day, especially when you reel it in yourself."

"And Bea is an amazing home chef. She spoils me." Jack set his mug on the table then banged his hands on the arms of the chair before declaring, "How about breakfast at Two Friends Patio? Then I need to stop in to see my barber and get rid of this ridiculous reverse mullet." He ran his hands through the hair on the top of his head. "I'll have him buzz most of it off so it matches the back. And after that, we can swing by the marina for a quick check."

"Are you sure?" He'd been warned not to let Jack overdo it.

"Listen, Mick. I appreciate you being here, but don't start tiptoeing around, all right? Jo and Bea have everyone watching out for me—I'll listen to my body and rest when I need to."

"Okay. I'll stop hovering."

A knock at the front door interrupted their conversation. Bea or Jo wouldn't knock, they would walk in, so who would be calling at this early hour? Cautiously, Mick looked out the front window and saw the sheriff standing on the porch.

Mick opened the door wide and invited him inside. "Good morning, Sheriff. Looks like you need a strong cup of coffee."

"Thanks." He immediately turned his attention to Jack, who stood to greet him with a handshake that morphed into a half hug.

"Ron, it's sure great to see you," Jack said.

"I was about to say the same thing. Welcome home." The sheriff accepted a large mug from Mick. "Have you heard?"

"Yes, Ruth called," Mick said.

"Heard what?" Jack asked.

The sheriff set his mug down. "About the guy that assaulted you—Morena."

"I didn't have a chance to tell you yet," Mick said.

"What the hell is going on here?" Jack asked. "No bullshit this time."

They all took a seat, and Mick shared the latest about Morena's multiple travel bookings and the FBI's plans to put him in custody. He contemplated holding back the part about Ruth's invitation to join the op in Miami, but since he'd already declined her offer, there was no harm in disclosing the details.

The sheriff raised his eyebrows. "You sure about that? I thought you'd jump at the chance."

Mick nodded but didn't reply until he noticed Jack's stare. "I'm sure," he said, though the words lacked conviction even to his own ears.

"I'm on my way to Miami to attend a briefing. But Jack, I want you to know I'm going to do everything in my power to make sure he pays for what he did. When I get back, I'll come by for your official statement about his attack. He's going away for a very long time."

"I never doubted you for a minute," Jack said.

"I don't think Mick would have agreed with you most days," the sheriff said with a smirk.

"I told him to trust you, but as you've already figured out, Mick can be like a dog with a bone."

"Well, I'm grateful for that. Mick, I also wanted to come by to thank you personally. Without your investigation and persistence, we might never have put all the pieces together in time."

So many things flew through his mind to say, but he landed on, "I appreciate that, Sheriff."

"Call me Ron."

"Okay, Ron. We always had one thing in common. Looking out for Jack. That's all that ever mattered to me."

Over his second cup, the sheriff filled them in on the details of Abe's plea agreement. "And we've moved his boat to the police lot. When the case is closed, he'll have to decide whether to sell it or put it up for dry dock."

"Good riddance. Ron, we were getting ready to head to breakfast to celebrate. You're welcome to join us."

"Thanks," the sheriff said. "But I've got to hit the road. I'll take a rain check though."

Mick followed the sheriff to show him out, and that's when Ron asked to speak with him in private. Mick had no clue what he'd done wrong this time, and since he didn't really have a choice, he stepped onto the front porch and closed the door behind him.

CHAPTER 39

"A couple things," the sheriff said. "I want you to call me if Jack needs anything. Anything at all. Don't hesitate, okay?"

"I will. It'll probably take me some time to sort out my role here." He chose not to mention the gun concealed in his waistband. Not after they had found common footing only minutes ago.

"And that's the second thing I wanted to talk to you about—your role here. I have to tell you, I was pretty pissed when the naval base commander mentioned the two of us were working together on this case, referring to you as my colleague. Impersonating a law enforcement officer is a felony—"

Mick interjected. "I know. I should have made it clear to him—"

The sheriff held up his hand. "Let me finish. It's a felony, but it got me thinking. I realize we got off to a rocky start, but I wondered if you're planning on sticking around town for a while."

Mick cocked his head to the side, trying to figure out where the conversation was headed. "That'll be up to Jack. I really haven't thought about anything long term. It's only been a couple weeks since my retirement, or whatever you want to call it. Why?"

"Well, if you were ever to consider making Key West your permanent home, I'd be part of your welcoming committee. I'm sure a job as a sheriff's detective is below your pay grade, especially after leaving your role as a special agent, but I hope you'll consider joining our team. I've been wanting to expand the department and could really use someone with your investigative skills. Someone I can trust."

It took Mick a few seconds to find his words. Things sure had come a long way. The sheriff began their relationship by obstructing his every move. Now he stood in front of him, offering him a job.

"Wow. It's hard to surprise me, but you just did. I'm not sure if I'm interested in another nine-to-five, at least not right now, but I really appreciate the offer. Can you give me a few days to think it over?"

"No rush—my door is always open. You just take care of my friend in there. Stay in touch." The sheriff firmly shook his hand and turned to walk to his patrol car.

Mick must have had a dumbfounded look on his face when he went back inside because Jack asked, "What was that all about?"

"You'll never guess. He actually asked me to join the sheriff's department as a detective. I didn't see that one coming."

"No kidding. What did you say?"

"Well, I stood there with my mouth hanging open, then I told him I wasn't looking to start a new, full-time career, but I would get back to him soon."

"Well, it's always good to have options. I'm not going to need a babysitter forever."

"You're right. I'll give it some thought. But first, let me call Bea. I promised her I would tell her and Jo when you were awake."

Jack took charge. "I'll call Bea, and you can call Jo," He smiled at Mick. "Then let's head to breakfast. I'm starving."

. . .

During the short, golf cart ride to the restaurant, Jack greeted a handful of locals. On two occasions, Mick had to pull over to the curb for extended conversations. He had never experienced that same sense of community, no matter how long he'd lived in a place.

Things felt like old times. The events over the past few weeks had robbed them of a proper reunion, and they had lots of catching up to do. As they did so, more acquaintances dropped by their table to chat with Jack. He wore his ball cap, hiding any signs of his recent injury—so the topic never came up. They'd been busy with their own lives, cleaning up from the hurricane.

After paying the bill, they stopped at the barbershop on White Street. A true professional, Omar the barber didn't ask questions but worked efficiently to blend Jack's crewcut to match the new hair growing on the back of his shaved head.

The sun had started its climb by the time Mick pulled into the marina lot. He chose a parking spot close to the harbor in order to minimize Jack's walking distance, deciding against offering any help, unless Jack asked for it. But he stayed close, just in case. Jack carried his cane to the dock but didn't use it until he stepped onto the boat, leaning on it for a brief moment. He climbed into his captain's chair and looked out toward Abe's empty slip, staring but saying nothing.

"You okay?" Mick asked, breaking the silence.

"I will be." He turned his attention away from the end of the dock. "Sure is quiet, even for the slow season."

"Yeah, I don't even see Earl and Betty moving around. It's still early though."

Jack looked at Mick. "I can't stop thinking about Ron's offer. Only you can decide if it's a good fit or even something you're interested in, but why *don't* you consider a permanent move to Key West. Hear me out. I get that Frank and Bryce are a big part of your life, but they're busy with their careers and probably have as much free time as you did before you retired. You told me you weren't sure if there was anything left for you in Tallahassee, but I can think of a few reasons to keep you in Key West." Jack pushed himself up and stood to face Mick.

"I'd like to add another job offer for you to consider. I could use a hand running fishing charters once the season picks up after Thanksgiving. The pay is crappy, but the job satisfaction is tough to beat."

Mick laughed. "Thanks, Jack. I'm here to help you get back on your feet, whatever you need. When you're up to booking charters again, we'll figure it out. Until then, let's take it one step at a time. That'll be best for both of us, right?"

"I guess so. You're welcome to stay with me till you work it out. The more time you spend in town, the harder it will be to leave. But there's one more thing." Jack looked uncomfortable as he shifted his weight from leg to leg.

"I know you and Jo have gotten real close. I can see it on your faces. Whether it's only friendship or more than that, I'm okay either way. I want you both to be happy." Jack patted Mick on the shoulder. "Okay, I've said my piece. We don't need to discuss it again."

Mick had contemplated asking for Jack's blessing to date Jo, but when he imagined her response to learning of his old-fashioned approach, he thought she might be annoyed he didn't ask her first, so he said nothing. Now, he didn't have to worry about it.

"I appreciate that, Jack."

"And about that offer from your FBI friend—you need to go." He spread his arms wide and grinned. "I'm all good here."

Mick put his hands up to halt the conversation, but Jack pushed on.

"I know you. It's killing you not to be involved in bringing Morena down. You need to do this. Make the call."

Jack had a way of dissecting away all the extraneous crap and getting to the crux of the matter. Mick wanted to join the op, but he had made a commitment and never went back on his word.

"I told Bea I'd drive you to your first few therapy sessions."

"I might be a little off pace, but I can handle arranging my ride just fine."

Mick fixed his gaze on his friend for a good long while, prompting Jack to say, "But if it makes you feel better, I'll clear it with her."

Mick shook his head. "Now is not the time to let our guard down. If Morena doubles back to Key West, we need to be ready. I need to be here."

"You said it yourself—you don't think he'll do that. And I have other friends with skills you know. They can take over until you get back."

With raised brows, Mick's eyes opened wide. "You don't mean Wayne, do you?"

"Hell no. He's a numbers guy. The only weapon he carries are his golf clubs, and he sticks to using them on the course."

"Who then?"

"Little Jimmy. Actually, that would be Sergeant James Coffey, U.S. Army Ranger."

"Holy shit. You do have friends with skills."

"Yup. Did tours in Afghanistan and Iraq before landing back in town at the Green Parrot."

"First things first. You've got your therapy appointment this afternoon, so let's focus on that."

"If you say so." Jack's grin stretched across his face. Mick knew that look. In the past, it meant trouble. Usually good trouble, but nonetheless, Mick had lots to think about.

CHAPTER 40

They stopped home to swap vehicles, and since Jack's first session would last two hours, Mick had some time to kill. Surrounded by a team of therapists and doctors, Jack would be safe until he returned.

To help focus his mind, Mick laced up for a run but not before clearing his gun and placing it in his bedside table. His route took him through the narrow, grid-like streets of Old Town. He passed by a small Conch-style cottage he'd seen before. Previously a chiropractor's office, now a realtor's sign stood in the front yard, listing the property for lease. That sign became the catalyst for a steady stream of thoughts.

He'd been contemplating Bryce's suggestion of packing up his home in Tallahassee and moving to Key West. He was happy here—content in a way he'd never known before. He wasn't quite ready for retirement, and soon, Jack wouldn't need his help. While he'd be welcome to stay as long as it worked for everyone, Mick wondered if it was time to find a place of his own.

The sheriff's job offer had sparked an idea. Mick had spent his entire life working in law enforcement. It's all he knew. He loved putting criminals behind bars. The recent run-in with the governor that inevitably ended his career left a sour taste in his mouth. And after bumping heads with Sheriff Wheeler, he never wanted to be in a position again where someone else controlled his investigation.

Branching out on his own never crossed his mind before because he'd always been a government man—until the organization betrayed him and forced him out. If he were to start his own business, he wondered what it would look like.

Mick finished his run, showered, retrieved the Sig, then drove across town to the therapy office. While he waited for Jack to finish, his mind wandered. Never one to daydream—a faint idea lingering in the back of his mind moved to the forefront, triggered by the For Lease sign on the chiropractor's cottage.

He had always enjoyed the investigative aspect of his job, more than any of the legal roles his law degree qualified him to pursue. His career and credentials would be a valuable asset in private practice. If he had his own investigative and legal practice, he could work for himself and pick which cases he took on. Thanks to a cushy pension, he wasn't desperate for money, and that financial freedom would allow him to be selective with his clients and only work when he wanted. It would be a new challenge, one he looked forward to.

Suddenly overcome with a sense of urgency, he reached out to the realtor for the chiropractor's cottage to inquire about the terms of the lease. She called him back within minutes. A few details needed to be worked out. But with no further analysis, he had her send over the lease agreement. She would be available to meet him for a walk through later that afternoon where he would sign the document, pay the required security deposit, and get the keys to the place. A background check would be a formality. The place was his if he wanted it.

For the first time since retiring, his future came into focus.

■ ■ ■

Jack settled into the passenger seat and leaned back on the headrest. "They kicked my butt," then he opened his eyes and smiled. "But it's all good. The head therapist is the daughter of a friend. I think she'll have me back in shape in no time."

Mick nodded but said nothing, still preoccupied with Morena's pending arrest and his rash decision to pull stakes and move to Key West.

"I can see you thinking. Have you reconsidered joining your FBI friend in Miami?"

"Yes, and no." Mick told Jack about the lease on the cottage and his idea for a new business.

Jack sat forward with an incredulous look on his face. "You did all that while I was at therapy?"

"Yeah. I know—it's sudden. It just felt right. But it means I might not be able to help you with future charters."

"Are you kidding me? I was half-ass offering the job to keep you around. I've been hoping you would decide to stay in town, but I wasn't sure where your head was. You've got a lot you're working through, and I didn't want to add any pressure."

"To be clear—I'm not going anywhere until Morena is behind bars. It sounds like I can get the keys right away, but I don't have any furniture, so it'll take me some time before I can move in. You know I wouldn't make these plans unless I thought you were well on your way to a full recovery."

"I know that. So, when can we see the place?"

"The realtor said she could meet me anytime to sign the lease. But I figured you'd want to rest first. We can go later."

"No way. Why don't we run by your new place now? I know the house, but I've never been inside. Let me see if Bea can join us. She'll be upset if we don't include her on the tour. Wait, did you tell Jo?"

"Not yet. I prefer to tell her in person."

"Good luck. I'll be staying out of it from here on in."

. . .

It was a short drive over to Bea's gallery. The moment they walked through the front door, it felt like stepping into a chic Manhattan art show—or at least how they were portrayed in movies, since Mick had never actually been to one.

"Well, this is a great surprise. Everything okay at your first appointment?" Bea greeted them from her corner desk.

Jack kissed her on the cheek. "Therapy was great, but that's not why we dropped by. Mick has some exciting news to share. Can you get away for an hour?"

"You've piqued my interest. Let me check with my assistant. She's inventorying some new pieces in the storage room. I'll be right back." Bea stepped from around the desk. "Jack, why don't you show Mick the gallery."

Mick wandered through the large, open floor plan, stopping to look at each of the pieces, while Jack took a seat on a bench in the middle of the room. Bea joined them and expounded on the background of the artists she represented. One particular artist who painted large, graphic watercolors of tropical fish and seabirds impressed Mick. When he learned the price, it confirmed he couldn't afford to hang any of this art in his own home, especially now that he was on a fixed income. He could dream, though.

■ ■ ■

After a quick walk-through, his friends were excited about his new place. The classic white cottage with its royal blue Bahamian shutters had a small front porch with just enough room for a couple chairs. Inside the business entrance, a welcoming reception area led to one large office and a separate half bath.

Similar to how Bea's gallery was set up, a small apartment occupied the back half of the cottage. Its high ceilings, open beams, and weathered, original Dade County pine floors added tons of island charm. It was perfect for Mick. The updated kitchen and bathroom had modern touches, but the living area maintained all its historical Key

West charm. He found it strange to have a fireplace in such a tropical climate, but it added to the style of the living space.

When they finished touring the property, Mick concluded his business with the realtor. He signed a one-year lease with an option to purchase at the end of the year. He'd never made such a big decision with so little forethought, but after signing on the dotted line, there was no turning back.

CHAPTER 41

While Jack inspected his back yard for storm damage, Mick spent the morning in front of the computer, planning his move. Putting his Tallahassee house on the market would be a simple task, since he was almost never home. It already looked decluttered and staged for sale. After spending years working day and night, his place looked like a corporate rental, devoid of any personal effects except the single framed photo of him with Frank and Bryce on a recent fishing trip. It never bothered him before, but now he realized how depressing it was.

He looped Frank and Bryce in on his decisions since he didn't want them to drive by and see the *For Sale* sign on his front lawn. As if they both knew that moving to Key West would be his ultimate decision, they didn't act surprised when he broke the news. His neighbor, Mrs. Beckman, would help coordinate the hand off of his house keys, and his realtor assured him the place would sell fast. Mick arranged for a moving company to pack up his Tallahassee things the following week, leaving behind just enough furniture to keep the agent happy. It gave him some time to get his new home ready to move in.

Mick still needed to have two important conversations before publicly announcing his plans, and they were with Jo and Sheriff Wheeler. He planned to tell Jo in person, but the sheriff would be the tricky one. The hardest part would be keeping it all under wraps until then.

Mick was emailing his Tallahassee realtor when Jack walked in the back door.

"It's a jungle out there," he said. "I'm going to bite the bullet and hire someone to clear the over-growth so I can get started on my landscaping project. Life's too short."

"You're right." That statement had more meaning these days after everything they'd been through. A life-threatening injury put many things into perspective.

"Mick, I called Little Jimmy. He's coming by tonight before his shift starts. I'm going to tell him everything about Morena, but he's already agreed to stay here with me while you're working the op in Miami. No questions asked."

"You don't need to—"

Jack interrupted him before he could finish. "Yes, I do. My house, my rules. Be honest with me—you want to go, don't you?"

Mick rolled his eyes. "Hell, yeah. I've been wondering if my impulse decision to sign the lease was a distraction of my making."

"Jimmy will be here around six. Why don't you catch up with Jo over dinner? I can't keep your move under wraps. You need to tell her."

"You sure about all this?"

Jack nodded. "Call the FBI and make it happen. I'll work on Jimmy, and we can regroup after dinner."

"Okay—you're right. I'll reach out to Ruth to see if her offer still stands." While Mick waited for her response, he processed his next move. He had no illusions about the fact this was a onetime deal and not a reboot of his career. It would feel good to be part of the team. A final swan song.

Ruth called, expressing her gratitude for his support and took no time before diving into the details. They had teams at the three airports, and Ruth planned to lead the Port of Miami operation. Moving gold through airport security was risky. Morena would be forced to conceal it in his checked luggage. Screening at a cruise terminal involved similar check points but with fewer hands involved and only one destination—the cruise ship stateroom.

The passengers would begin embarking at eleven o'clock, so if Mick left before sunrise, he'd arrive in time to attend the team briefing. Ruth had negotiated with the cruise line and the port authority to allow her team to be staged throughout the terminal.

Mick had been directed to dress as a tourist to blend in with the other cruisers. Not his usual style, but thankfully Jack had a closet full of Hawaiian shirts. He told Ruth he didn't have his personal firearm with him since he had to relinquish it at retirement. He didn't mention the Sig since he wanted Jack to keep his pistol nearby. She confirmed she would handle procuring him a weapon.

With one task complete, he moved on to convince Jo to join him for dinner. He told her he felt like a third wheel when Bea was around and wanted to give Jack some private time. She laughed and agreed to meet him at seven.

. . .

After sitting in on Jimmy's briefing, Mick walked to Antonia's restaurant, arriving early to enjoy a cocktail at the bar while he waited for Jo. He couldn't remember the last time he'd been on a proper date. Uncertain if this counted as an official date, it seemed different from their previous meals together. More formal and definitely layered with some expectations.

Jo came breezing through the front door a few minutes after seven. When she spotted Mick at the bar, her face lit up, then she smiled, leaving him breathless. Mick hadn't felt like this about anybody in a long while. Jo greeted him with a hug and ordered a spicy margarita on the rocks to join him in happy hour.

"It felt good to put on something other than my scrubs. And a sit-down meal is a nice reward after this past week," she said.

"Jack's on a health kick and plans to eat all his meals at home, avoiding any side trips to the bars, even Turtle Krawls."

"He's working so hard. I'm really proud of him. He told me he wants to drive himself to and from his therapy sessions if he's not too exhausted. He'll have to get medical clearance from his doctor, but what do you think?"

"He doesn't need my help for much of the day-to-day stuff, and I trust him to make the right decision based on how he's feeling. Working on *Zulu* is a bit of a different story."

They were soon seated for dinner and enjoyed a relaxed evening, laughing and telling stories over a delicious meal. Being with Jo was effortless. She was funny, wickedly intelligent, and beautiful. Mick thought her ex-husband must have been a complete ass to let her get away. After sharing a dessert and finishing their bottle of wine, Jo offered to walk Mick home. She'd taken a ride share to the restaurant and would order a car to pick her up at Jack's.

She hooked her arm through Mick's as they strolled through the back streets of Old Town. He leaned to his side to draw her close. Her perfume had a heady effect on him with its notes of citrus and spice. She smelled so good. As they approached the front of Jack's cottage, they both stopped talking. The expectations and tension building with every step.

"I'm glad we got a do-over on this dinner," Mick said. "The last time, you found me knocked out in the driveway. Not my best look."

"But finding you that night made me realize how important you were to me." Jo grabbed his hand and pulled him into the shadow of a Gumbo limbo tree, running her hands up his chest before kissing him. "I think you know this, but in case I haven't made myself clear, I'm grateful you've come back into Jack's life and into mine."

"About that," Mick said. "I have a few things to tell you." Mick kept his hands on her hips but leaned back so he could see her face while he told her about his plans. Any concerns he had about her reaction to his move were pushed aside when she began kissing him playfully.

"I've been dreading the day you would tell me you were moving back to Tallahassee." Jo kissed him again. "I'm so happy that day won't come."

"I didn't want you to think I was suggesting anything between us. You're one of the main reasons I want to stay in Key West, but I don't want you to feel any obligation."

"I don't. I understand it's about more than just me. Have you told Jack and Bea yet?"

"Yeah, I showed them around my new place earlier today. I wanted to tell you in person. Bea's going to be my interior design consultant."

"Lucky man."

"There's more," Mick said. He told her about his decision to join the FBI operation, but based on the strained look on her face, he left out many of the details. Instead, he worked to convince her Jack was in expert hands until he returned.

"I don't like this. This guy's a murderer. It's dangerous."

Mick leaned over to kiss her, to reassure her. She immediately kissed him back, intensely, pulling him close. Weeks of pent-up desire were beyond their control. When they eventually let go, they both smiled and started laughing.

"I know this is normal everyday stuff for you, but please stay safe."

"Always."

When Jo's rideshare pulled to the curb, they reluctantly parted ways. Mick didn't move until she was out of sight, then he sighed, turned, and walked into the cottage. He was fully committed to moving, but his date with Jo added to his motivation.

"It's about time she took a night off," Jack said when Mick walked into the living room. Little Jimmy stood at the kitchen island in front of an impressive collection of weapons. Two pistols, a rifle, ammo, a speargun, tactical knives, and zip ties for securing prisoners.

"Don't worry. They're all legal," Jimmy said, displaying a wide smile.

"I need to be on the road before six. Is that still good for you?"

"I'll be here. I'm working the early shift tonight, and I can call out tomorrow if you're not back yet, or this jackass is still at large."

Mick contained a smirk. Jack was most definitely in good hands.

...

Waking before his alarm, Mick showered then made a lumberjack breakfast to fuel the day ahead. Jimmy arrived early, his duffel bag weighed down with enough firepower to fend off an insurgency.

Jack joined them in the kitchen, handing Mick a red Hawaiian shirt covered in large, green palm fronds and white and yellow tropical flowers. "It's my lucky Magnum P.I. shirt."

Mick put on the last piece of his undercover attire.

"You wear it well, buddy." Jack patted him on the back.

In exchange, Mick returned Jack's handgun. "I don't think you'll need it, but be on the ready and keep it close." He grabbed his keys and coffee thermos.

"Don't worry about us. Just watch your six," Jack shouted as Mick walked out the door.

CHAPTER 42

After passing Summerland Key, heading north on the Overseas Highway, Mick called Ruth to review the plan. The final details would be covered in a team briefing once he arrived at the Port of Miami. When he crossed the Seven Mile Bridge, he phoned Frank and Bryce to update them on the operation. They had a shared understanding and common language that allowed him to keep it short. There was no need to remind him to stay safe—it went without saying when they were in the field.

He used the rest of the drive to get his head straight. After only a few weeks of retirement, he found himself out of practice and needed to shift back into law enforcement mode—to focus.

Heavy traffic delayed his arrival. On Biscayne Bay, east of downtown Miami, four massive cruise ships were docked end-to-end, towering over the surrounding area. Mick kept glancing at his watch—he was cutting it close. Passengers would soon start boarding.

. . .

Mick located Ruth in the team's staging area inside a security office in Terminal B.

"Everyone, meet Special Agent Mick Nassau. You all know he's the reason we're here." The six federal officers in the room introduced themselves then returned to their own tasks.

Ruth pulled Mick to the side for a private conversation. "It really is great to see you. And nice choice with the shirt." She straightened his collar. "But I have to say—you're looking a little worse for wear."

Mick instinctively ran his hands over his day-old stubble. "Nice to see you, too. You haven't changed a bit."

Standing at 5'3" with not an ounce of fat, Ruth had an impressive athletic background. After medaling in archery at the '96 Olympics, she moved on to earn black belts in multiple martial arts. Mick had witnessed her take down a suspect nearly three times her size.

"I'd love to catch up, but we don't have much time." She stepped in front of a mounted schematic of the terminal. "We have agents posing as porters stationed near the check-in counter. Here and here." She tapped to show the locations. "Based on Sheriff Wheeler's intel, Morena may be carrying up to thirty pounds of gold coins—difficult to hide in a carry-on, as those are more likely to be searched. A checked bag would make it easier to conceal the stash, even though letting it out of his possession is riskier. Once checked, the bags are sent straight to the passenger's cabin, involving fewer handlers compared to an airport."

Mick believed Ruth had a solid plan—let Morena check in, intercept the suitcase, and inspect it before he boarded the ship. The cruise line made it clear they planned to set sail promptly at five o'clock, regardless of what happened. If Morena got on board, it would be easy to disembark during either port of call, Cozumel or Honduras, and disappear for good. The stakes were high—the arrest of a murderer carrying millions of dollars' worth of stolen antiquities.

"If he shows up, we'll let him pass through security screening to ensure he's not carrying a weapon. The terminal gets crowded and chaotic, so after he exits the end of the ship's gangway, we'll arrest him right before he boards. Familiarize yourself with his former disguises and aliases." Half a dozen headshots of Morena lined the board, and Mick committed the face to memory.

Ruth handed Mick a straw hat to complete his tourist apparel, his priority boarding pass, an earpiece comms unit to communicate with the team, and the requested Glock and clip-on holster. He checked the magazine and chambered the first round. It wasn't ideal to conceal a gun in his waistband, but he had no other choice given his attire.

"And confirming, my role is to surveil him inside the terminal, line up behind him at the boarding gate, and create a buffer between Morena and the other cruisers?"

"Yes. I've assured all parties the arrest will be seamless. We have to protect the safety of the passengers and crew as our top priority."

"Any status updates from the other teams?" he asked.

"I'm waiting for word from the Miami airport. The flight to Quito leaves first. The other two flights are red-eyes, departing after the cruise ship leaves port."

Ruth looked at her phone then whistled to get everyone's attention. "Someone using Morena's alias checked in for the Quito flight. They're trying to get eyes on him."

Ruth paced the room as the minutes passed by. When her phone rang, the team gathered around while she listened.

"Got it." She hung up. "False alarm. They detained someone matching Morena's description after he checked a bag using Morena's alias. The guy swears he doesn't know anything. Claims he's an actor paid through a third party for a role in a reality show. He kept looking around for hidden cameras because he thought he was being punked. Idiot."

The team returned to their previous conversations, speaking in hushed tones while they waited. Mick hated not knowing if they were any closer to making an arrest. To fill the time, he poured a cup of coffee, grabbed a sandwich, and continued reviewing Morena's many disguises.

"Yes! We have confirmation—Morena's here." Ruth called to her fellow agents. "Listen up. He's disguised with a mustache and long sideburns. He checked his bag and is moving toward security. Time to get into position."

The agents filed past—two dressed as porters, two as tourists, and two in branded FBI shirts. The last two would join the team at the bottom of the gangway, ready to execute the arrest warrant. Ruth alerted the airport teams to standby.

"Good luck, Mick. I'll see you on the other side," she said as they moved to their intended posts.

...

The terminal buzzed with excited travelers waiting to board their ship. A cluster of friends wearing matching T-shirts emblazoned with *Freddy's 50th Fiasco* stood out amongst a sea of elderly passengers. Mick sat near the boarding door with his hat pulled low over his eyes, seemingly focused on scrolling through his phone.

"We've got the gold. Go, go, go! I repeat, the operation is a go." Ruth's voice echoed in his earpiece. His training enabled him to absorb the news without reacting, despite the excitement in her tone.

Mick glanced up as Morena entered the waiting area. Even with the added facial hair, Mick recognized him right away. Dressed in a tailored linen suit and wearing sunglasses, his salt-and-pepper hair was immaculate. He carried himself with the air of someone who was accustomed to being in control.

"Target in sight," Mick said just loud enough for his comms to pick up and transmit to the team.

"Copy."

Morena took a seat, removed his sunglasses, and pulled a book from his satchel. Mick watched him scan the room at each turn of the page—constantly on alert. The ticket agent interrupted the instrumental steel drum music being piped in over the speaker system to announce the start of the boarding process, inviting priority-class passengers to approach first.

Mick spotted a fellow agent stationed ahead of Morena and quietly slipped into line behind him. Just then, a middle-aged woman abruptly cut in front of Mick. *Damn*, he thought, but he couldn't react without risking unwanted attention.

They moved through the maze-like gangway until a view of the ship opened in front. The glass and metal tunnel provided little cover for the waiting agents except at the exit closest to the ship. But something changed, causing Morena to slow his pace. Mick looked past the line of passengers at an adjacent exterior window, which reflected a distorted image of the agents standing on alert outside the tunnel exit. Morena was now only ten feet from the end when he stopped and turned.

The forward agent approached Morena from behind and flashed his badge. "Excuse me, sir. We need to ask you a few questions."

Morena looked past Mick toward the terminal, his eyes narrowed, but he didn't resist. "What's this about?" he asked, keeping his back to the agent as he casually reached for his satchel.

"Routine inspection," the agent said as he pocketed his badge and pulled his weapon. "Please step aside."

The woman ahead of Mick clutched her purse to her chest, screamed, and backed away. With expert speed, Morena spun his leg around, landing a kick that clipped the barrel of the agent's gun, sending it flying through the air, and the agent scrambling after it.

A nearby passenger shouted, "Gun!" as Morena grabbed the woman and pulled her in front of him, holding what looked like a ceramic knife to her neck.

"Back off, or I'll kill her!" he shouted at the FBI agent. Using her as a shield, he dragged the terrified woman backwards into the terminal, sending everyone in their path running for safety.

Mick had no choice but to put his hands in the air and let Morena by with his hostage. He couldn't risk reaching for his Glock. Morena turned the last corner in the gangway, allowing Mick to follow behind unseen. When Mick reached the gate, the terminal was in chaos. Passengers yelled and ran for cover as uniformed law enforcement rushed the scene, guns drawn.

Things were spiraling out of control. Mick knew Morena needed to make a quick getaway to avoid a long, drawn-out hostage crisis. He'd keep the woman close until he found an opportunity to make a break. Mick scanned the terminal's exit points and made a judgement that Morena was heading for the closest doors. All bets were off if he made it onto the road with access to the docks next to the ship.

Ruth shouted commands into his ear not to approach and instructed agents to create a perimeter.

Anticipating Morena's next move, Mick moved behind the boarding gates and headed toward the farthest exit door, away from the commotion. He managed to get outside the terminal and planned to double back and intercept Morena.

The sidewalk was choked with departing passengers. Mick shoved his way through the crowds and darted out into the street. Weaving between cars, he sprinted toward the exit where Morena had been heading. When he reached the doors, he ducked in behind a van parked at the curb. Through the window, he saw Morena approaching the exit as he struggled to hold the weeping woman in his grasp. He faced the terminal but kept checking over his shoulder.

"I've got Morena," Mick said into his comms. "I'm moving in." Uniquely positioned to blindside Morena when he stepped outside, Mick maintained his cover using an exterior wall located feet away from the exit door.

When Morena moved into the breezeway between the two automatic sliding doors, he shoved the woman to the ground and turned to run for it.

Mick was prepared for what came next. He dropped his shoulder and tackled Morena, lifting him off his feet before piledriving him into the pavement and knocking the knife from his hand. Stunned and winded, Morena looked at him wild-eyed as Mick pulled his Glock and aimed it directly at Morena's face.

The freed hostage started screaming as Ruth and the rest of the agents funneled through the doors, their guns pointed at Morena. Ruth approached, holding her credential case in one hand and her gun in the other.

"Alejandro Morena," she shouted, "you're under arrest for the murder of Scott Bainbridge, conspiracy to traffic in stolen antiquities, kidnapping, and assaulting a federal officer."

Morena's face hardened as he glanced at Mick then back at Ruth.

Ruth handed the cuffs to Mick to do the honors.

Mick rolled Morena face down, securing his arms behind his back, and pulling the cuffs tight. "This is for Jack."

CHAPTER 43

Morena was loaded into the back of a black SUV and hauled off to the FBI Miami Field Office. Mick found the closure he needed the moment he cuffed Jack's attacker and had no desire to be part of the interrogation. Besides, Moreno was an experienced criminal, he wouldn't talk to anyone except his lawyer.

Mick made his way back into the terminal, now swarming with law enforcement who had the unenviable task of restoring order. Motivated by the prospect of their cruise departing on schedule, most cooperated without hesitation. Refunds were offered to those too shaken to continue, but from Mick's perspective, the majority seemed to press on. Even the woman whose pushy behavior had landed her in harm's way appeared to relish her newfound celebrity status as EMTs attended to her. The promise of an open bar once on board eased any lingering unrest.

Back in the terminal security office, the team conducted a thorough debrief. Mick assumed a more private conversation would take place between Ruth and the agent disarmed by Morena's ninja kick.

The confiscated gold was under guard, and Ruth planned to handle its admission into evidence. The coins were spread across the desk as they were cataloged and photographed. They had been sealed inside antique, toy train cars, complete with certificates of authenticity. Even if the metal cars triggered a visual inspection of the luggage during security screening, the toys would likely be dismissed as harmless.

Ruth commended the team for keeping their cool under pressure, but she saved her highest praise for Mick. Agents finished gathering their gear, when Mick approached Ruth.

"If you're all good here, I'm going to head out," he said.

"I'm leaving soon, too. I need to smooth things over with the cruise line. They're not happy." She shrugged with a grin.

Mick laughed. "It could've been worse." He handed her the Glock and earpiece. She let him keep the hat.

"So, what's next for you?" she asked.

"Back to Key West to help my friend during his recovery. After that—I have a few ideas."

"Ever think of switching agencies? I could put in a word for you with the FBI."

A faint smile tugged at the corner of Mick's lips. A few weeks ago, that offer might have been a lifeline as he fought to save his career, but things had changed.

"Thanks, Ruth, but I'll have to respectfully decline. My plans don't include working in another bureaucratic chain of command."

"I get it. If anything changes, you know where to find me."

Mick left the team as they wrapped up the operation and walked back to his jeep. A long list of people would celebrate Morena's arrest, but Mick felt little like talking—except to Jack who would be waiting for his call. Even though the threat had faded since Abe's arrest, this removed that last layer of doubt.

Jack volunteered to call Jo, Bea, and Wayne with the latest update and had to be convinced not to wait up for Mick who wouldn't arrive until almost midnight. Jack put Jimmy on the phone so Mick could convince him the coast was clear. Jimmy still had enough time to pick up a late shift at the Green Parrot. A quick text to Frank and Bryce covered the basics and a commitment to call in the morning with more details. Faced with a long drive back to Key West, Mick pulled out of the terminal, weaving his way through the streets of Miami.

...

Returning to a darkened cottage, Mick quietly washed up before collapsing in bed. He woke the next morning well past sunrise and stumbled into the kitchen to find Jack sitting at the island.

"Morning, Mick. Got your coffee here." Jack passed him a steaming mug.

"Thanks. I need this."

"I've been playing the scene in my head ever since you called—tackling Morena and cuffing his ass."

"Yeah, it felt good." Mick recapped a play-by-play of the arrest for Jack's enjoyment.

"I hope the bastard gets locked up for the rest of his life." Jack leaned on the kitchen island, balancing his cane on the edge.

"He will. The murder charge should be an easy conviction with your testimony, Abe's, and all the forensic evidence against him. And there's still the outstanding investigations surrounding his past illegal art deals. I'm sure Interpol will want their crack at him, too. But most importantly, he'll have to answer for your assault and attempted murder. That'll cinch the case for the prosecution."

"I'm looking forward to my day in court. I want to look both Morena and Abe in the eye when I testify against them." Jack refilled their mugs. "After you called with the good news, Bea and I got talking. She wants to have a party at her gallery to thank everyone for all their help. I think I'm finally ready to celebrate."

"That sounds like a great idea. And I agree—it's time. Are you thinking a small gathering or a big bash?"

"Somewhere in the middle. But it's all centered on one key invite. I'm hoping Frank and Bryce can be here for the entire weekend. It's my treat. I don't want them paying a penny for this trip. I'm confident I can handle hosting them for a full day on the water with your help, and it'll be an excellent test to see if I'm getting close to accepting charters again."

"I'm sure they'll be here unless they already have previous commitments. Who else is on the list?"

"Wayne and Michelle, Ron Wheeler, Earl and Betty, Little Jimmy, Captain Phillips, Alex Balfour, my physical therapists, the four of us of course, and a few other friends from the marina and around town. It should be a good crowd."

Mick finished his second cup. "Do you need me for anything right now? I thought a run might help clear my head."

"I'm good. Our morning is free, but I'd like to swing by the marina before my therapy session this afternoon."

"I'm going to run by Jo's place, but I won't be long."

"She'll be glad to see you. I told her about the arrest, but she had lots of questions."

Mick nodded. He owed her a personal account of everything that had transpired. As a bonus, it would give him a chance to take Bob for a walk. He cherished every chance to spend time with two of his favorite people in town.

It only took a few minutes to confirm both Frank and Bryce would be there for the party. Apparently, they'd been waiting for the invite and cleared their calendar. He placed another call to Ruth for a status update.

"Did you have a late night?" Mick asked when she answered her phone.

"Not really. Morena's still refusing to talk, so I made it home in good time. I always sleep like a baby after a big arrest."

Mick laughed. "You're hard-wired for this life. Has Peter Harley from Deep Water Salvagers been told about the recovery of his coins?"

"Yeah. Of course, he's ecstatic," she said. "They'll need to stay in evidence for now but will be returned to him as soon as possible. He's agreed to be an expert witness as to the provenance of the coins."

"I'm sure he's already planning a new salvage operation in that area of the Shoal to search for more of the treasure," Mick said. "And kudos to you for getting your man."

"I owe that one to you, Mick. Listen, I've got to attend a briefing soon, but I promise to fill in the details once the dust settles."

"I'm going to hold you to that."

. . .

When Mick arrived at the back door of the hospital drenched in sweat, Jo's technician informed him she was in an appointment. He understood she had to make up for the delayed opening and hoped these brief visits wouldn't be the only times he saw her.

Mick chose one of Bob's favorite routes in the neighborhood, and after their walk, they both sat to cool off in the treatment area. Jo walked out of an exam room and when she saw him, her face lit up and she ran across the room.

Before she could hug him, he put his hands up to block her. "I'm soaked in sweat."

"I don't care." She held him tight.

"What's that all about?"

"Okay, you're just being humble now, right? You keep telling me it's just what you do—taking down bad guys—but I was really worried."

"I was part of a team with lots of back up."

"Doesn't matter—you're my hero. It's because of you that Jack can get closure. And this Morena guy can't hurt anyone else."

Bob interrupted to paw Mick's foot, prompting him to hand over the last cookie. Mick had stopped asking Jo whether anyone expressed an interest in adopting him. He selfishly hoped she wouldn't find Bob a new home because he would miss seeing him.

"My appointment schedule looks light tonight, and I think we should celebrate. We need some alone time now that you're free from your bodyguard duties. I'll pick up the food if you can be here at eight. You might want to pack a toothbrush." Jo pulled at the waistband on his running shorts, making her intent crystal clear.

CHAPTER 44

The morning after his sleepover with Jo, Mick woke up feeling invigorated. He owed his unusually cheerful mood entirely to her. Had she not nudged him out the door to get ready for work, he would have gladly stayed in bed with her all day. Any lingering doubts he had about this move had vanished, thanks to Jo.

Jack and Bea spent the day party planning, so they never noticed when Mick came home after sunrise only to shower and change his clothes before setting out to tackle one of the last things on his list. Having made an appointment this time to meet with Sheriff Wheeler, he used the drive across town to rehearse his message.

The sheriff had called after Morena's arrest to congratulate Mick on the take down. He seemed up to date on the status of the federal case as he was forced to wait his turn at prosecuting Skiff's murder and Jack's assault. Mick let him know he appreciated the sheriff's job offer, but in the end, it wasn't the right choice for him. The sheriff wasn't surprised but hoped he'd consider staying in town.

"Morning, Mick." Sheriff Wheeler stood and motioned for him to take a seat.

"Hi, Ron. Frank and Bryce are flying in to attend Bea's party. I assume you'll be there."

"Wouldn't miss it."

"Thanks for meeting with me." Mick sat in the chair opposite the desk. "There's something I want to run by you."

The sheriff's brow furrowed. Their conflicted history ran deep despite their recent friendship.

"I've decided to move to Key West. My Tallahassee house is on the market, and I expect to be settled into my new place in Old Town over the next week."

"Congratulations! That's great news." His face lifted. "I'm sure Jack's happy about that decision. Where are you going to be living?"

"Well, that's part of why I'm here. I'm moving into the back half of the former chiropractor's office in Old Town. That little white Conch cottage with the blue shutters."

"I know the one."

"The front half was the original doctor's office, and in that space, I plan to open a new business—a private investigation and law office. I've maintained my license to practice law in Florida, but I'm most looking forward to being able to choose the cases I take on. As you're aware, we don't get that liberty in law enforcement."

"Ain't that the truth. Congrats again, Mick. I can help you out with any license applications. A few reputable private investigators are in town but none that also practice law. You'll have that market cornered. I'm sure you'll figure it all out soon enough, but you should also be aware, a couple unsavory characters operate in the area. Watch out for them."

"Thanks for the heads-up."

"Now and then, a case comes through here that isn't quite a police matter. I'll be glad to have someone I trust to refer them to."

"I appreciate your endorsement." Mick reached across the desk to shake the sheriff's hand. "Now that we have that out of the way, do you have any updates on Morena or Abe? I talked with Ruth Pender, and she told me Morena's still in federal custody while all the powers to be fight over him."

"I want him back here to face murder charges, but now that the FBI and Interpol are involved, well, that's a little over my pay grade."

"You'll get your crack at him, but it might take some time. What about Abe?"

"The judge just signed off on his plea deal. He's still here in jail and will soon be transferred to a state prison to serve out his sentence."

"Must feel good, closing the file."

"It does but only because Jack is still with us."

"I'm looking forward to celebrating his recovery. And thanks again for your support. See you Saturday."

That went better than expected, Mick thought to himself on his way out of the sheriff's office. He could now spend the day getting ready for Frank and Bryce's arrival. Jack and Bea planned to join him at the airport to meet them when they landed. They wanted to express their gratitude for all they had done for Jack and were eager to thank them in person.

▪ ▪ ▪

They stepped off the jetway stairs onto the tarmac dressed in touristy vacation gear. Frank wore his fishing shirt, and Bryce was decked out in a tropical Hawaiian shirt. A contrast to the last visit that had been all business. Before they even made it out of the airport, Jack and Bea had created lifelong friends.

Frank pulled Mick aside to tell him Jack was everything they thought he would be. He now understood how one person could invoke such loyalty and friendship.

"Bea and I have booked you each a room at a resort on the harbor. You're already checked in, and we've taken care of the bill." Jack handed them their room keys. "You'll be close to the marina so you can walk over early in the morning for our fishing trip. The marine forecast is looking good."

"Jack, it was torture to spend so much time on *Zulu* without leaving the dock. We've been talking about this day since we got back home," Bryce said.

"Well, you have an open-ended invitation to join me on the water any time you want. You're both family now."

"I volunteered us to get the boat stocked for our fishing trip." Mick said. "Tonight is low key since we'll be out on the water early in the morning. If you're up for it, Wayne has invited Alex Balfour and the two of you for a round of golf at the Key West Golf Club day after tomorrow. He's got rentals reserved and will set you up with any gear you need. I've left Sunday wide open since who knows how late things will go at Bea's party."

Bea laughed. "I can't be responsible for whatever trouble you boys get into."

"We'd love to check out your new place," Bryce said to Mick. "Is it on the way to our hotel?"

"Old Town is so small, everywhere is on the way," he replied.

Jack and Bea said goodbye at the terminal to attend to their errands while Mick took the boys on a quick tour of his new home and office. After lots of internal debate, he ended up calling his new business the Nassau Investigations and Law Office and had ordered a sign to be mounted on the front of the cottage. His friends could appreciate his vision for the place and looked forward to returning once he settled in.

Next stop—Zero Duval Street so they could drop their luggage in their hotel rooms. Jack had not skimped on the accommodations. Each of them had an oceanfront view looking out over the Gulf.

They brainstormed Mick's new business plan while drinking rum runners around the resort pool. After feasting on fresh seafood, they stocked up on fishing supplies of beer and bait and landed back on the deck of *Zulu* for sunset. Just like old times, but without the piercing stares from Abe or the threat of an unsolved murder hanging over them. Jo got away from the hospital at a reasonable hour and joined them for a nightcap.

Mick had updated Frank and Bryce on their new dating status, and the entire time she sat tucked in next to him on deck, the two men grinned at Mick. He was head over heels for Jo but tried hard to play it cool.

The next morning, the three men arrived at the marina and found Jack busy on board. He'd already prepped the boat for their day of fishing. Mick could see a renewed strength in him. He'd come so far in such a short amount of time.

They had an epic day cruising around the Gulf of Mexico. Frank and Bryce took turns reeling in a prize tuna, and Bryce added a wahoo to the day's catch. To Mick, it seemed like the four of them had been lifelong friends, reuniting after an extended absence. He expected them to hit it off, but it was more than that. The bond they had formed after the events of the past few weeks propelled their friendship to a new level.

Jack easily handled all his captain's duties, leaving the heavy lifting for the others. After they returned to port and cleaned up the boat, he headed home to rest, leaving the three of them on their own for dinner. Bryce fixated on having another slice of Blue Heaven's key lime pie. After a day on the water and an enormous meal at their new favorite restaurant, they followed Jack's lead and returned to their hotel, steering clear of the bars on Duval Street.

■ ■ ■

Mick didn't see his friends again until Saturday evening. Wayne had treated them to a lobster lunch at the golf club after they finished their round, and Frank and Bryce closed out their afternoon napping poolside at their resort.

Mick waited at the hotel lobby entrance in the golf cart, and once all three men were on board, he drove across town to Bea's place.

"Her gallery is at the other end of Duval Street. I think you'll be impressed." Mick said. "I'll drop you off, and I'll be right back after I pick up Jo."

"You don't need our approval, but we're happy for you, Mick," Bryce said. "Jo is the real deal. Just don't mess it up."

"I don't plan to. Not this time."

Mick didn't have the best track record with long-term relationships, but everything about his new start in Key West felt different—in a good way.

CHAPTER 45

Bea and Jack created a magical evening in her gallery. They hired a bartender and caterer, allowing them to relax and enjoy the party with their closest friends. This was a celebration of Jack's recovery and a way for them to thank everyone who'd supported them over the past few weeks.

When Mick walked in with Jo, he noticed Frank and Bryce chatting with the sheriff. By the time he caught up to them, Little Jimmy had joined the group and encouraged everyone to stop by the Parrot sometime that weekend for a round on the house.

Mick and Jo stayed close to each other as they mingled with the guests. It was easy being with her, but not in a boring or predictable way—instead, in a way that made sense because of how well they fit together. She would catch him staring at her across the room and would smile back. How could he be so lucky?

"Everyone, can I get your attention for a moment?" Jack said.

His powerful voice once again easily filled a room.

"Thank you for coming tonight. More specifically, thank you for the love and support you've shown us during these difficult few weeks. I'm standing here today because of that love." Jack turned to kiss Bea then walked across the room to give Jo a brotherly hug.

The friends gathered around and raised their glasses in an impromptu toast. "To Jack!"

"Thank you." Jack acknowledged their cheers then motioned he had more to say. "I want to mention one other person in particular. You've all gotten to know Mick, and in case you haven't heard, he's becoming an official Conch and making the permanent move to Key West. We couldn't be happier."

"Mick, when you toured my gallery, you seemed quite taken by this piece of art on the wall behind me. Jack and I want to give it to you as a gift. It'll look great above your new fireplace mantle. It's our way of saying thank you for everything you've done for us. We hope each time you look at this painting, it'll remind you of our friendship." Bea smiled. "Everyone, raise a glass!"

"To Mick!" was the collective reply.

He was speechless. Knowing the value of the art in Bea's gallery—it was beyond generous. Jack and Bea told him they would hang his new painting when he was ready. Mick's apartment would immediately transform into a home with this gift taking center stage. Jo hugged and kissed him, announcing to the entire group they were a couple.

"Jo, did you know about this?"

"I did. Bea's been busy. She's picked out a bunch of furniture for your house as well. I'd just stay out of her way if I was you."

"I've been thinking about another addition to my new place that would really make it a home," Mick said. "It's been on my mind for a while now, but I'm finally ready. I'd like to adopt Bob."

Jo gasped, drawing her hand to her mouth. He'd surprised her in the best possible way.

Mick kissed her. "I assume that means you approve of the adoption, Dr. Barton?"

"Yes, I approve! And Bob will approve as well. I'm so happy.

"Thanks, Jo. Having a dog has been a dream of mine for a long time. But I might occasionally need your help if I have to be out of town for work,"

"Anytime."

Frank and Bryce joined them, and Mick shared the good news. Frank, a dog person, had considered adopting Bob himself and supported Mick's decision. There were so many things to celebrate, but eventually the party wound down, and the guests made their way home. Jo stayed behind to help Bea and Jack clean up the gallery so it would be ready to open for business in the morning. Mick left them, thinking they could use some private family time.

Mick, Frank, and Bryce eventually worked their way back to the hotel via a Duval Street bar crawl that lasted into the early hours. Little Jimmy joined them until they landed at the Green Parrot then left the three of them to finish out their night at the iconic Hog's Breath Saloon. When Mick finally arrived at Jack's, he collapsed into a booze-filled sleep. The end to one of the best days of his life.

Sunday became a recovery day. The three men slept late then feasted on a big, greasy breakfast to counter their lingering hangovers. Jack sent Mick a text inviting them to join him, Bea, and Jo for a sunset cruise. Frank and Bryce would be heading home in the morning, and he wanted the six of them to spend time together. That gave the boys the rest of the afternoon to fully recuperate, so they opted for napping in the shade by the pool.

· · ·

Mick arrived first at the marina, followed shortly by Bea and Jack. He helped load a cooler full of food and drinks.

"We had tons of leftovers from the party," Bea said.

Mick turned to see Jo walking down the dock with Bob on his leash. She carried a large bag full of dog food, bowls, toys, and treats. When Bob saw Mick, he pulled, forcing her to drop the leash. Bob's entire body wagged uncontrollably. He loved being at the marina, but this time was different. This time, he'd be going home with Mick.

"What a great surprise. Thank you," Mick said.

"I checked with Jack, and he's okay if Bob stays with you at his house until you officially move in to your new place in a few days. It's time for Bob to say goodbye to the kennel."

"Thanks, Jack." Mick sat to pet Bob, his dog, not the Dog, as Frank and Bryce arrived and joined them on board. Bob greeted everyone with a happy tail, but he always returned to Mick's side.

"Let's get underway, or we're going to miss an amazing sunset," Jack said.

With five available deckhands, they deftly moved off the dock and spent the next hour cruising outside the harbor. Once they'd passed all points of land, only the ocean separated them from the setting sun.

Key West was famous for its sunset celebrations, but tonight was shaping up to be particularly awe-inspiring. Frank, Bryce, and Bea were on the stern deck while Jack sat in his captain's chair. Mick and Jo had climbed up the tuna tower to get the best view, but he struggled to pay attention with her so close. As the giant red ball of fire dropped off the horizon, Jo pulled Mick into a long, passionate kiss. Out of the corner of his eye, he saw the elusive, green flash of light streak across the sky, confirmed moments later by the erupting applause below deck.

The End

ABOUT THE AUTHOR

DL Mitchell is the award-winning author of the *Coral Shores Veterinary Mystery* series and a 2024 Nominee for Georgia Author of the Year.

In *Untied Lines,* Mitchell draws upon firsthand experience with South Florida hurricanes and her love of the Florida Keys. Time spent above and below the turquoise waters around Marathon and Key West inspire her storytelling.

She lives with her husband, daughter, and their menagerie of pets and is constantly planning their next adventure. She's a scuba diver but gets seasick, and when she's on the road, she travels with her espresso machine and her blow-up, stand up paddle board.

Other Titles by DL Mitchell

Note from DL Mitchell

Word-of-mouth is crucial for any author to succeed. If you enjoyed *Untied Lines*, please leave a review online—anywhere you are able. Even if it's just a sentence or two. It would make all the difference and would be very much appreciated.

Thanks!
DL Mitchell

We hope you enjoyed reading this title from:

BLACK ROSE
writing™

www.blackrosewriting.com

Subscribe to our mailing list – *The Rosevine* – and receive **FREE** books, daily
deals, and stay current with news about upcoming
releases and our hottest authors.
Scan the QR code below to sign up.

Already a subscriber? Please accept a sincere thank you for being a fan of
Black Rose Writing authors.

View other Black Rose Writing titles at
www.blackrosewriting.com/books and use promo code
PRINT to receive a **20% discount** when purchasing.